S.L.Mason

KILLING GODS

ALETHEA

CALYPSO

HERA

FATES

UNDERWORLD

ELYSIUM

POSEIDON

NOVELLA

EMMALINE

BLOOD OF THE GODS

ELYSIUM

This Book is a work of fiction.

All of the characters, organizations, and events portrayed in the novel are either products of the authors imagination or are used fictitiously. Its not about you.

DEDICATION

To my brother and his wife, who I consider my sister. Thank you for allowing me to stay at your home and finish this book. And for helping me become a better parent.

TABLE OF CONTENTS

PROLOGUE

Thebaid

The lord of Erebus Hades, enthroned in the midst of the fortress of his dolorous realm, was demanding of his subjects. The misdoings of their lives, pitying naught human but wroth against all the Shades. Around him stand the Furies and various Deaths in order due, and savage Vengeance thrusts forth her coils of jangling chains; the Fates bring the Souls and with one gesture damn them all.

Too heavy grows their work...

Statius

CHAPTER 1

SYDNEY

It's funny how something so small could hold all your dreams and future at the same time as if your very life depended upon what it held. In our case, I was not so sure our lives depended upon it, but our future for sure.

It didn't look like much - a little electronic doodad, similar to a flash drive or a mini san-disc. It certainly wasn't any bigger than a sim-card. Yet, the moment Adrian put it into my hand, I knew it was the most important thing on the ship.

Other than our lives themselves.

I wanted to live in this moment. I wanted to eat it up until my belly was full, using it to ease my guilty conscience. I wanted everything we'd been through to be worth — *this!*

Life had taught me that putting so much emphasis on one *'thing'* was a sure path to disappointment. So I bit back that desire, that need to control our future, and braced myself for reality.

Whatever that reality is

"How do we hook this thing up?" I asked with as much control as I could muster, impatience lining everything I did. I paced by the main display. Hoping the holo would light up, I huffed and sighed, then crossed and uncrossed my arms.

"Hand it over! I'll fix ye up," Emmaline thrust her hand out. Her teeth clenched the cigarette that a moment before was held between her fingers, the ash at the tip clinging to the end for dear life.

Trust Emmaline to know what to do.

In the few short months since I'd left Emmaline in charge on Odyssey and Charon had shifted Prometheus away, she had grown into her role as leader. The ship had taken on a life that revolved around her. Everyone genuflected for her, and I was actually good with it. I didn't want to run the day-to-day bullshit of a ship or a civilization. The boring amounts of paperwork and the bureaucracy of life were beyond my tolerance level.

If it was stock trading, I'd feel different.

Emmaline could run Odyssey all she wants, as far as I was concerned. Hercules and Isolde could run Prometheus. As for Ares, he only wanted the Argos and all the space shuttles he'd acquired from Astrodel.

He viewed it as his own little fleet of attack ships. His mini navy was a means to an end. They kept him out of my hair and provided an additional blanket of protection for our growing fleet.

My eyes settled on the space outside. There were at least a hundred ships floating around out there. If you stared long enough, you could pick out sparks on a few. Those were the work crews.

All I wanted was my children's and Adrian's safety.

I was still in charge of everything. Yet, I couldn't say I liked it. Truth be told, I didn't. I hated it.

This wasn't how I envisioned myself. I'd never thought of myself as a leader, but there I was with thousands of people looking at me for safety, comfort, and the promise of a home.

I only hoped I could deliver.

A holo image of a star chart appeared in the center of the shifting room. One of the things I admired about Themian technology they didn't leave out the colors. Things weren't in black and white or variations of red, blue, green. Everything was full of bright, brilliant techno-colors.

When you examined a star chart and its planets or a nebula, you saw the actual colors of the nebula as seen with the naked eye. You got a real visual of what that area of space looked like. This version of sight was more Themian than human. Humans missed half the detail.

Shifters can see in three dimensions with a rainbow of colors. Every image, every detail of that image, is important. When they make a shift through subspace, they move safely from point A to point B because of those details.

Or at least that's how Adrian explained it to me.

There were a few instances where I was pretty sure I had moved someone.

Shifted?

However, I had no idea how it happened. I didn't picture them. It wasn't like drawing a line from point A to point B. I simply wished for their presence, and there they were.

It worked like my knowing-power. I knew where things were. I could find them with a thought. Their location just came to me.

It felt as if I'd pulled Hera out of her existence and moved her with desire alone.

Now I needed to figure out how to make that desire work again.

"Do we have an ETA, Odyssey?" I asked. The onboard computer interface answered with her usual flat-tonal, simulated voice.

"Based on our current engine capacity, without a visual to perform a shift, it will take us six years, three months, seventeen days, four hours, and 53 minutes, Earth-time to reach Elysium."

My heart fell into my shoes and out the bottom of the ship.

Yeah, six years doesn't really work for me.

I could be a grandmother in six years. *Ugh, why did I think of that?*

I wouldn't look like a granny, but then again, the average physical age of anyone on the ship was about 23, excluding children.

Adrian, I'm assuming, resembled a 24-year-old.

Not that I ever saw him at 24.

< Stop musing, *beautiful girl*! Let's get on with it. > Adrian broke in.

I glanced at him out of the corner of my eye, throwing him a half-smile. It was still one of my favorite things to hear - the caressing tone of his voice in my mind, calling me '*beautiful girl*'.

I know it's stupid. I'm old!

According to human standards, I was an old lady, or at least should have been. Inside I was an old lady. The idea that anybody would think I still looked like a girl was ludicrous.

Being the mother of two grown children, one of which is technically married...

Not that I liked to think about Hercules and Isolde together. I was happy for her. She was loved and in love.

There's nothing more important than that.

But I still didn't want to think about the intimate meaning of that love.

"All right! Get us going! I want to get there before I die. Move the Phaedra ship to Prometheus' shuttle bay and seal them in. Tell Ares that if he doesn't have the Argos inside Odyssey within the next 15 minutes, I'm going to leave his stupid ass behind!" I ordered.

Eris nodded her head as she sent to her brother, using nicer terms than I, or maybe not. Ares liked a good fight, and Eris liked to antagonize everyone, including him.

I could only imagine being Ares' twin. Everything between the two siblings would be a fight, and he'd always win. Or would he?

Phaedra — all the people from Phaedra were descendants of criminals. As they put it, some were original sinners, people who committed their own crimes and weren't paying for someone else's.

I'd already tapped the android, Jorhan, for as much information as he carried.

'He' it's an it.

I didn't know why I was referring to *'it'* as if *'it'* was a he.

Robots don't count as people in my world. Jorhan will always be a machine to me.

< Adrian, let's go to see Melinda. >

I didn't have to say another word. That was one of the beauties of sharing each other's lives inside our minds. You could say you're sorry without having to literally say the words. The other person knew exactly how you felt, what you were thinking and how.

It's an alien thing.

The only time I'd been scared wasn't because of the voice in my mind but because I thought I was cracking up.

The scene in front of me shifted from the bridge of our ship to Melinda's laboratory.

"I'd try knocking before you jump into my personal private space, thank you very much," Melinda called out.

Shit! That is kind-a crappy.

"Sorry, Aunt Melinda. I guess I wasn't thinking about your privacy. You're right. You could've been changing, and I would've seen something that would've scarred me for life," I demurred while looking around at the floor.

She threw her head back and barked out a laugh. "Or you might have learned something for once in your life. What did you come to see me for, girl?" Melinda was never one to mince words. She liked to get right to the meat of the bone and chew it to bits, then move on to her next victim.

"All those people we pulled off Phaedra, I need to know if any of them have seen Elysium. According to the star charts, it'll take us six years to get there. I'm sure that when Hephaestus finishes those two extra engines, we'll move faster. But to tell you the honest truth, it'll only cut our time in half. That's still three years. I don't know about you, but I don't want to spend that much time looking for a planet." I chanced a glance at her face to gauge her reaction.

She leaned back against the laboratory counter, crossed her ankles and arms, tilted her head to the side, and smiled broadly at me. "You don't want to spend that much time looking for a planet. Am I wrong or what? Have we not spent the last year searching for this planet going through heaven and whatever the underworld held just to get this far?" She moved a lock of hair behind her ear. "And now you're suddenly upset about perhaps it being another six or three years? Listen, honey, if you were just looking for a home planet, you would've picked one of Ixis pet projects." She began tapping her fingers on the counter.

"He would've shifted us all down. We'd have crops planted somewhere by now. But that's not what you did. What you did was decide that we needed allies." Taking a breath, she ran her tongue over her lower lip and hitched a half-smile.

My mouth dried. I opened it to retort, her hand came up to silence me.

She continued. "Now, I don't know why you got it in your head that somehow or another, we need to bolster our numbers and have friends. But I cannot argue with you or your abilities. I don't have your gifts. You want me to talk to those folks from Phaedra and find out if any of them have been to Elysium or have seen it. That's really what you're looking for, isn't it? A visual?" she crossed her arms again.

"Yeah, I'm looking for a visual, a picture, or something." I searched her face as desperation welled up in me. I pushed it back. The need to find this planet pulled me to take action. Explaining the fates or what had happened on Delphi was not the top priority on my list.

I couldn't even think about Ixis and the jackpot he put us in. He saved our lives for the moment.

That is the only reason we have a chance to find allies.

"Well, I'm afraid that getting a visual from one of the Elysians will be mighty tough. They have zero telepathic ability. If they have any at all, it's so minuscule and latent, I'm not sure they could send anything to you. In other words, the only way for you to get it would be to judge them, which I don't know how fair it would be. Seeing as with you, it's a 50-50 chance whether you're gonna kill them or not," she sighed.

I shook my head and cringed. She was right. Well, maybe not precisely correct. It was more like a 72% chance of living and a 38% to 28% chance of dying after my judgment.

I was not even sure that math was correct.

That's one of those things we have Professor Michelson for.

Math just wasn't my strong suit unless it involved money.

"Okay, well, what about the old guy? He said he was willing to be a guinea pig. Did you try Primordium on him?" I asked, groping for a better outcome.

"Well, now there's something really interesting. He comes in here old as the day is long, hobbles along with his cane, carrying a lot of arthritic pain and all that. I felt for him. I truly did. Because I've been there. I handed him the Primordium. *'It looks like a regular cup of water,'* he scoffed at me, *'I thought it was a tonic.'* I told him to just take a drink and sit back and enjoy. He sat down over there," Melinda indicated a reclining chair with a footrest that she kept off to the side.

I always thought she sat there and drank coffee in the morning while she went through her email.

We managed to enact a server like-system here, so we had our own form of Internet. It had all of the human information, but it was also filled with all of Themian history and data. The only difference was that the Themian data was right, while the one from Earth humanity was under review.

"So, he sits there, takes a big swig of his glass of Primordium, then remarks and says it tastes like water." Melinda's eyes twinkle.

"But it does taste like water. What's the big deal?" I crossed my arms.

"Nothing happened. So it got me thinking. Why is it that nothing happened when we gave him Primordium, but when we, hybrids, use it, it's like the elixir of life? Why is it ambrosia that fixes everything? Earth's water doesn't work that way on us. Water from any other planet in the universe doesn't work that way on us. Yet, it works like regular water on him." Her smile grew. "So, I gave him another glass and said it was regular water. One of his kids said they were thirsty, and he shared it with them."

I gasped, "Melinda, you cannot test on people without their permission. What the fuck? And a kid! I mean, really, on children?" I yelled at her in shock.

She shook her head. "I said it was one of his kids. I didn't say it was a kid. The guy had to be 40. I tested it on him without his permission. If it didn't do anything to the old man, it probably wouldn't do anything to him either. I've already taken a blood sample and started testing. Their blood is filled with a liquid similar to Primordium. Primordium is water to them, Sydney. It's the same thing. There's no difference." Her excitement grew, and she skipped to her microscope. "I still haven't figured out exactly what separates Primordium from

Earth water, but there are a few components in it that I cannot identify. It's something to do with the creation process in an infinity pool that changes the chemical compound. You can put Earth water in an infinity pool all you want."

Now, she's rushing on with her discovery.

"What comes out the other side will be Primordium every time there is a process changing it, and I just can't figure out what it is. No one on the ship understands the technology, including Hephaestus," she finished, her excitement electrifying the room.

It was almost like a blow. I was so hoping that we would be able to do something for these poor people. "Alright, well, which one of your laboratories is the best shielded here?"

Moving on to our next item on my made-up list that never gets shorter.

"The one next door's got the best shielding. It is also where I can keep a close eye on whoever it is you decide you want to put in there." She tipped her chin at the room.

I nodded absently, looking down and around. I did that when I was thinking.

< Adrian, please transfer Charon. I want him next door to Melinda. > I sent him a visual of the room I wanted the man in.

< Anything your heart desires, *beautiful girl*. > Adrian responded.

A moment later, Charon's sleeping form appeared in the lab next door.

"I always wanted to meet the mischievous Mr. Charon." Melinda's eyes glistened with delight as she rubbed both hands together, like a chef with a new ingredient to use.

"He said something about giving everyone gene therapy. That's what started this shit show," I grumbled, though none of us would be here without him and his genetic meddling.

Melinda was always looking for someone to talk science with. If you let her go, she would talk until your eyes glazed over.

I think she'd be happy to settle for anybody who has a scientific brain.

Her face had to hurt with the stretch of her smile. If I didn't know better, I'd think it was Christmas.

"You can ask him all the questions you want. He's a shifter, so you cannot allow him out of that room for any reason. I don't even want you opening the door. He can shift out as soon as you break the seal. You know, like a Faraday cage. Use the intercom. Try and find out how the fuck he changed them. Find whatever he did to his group of Themians. He's the one who created all of us. He instigated it. He's brilliant. You'll love him and hate him. Again, don't let him out of that room! I don't trust him. He's already tried to fuck me over three times," I grumbled.

Melinda walked over to the glass and trailed a finger across the clear surface. "Oh, I won't let him out. Don't you worry about that. I'll be, however, up close and personal with him. I'll make sure someone shifts me in." Her eyes never left the sleeping form in the next room.

"No, you can't be shifted in. No one will be able to shift you out, and you'll have to open the door. Unless you plan on sedating him, and you're absolutely certain he's sedated. I don't want you to go in there for any reason." I informed her.

"Yes, mommy. Boy, you got bossy britches! So, what exactly am I supposed to find out here?" she demanded after brushing my warning off.

"We need to know how he changed us or them," I said, rubbing my temples with all the us's and them's. "Obviously, if the Primordial water doesn't work on the Elysians and they are the original Themians, Charon and all of his people and, of course, their descendants IE us were hybridized. We need to know how he did it. Maybe, we could change the people from Phaedra," I shrugged.

I didn't like the idea that we were all a cut-and-paste version of life, the use of CRISPER on a grand scale.

She tilted her head several times in agreement, then crossed her arms, putting her index finger up over her mouth and tapping it on her lips. Her eyes had taken on a faraway look as she was off on a mental mind puzzle.

"Okay, get out because you're distracting me. I got a lot of big brain thinking to do." She turned away from me, still tapping her lips.

I gave her a half-smile, walked over, and threw a peck on her cheek. "Thank you, Aunt Melinda!"

She threw up her hands. A moment later, I was back on the bridge of Odyssey, standing next to Adrian. I glanced over at him, "You know, I don't like you doing that without warning."

His face curled into a crooked smile, and he simply replied, "I missed you."

I wanted to give him a kiss, but someone behind us cleared their throat. "If you two are done with your protestations of love... I've got better things to be doin'. Your aunt just asked if we could shift her over to Prometheus. She wants to look at the labs there."

"Move her wherever she wants to go. Hephaestus movements are a priority. I don't care how long anybody else has to wait. What they're doing will make a difference in everyone's lives. Whereas anything else might not. Ares is going to take a backseat, and he's gotta suck it up."

Emmaline liked telling Ares what to do, and I was almost sure that Ares secretly liked her doing it. She didn't threaten him. She didn't bully him. She ordered him, crossed her arms, and waited for him to protest. So, she could just calmly tell him no.

It was actually kind of funny. They both enjoyed the sparring of words every now and again. If they didn't, Ares wouldn't come back for more.

"What do you mean? I have to wait. I need Hephaestus to come back and upgrade the Argo's engines. If we're attacked, we need to be able to defend ourselves!" Ares raged from the arched exit to one of the hallways.

"Our?" Emmaline turned on him.

Every eye in the room was now fixed on the standoff.

< We could leave and leave her to it. > Adrian supplied.

<Yes, I know, but that would just be kind of mean.> I snickered.

< Okay, say the word, and we're outta here.> Adrian's offer was tempting.

Leave Emmaline and Ares to fight it out amongst themselves.

"Yes, whatever it is that you need, needs to wait. At this rate, we will be lucky to make it to Elysium in six years on the outside and three years, perhaps on the inside. I need

Hephaestus upgrading engines for the big ships first. You really want to help? Find me a visual of Elysium. Then, we can shift our happy asses there, and you can have the first upgrades." Emmaline ended with a tight-lipped simpering smile.

Ares stood stock still like a statue. "Six years on the outside? I'm not keen on being imprisoned on this or any ship for that amount of time," he retorted as he leaned down as his eyes bored into her oh-so fake smile.

"Neither am I! So either you are helpin' or hurtin.' Pick your poison!" She finished, holding her hand up and inspecting her nails as if they'd just been painted.

"I'll just go work on the weapons arrays," he growled, "none of our ships are armed, and they should be, first!" Ares didn't back down, even though he'd been outmaneuvered.

"That's all fine and dandy, Ares, but remember, when it comes time to use a 3-D printer, you only get one. All the rest are dedicated to your brother and his work. It's more important!" Emmaline cut off his flanking tactic.

"You didn't think his work would be more important when we went to Phaedra. You made it very clear that having

Armed Forces could be extremely useful and important," Ares roared back.

"Yes, you're right. Having Armed Forces is important and especially handy when you're goin' to meet strangers. However, we need to get somewhere safe first. We haven't come to a planet yet that we could harvest anything off of. And you can't eat an asteroid."

Awe! Emmaline's voice of reason wins the day again.

I melted into the background to enjoy the show. I wanted to kiss her for taking Ares on.

"Obviously, you haven't been to one of the Biodomes lately. Because if you had, you would have seen we have plenty of food, and the likelihood of running out is extremely low," Ares hissed through his teeth.

"Why, I'll make sure that's the first thing I do before I go to bed tonight. I'll stroll right down to one of the Biodomes. Which one should I pick first?" she challenged, with her eyes lighting up with static electricity. She was a vampire, and Ares was her next victim.

"Biodome two. They practically turned the entire thing into an agriculture farm. I actually think some of the other hybrids enjoy it," he scoffed.

Part of me thought he was going to spit on the floor. Then the real fireworks would have started. Emmaline would have killed him for that.

She hates spitting.

"Fabulous! You're dismissed!"

The muscles in his jaw worked over the bone as he clamped his teeth down. Then with a curt nod followed by a swift pivot, he left the room. Everything about him screamed, barely under control.

We didn't need him to like us, only obey.

He can go 'like' his mother.

CHAPTER 2

PERSEUS

Hercules and I had always been close. That feeling of brotherhood never changed for us. We were always of the same mind.

We, my siblings and I, all sat on Homeworld 12 for thousands of years, waiting. Waiting for a chance to be free. Waiting to be reunited with our mother and waiting to be mated.

And now Hercules is.

I was jealous. I had hoped that we'd be freed from that long imprisonment and sent back to Earth, that blue ball floating in the cosmos. I thought I'd see oceans, mountains, and snow again. Instead, I was stuck with lakes and hills artificially created inside the Biodome of this spaceship monstrosity. I couldn't say that I was not resentful.

I am!

Mother kept her own counsel, never telling us the truth, not until my father became a monster.

How could she not have known what would happen?

These musings amounted to nothing. I didn't even know why I kept going over them in my head. It was not my mother's fault that Zeus was an animal. Really none of this was her fault, and yet it all was.

But Hercules and his mate, Isolde, say it's fate that it was meant to happen.

I was tired of sitting on the sidelines, waiting for my turn at life to happen. For Fate to finally find me and let me live.

I must get off this ship somehow.

Ares had his spaceships, and Hercules had his adventures.

Finally, that blow-hard has lived up to some of his braggings.

Hephaestus was perfectly happy inventing anything, and the girls had always had their own plans. Eris had somehow insinuated herself on the bridge. She was probably there to keep Ares under control which is a comedy in itself.

Discord controlling war.

Hebe spread happiness like butter over the children of this ship, giggling and laughing her way through the cosmos. Eileithyia was mothering all the babies and helping Hephaestus as usual.

I gazed into the mirror of my life. I saw myself not as who I was but as who I wanted to be.

Free, mated, a hero?

Most of the hybrids already believed me to be a hero. All of those acts described in their stories — I never performed any of them. At least not for the reasons they believed.

I failed to stop my father. My father destroyed hundreds of nameless cities, killing thousands of faceless people. He was the monster of the ancient Greek world.

I wasn't able to stop the wave that destroyed Joppa. I didn't become a king. I spent 100 years hunting down my own father, saving humanity just so I could watch him beheaded. Only then, for my siblings and I, to be treated like pariahs.

Does that make me a hero?

I didn't think so. The only reason humanity remembered me was because I hunted my own father. They made-up stories as to why I did it. They called it a quest to save my mother and find my true love.

Only to change mother's name, making her someone else. The truth is that the monster I fought was my father. As for love, I never found it, only heartache.

Sydney said she didn't believe in fate. However, I always believed my mother had a higher calling, a greater purpose. If it's all meant to be and it was fate. *The question becomes what is my fate? And how do I accomplish it?*

"Are you still musing, brother, always so thoughtful and reflective?" Ares elbowed me with his sense of humor, returning after Emmaline's verbal lashing.

"Yes. I'm always reflective. One cannot learn from their mistakes without first meditating on what they are. You wouldn't understand that. I love you, brother, although you are blind to your own missteps. Your thirst for war will only lead you to chaos and trouble." I heaved a sigh.

This ship has become a new prison. I've turned it into one.

"That may be so, Perseus. It may be that my thirst for war will lead me to nothing but chaos and trouble. But at least I'll be alive. You," he poked a finger into my chest, "need to leave this room." His nose curled on one side as if a foul smell had reached him.

"I say this not because I wish to kick you out. You need to live. You need to find that which fuels your fire. Hercules found it. Honestly, I never thought he was that bright," Ares murmured under his breath and glanced away. His head then whipped back to stare me down, his blue eyes hard as granite. "I, too, feel the emerald-colored jealousy regarding Hercules having found his mate. That feeling of love and satisfaction that bleeds through when he's around, it makes me want to pummel his face, to pulverize him. If it wasn't for Eris telling me constantly that my turn would come, I'd wipe that smug look of happiness off of his hair-covered jaw." Ares guffawed at the idea of belting our brother, then slammed his fist into the opposite hand.

Ares may be the God of War, but Hercules is a mountain too high to climb and kill.

He was a full head higher than the both of us. Even a few inches above Hephaestus.

A smile curled my cheeks. I wasn't alone in my feelings.

"Ares, if I must leave this room and find something to occupy my time until my lady love arrives, what should I do? Where should I go?" I asked and waved my arms around to indicate the visage from our view-ports.

Other than stars and rocks, there was only the wide empty space of the cosmos. "Odyssey is a circle, and I have no desire to go round and round as a dog chasing its tail."

"Go to Prometheus," he shrugged. "The ship is practically unoccupied. I know Sydney's aunt's over there, poking around in all the laboratories. Perhaps, you may meet her and fall in love," he chuckled, at what he found to be amusing.

I felt no mirth at his jest.

"Take our sisters, put them to work. I am tired of their twittering. However, leave Eris here," my brother added.

I scratched my chin. Hebe would not be thrilled about being dragged over to Prometheus and pulled away from all the man-flesh around here. But I was sure that Eos would be willing to go.

She says she will follow me anywhere.

I decided to put that sentiment to the test.

<Of course, brother. I will follow you, let's go. Contact Sydney's son. He'll shift us. > she giggled.

There was a secret there.

<Only if you truly desire to accompany me, sister. > I replied, throwing her bait of a secret back at her.

<Perseus, you will never be happy until you've found your way. Mother has her fate. Let's go find ours.> Her steady voice nudged me into action. I, in turn, took the bait for that one. Eos was almost never wrong.

Not having the ability to shift and not wishing to use the forces inside the ship unnecessarily, I allowed my feet to lead me to the great shifting room on Odyssey.

Upon entering, I spied Eos on the other side of the room, standing next to Eris. She nodded her head and winked at me.

Looking around, I knew most of the players. Tristan was off to the side, fiddling with some globe-shaped star chart. He and his father, Adrian, were of my line. If I was going to get anywhere, he would give me what I wanted.

I hoped he would.

Like two moons in perfect gravitational unity, my sister and I converged on Tristan.

"May I inquire as to what you're doing, grandson?"

He never even looked at me.

"Perseus, you remind me a bit of Adrian. Are you Emmaline's great-grandfather?" Tristan inquired. His serious tone and lack of reaction struck me as odd in one so young.

"No, Hephaestus re-seeded my line for her grandmother," I supplied.

Tristan removed his hands from the ball, and I felt his inquisitive blue eyes settle upon me. He looked remarkably like his father. Although I knew that they were closest to Hephaestus, they both resembled me.

A smile worked the side of my mouth. Part of me wanted to quash it. It was pride, and I had never been one to exhibit pride if I could avoid it.

Eos placed her hand gently on my shoulder, bringing me back to the task at hand. "We are here because we wish to ask something of you. Will you shift us to Prometheus? We may be of service to Melinda or Hephaestus. We feel our fate requires us there." Her artful use of implied destiny and emotion caused me to hold my breath. Eos always brought that on. It was one of her abilities - the bending of emotions.

She, like Hercules, had a way of knitting words into a fabric you couldn't turn away from.

Tristan's brows knotted together, "Emmaline and my mother said that all shifting must be focused strictly on Melinda and Hephaestus and whatever they're doing. I can't shift you without permission, and I have my own job." Then his eyes glanced left and right, staring off into the distance.

A peace broke over his face and he refocused on me. "Isolde says that I should move you. Apparently, the fates have decided you must go." He wagged his brows at us conspiratorially.

I didn't think he believed the hype any more than his mother did.

"So, you won't do it because I asked? But you will because your sister told you to?" I scoffed. As if I, too, wouldn't do as my sister asked or told me as needs may.

"Wouldn't you, *grandfather*?" he asked.

I would!

Eos laughed, and I side-eyed her. She had the back of her hand covering her mouth.

"Touché! I do almost everything my sister asks of me. Thank you! Will I see you on Prometheus?" I inquired.

The question was meant to be polite, but in truth, I was indeed interested in his reply.

"Of course, you will, *grandfather*. I am the shifter for Prometheus. I'm only here studying star charts that haven't been transferred. Don't worry! I'll be on deck soon."

I never heard another word. We appeared on the bridge of Prometheus, next to a funny-looking man with an ascot.

He cleared his throat, "I'm Professor Michelson, and you must be related to Adrian?" he chuckled with glee while rubbing his hands together.

Eos burst out laughing, and the sound filled the small space. It resembled the musical notes of a perfectly tuned instrument more than laughter.

"Yes, I am Perseus," I remarked without all the laughter or belly shaking.

"I'm sure you're going to hear this a lot, but I heard that you haven't joined the hybrid population on Odyssey. So, I have to know." He leaned in, "Did you really do all those things in the mythological stories or are they just stories? Like Hercules?" His mouth hung open with some awe as he awaited my answer.

I wanted to grind my teeth, but he was direct, and he hadn't exactly called my brother a liar or blow-hard.

Which he was. Both.

I found myself smiling at him, "No, the stories are true. I did things that were similar, but not for the reasons they say. I certainly didn't slay any woman with snakes on her head. I am pretty sure no one like that even exists. I never flew with winged shoes, only the forces. Wind comes at my call rather easily." I said, shaking my head at humanity's ridiculous ideas.

I continued, "The Gorgons are mythological sisters. It's a story from Elysium, and nothing about that story ever said any of them were mortal, immortal, or grotesquely ugly. I don't know if you've gone through the files, but I'm sure if you do a little research, professor, you will find out that Themian mythology is a little different from the human one. Now, the story of someone slaying some woman named Medusa, well, it's just a story told by Pythia probably to scare children." I leaned in with my fingers curled as if claws were coming down to tear the man apart.

"My mother told it to me, and it scared me." I laughed. It was an honest laugh, good and clean, without the normal reserve and worry of causing offense or slight. Our time on Homeworld 12 had left me even more jaded than my time on Earth.

The freedom to share a momentary comedy with a fellow hybrid was a relief I did not think I needed. And yet, it was there, and I did indeed need it.

Professor Michelson's arms were crossed, and he nodded while scratching his chin, "No, I researched all the files. I like to read. It's refreshing to know someone wouldn't want to take credit where credit wasn't do." He smirked and tilted his head down to look at me through the hair on his brows.

I smiled broadly back at him. He was politely testing me, but it didn't annoy me. His battle of wits was worthy. "My sister and I are here now. What can we do to be of help?"

"Hephaestus is down in what is now called the engineering sections. He's installing one of the new engines. I don't know if you're good with technology. However, you're welcome to go down and help him." He waved at the arched opening onto a companionway.

"Or if you are better with computers, you can stay here and help me." He turned away from me, giving his full focus to Eos. "Your lovely sister is welcome to stay with me for all eternity. I would be most happy to stand next to her forever," he said and blushed right down to his toenails.

I was not sure that he meant to announce that to the room.

Eos reached out to take his hand. Blue electricity shot around the room. The fingers of it rushed over my skin, zapping me. The mental conduit between my sister and I slammed shut. I was viciously pushed out.

Both of them gasped, their eyes widened, and broad smiles spread across their faces.

I staggered back and sat in one of the chairs, waiting for whatever was happening to end. A moment later, the buzzing in the back of my mind changed.

Eos' hand released Michelson's arm. Her eyes landed on me, "Perseus, I was right! My fate lay here all along," she gasped.

The fluttering in my belly turned into a tornado.

My sister, my twin, my best friend! She'd always relied on me and I on her.

The realization that I had relied more on her than she ever did on me hit me hard.

How is it that she was the stronger of the two of us?

"Perseus, I've mated," she said as her gaze whipped back to Michelson.

He stepped forward and put his arm around her waist, "When I said she could stand next to me forever, I was joking. At least I thought it was a joke." His eyes never left her.

He smiled. "Sydney said I was here for a reason. I know she doesn't believe in this fate stuff, and says it's all malarky. Did you even know why you wanted to come here?" he asked in a husky voice.

"I came here to find something to do and Eos came with me. She said she felt like our fate lay on this ship." I cleared my throat to push back the lump housed there.

"I'm truly happy for you, sister. You were right." I kissed her temple, "Professor Michelson, treat my sister well. Not all of the stories are wrong. I am a fighter and I will kill you if you do anything to harm her," I stated.

Eos head whipped around, <You know that if you kill him, you kill me brother? Don't say such things.>

<Does he know that, sister?> I remarked.

<Yes! Of course, he does. He snickering to himself. He knows you're being a blow-hard, so stop. If you wish to hurt him physically, fine. But you're not allowed to kill him. > She returned.

Her simple sweet smile met my eyes. My sister's happiness was more important to me than mine.

My honor required I congratulate him, so I stood up and shook Michelson's hand, "Professor Michelson, you found your bride. Now, I suggest you find somewhere to get to know her. Somewhere I don't have to bear witness."

The man blushed, a fighter, I think not. I've been told that Professor Michelson was brilliant. Apparently not smart enough to keep from blushing in front of his wife's brother.

"May you find your mate, Perseus." Eos whispered and squeezed my arm. The two of them left, hand-in-hand. I sat down in the pilot's chair.

I was familiar with the controls; I could've flown this ship.

Pressure in my chest mounted. I went inside my mind and closed the empty door to Eos. Her voice was never going to be there again. It was nothing more than a door leading to nowhere.

A moment later, a voice behind me started talking, "You know that bull about my sister saying I should let you come over here? It was really my mother, my sister, and your mother who said you had to come here." Tristan plopped down in one of the chairs and threw a leg over an armrest.

His hair stuck out from the front of his head at strange angles as if he'd bathed and never brushed.

"I know you feel like your sister's been torn away from you, that things will never be the same. That you feel that your greatest friend and ally is somehow no longer with you, and you are alone." His nonchalant statement made me want to stand up and punch him.

Who is he to guess at my emotions?

He was no more than 18-19 Earth years old. I have lived thousands of years.

Why should I listen to the advice of Tristan?

My mind chewed it over.

"I've been where you are now. The feeling of my twin suddenly not being just mine. And if you think you love your sister more than I love mine, you'd be a fool. So, she mated," the man-boy shrugged. "Michelson's a nice guy. Not a bad choice. He may not look like a fighter, but he's got a pretty big brain. I'd be pretty scared to pit my wits against his. I think he could out-think all of us. And that, my friend, is a very powerful weapon. What I am trying to say is that this doesn't mean your sister's gone," he paused for effect. "It means you're now free to do whatever you want, and you don't have to worry about her tagging along."

His words rang through my mind.

I had never thought of my sister as a tag along. She held her ground. She was good with a sword and shield. Even though her heart was never in it, she stood by my side in every battle.

I took to my feet and faced the boy lecturing me about life. I crossed my arms, trying to push away that fluttering feeling of dread I had in my stomach.

"Will I need to worry about you tagging along?" I asked as a smile played at the sides of my lips. I was goading him for sport.

A grin broke over his face, "No, I've had my share of fighting. Thanks! My sister doesn't need me to protect her anymore. She's got Hercules, who I think is a pretty good warrior. Better than I am." Tristan pulled at the hair hanging in his eyes, "your brother can't protect your mother and my sister at the same time. And the Fates must go wherever. You wanted adventure? My mother's planning on going down to the planet as soon as we reach it." He released the hair, allowing it to stand on end.

He stared up at me through his eyebrows, "Be your mother's guard, her guardian, her protector." He rolled his head around on his shoulders to stare out the view-ports. "My mom's got Adrian. He was trained pretty well, tells me that Apollo trained him and that he's fought against Athena."

Both were worthy fighters. I fought them myself numerous times before the High Council chose to hide us away on Homeworld 12.

"Hercules has Issy. My mom's got Adrian. But Hera is alone. Don't leave your mother unprotected. I certainly wouldn't leave mine that way." His fingers danced over the controls on the console.

"For a child barely off your mother's breast, your wisdom surprises me," I replied.

Maybe Eos was right.

Finding our fate was something we would do on Prometheus.

She certainly found hers.

She'd probably never leave the ship without her mate. She enjoyed technology, and so does he.

Two peas in a pod.

At least I don't have to bear through her jabbering on about it anymore.

"You sure you won't be leaving the ship?" I inquired to assure myself of his relinquishment.

"No, I can't," he sighed, "We only have three shifters. Ixis, Adrian, and myself. Ixis is on Odyssey, Adrian will never leave my mother's side again," he shrugged, "...and he shouldn't. So, my place is here. Whatever I do, whether there's a battle, there's a planet, or whatever it is, for me, it's gonna happen here, on Prometheus."

He turned back to pierce me with his icy blue eyes. "My mom doesn't believe in all the fate crap. At least she says she doesn't." His face darkened. "I can hear everyone's thoughts. She knows something more is at work here."

He pulled at his bangs, making them stick straight out from his head again.

It must be a nervous habit.

"When we finally reach Elysium, and they go down to the planet, go with them. It could become our home. You can see those oceans you've been longing for." He turned back to the console.

I slapped him on the back "I didn't know you could read everyone's mind." I said as I was tightening my walls.

He shook his head, "Sorry, that shit wouldn't work. Throw up all the walls you want. It works against other people. Doesn't work against me. The only way for me not to hear you is to stop listening," he drolled.

That's frightening.

"Where is my mother?"

He went still for a moment, then he looked back at me. "She's on Odyssey but should be back here in a couple hours. She'll contact me and ask for a shift. Go down the main corridor about seven doors. On the left are your mother's quarters. I think the one next to it's empty. If you want to move your stuff from Odyssey, just let me know."

I thought about the few items I still had on Odyssey and made my decision.

This ship was as good as the other.

There were fewer distractions, "I'll inform you when I'm ready to move my things. Just because you plan on waiting for your fate to find you on the bridge of this ship, it doesn't mean you shouldn't train. I'm sure Charon installed an exercise arena. Meet me there in one Earth hour, as it probably will take me that long to find it. I'll show you some real swordplay, so you can stop the -- how do they say, *half-ass* sword work technique Hercules teaches."

He belted out a laugh, throwing his head back.

"Sure, *grandfather*, I'll go spar with you in about an hour. Course, if I get to the gym and you haven't made it there yet, I'll just shift you." He waggled his eyebrows at me.

I let the threat hang and left the bridge, following the hallway with the black spider-like crystalline along the walls.

Counting the doors, I found my mother's. She scrawled her symbol onto the surface. They were simple hearthstones. I certainly didn't want to intrude.

I strolled on by to the next door. It opened easily enough. I was sure that all the quarters on the ship looked pretty much the same.

I went inside and all at once felt a desire to see horses.

The horses on Earth didn't exist on Themian worlds. I missed the scent of them and the feel of their muscles under my hand. No matter how long I'd lived away from Earth, these feelings never went away.

That longing for a life I can never have.

I moved a few chairs around and played with some of the panels in an effort to make the space mine.

A tap came to the door, "May I come in?"

It was a feminine voice. The door slid to the side and revealed a blond and beautiful woman. I instantly recognized her.

Sydney!

She had a deep penetrating stare that reminded me of Tristan's. It's probably where he got it from.

"I hear Professor Michelson is now your brother-in-law," she remarked, and her glaze trailed around the room only to land on me again.

"Yes, so it would seem. I'm happy for my sister," but my automatic response didn't fool her.

She cocked a brow in disbelief. "Are you going to stay on Prometheus with her?" She inquired with a shrug.

It was an obvious probe for information. I waved her to a chair, and she sat down.

"No, I'm not staying on Prometheus for Eos. She doesn't need me. Your son Tristan said something about my mother being unprotected. And how a man divided can only protect one love. Hercules has your daughter, so I'm here for my mother." It was the best excuse. I could hide my aimless mind behind this curtain of order.

Sydney nodded her head, "I was hoping you'd say that. I'm glad we're of one mind. I thought I'd need to convince you." She kept nodding her head, "Your mom needs somebody to watch her back." She leaned forward, putting her elbows on her knees, looking up at me while clasping her hands. "Now, I do have a job for you."

I leaned back into the wall and crossed my ankles, "You are the lady with the plan. What would you have me do?"

Whatever it is, it will keep my mind off my aimless wanderlust.

"Board the Phedrain's ship and talk to every person there. Find out who's actually been on Elysium and seen it from outer space. We need a visual." She puffed her bangs out of her face. "Sorry, six years in space trying to get to Elysium doesn't sound fun. Do you want to sit around on Prometheus for the next six years, waiting for something to happen while watching your mother and your sister?" She asked.

Sydney went right for the jugular. I had no intention of waiting around, and she could see it. I would do anything to get off any of these ships.

Ares was already having his adventures. To him, building an army was fun. Hercules had his adventure and won the greatest prize there is to be had. Hephaestus would be eternally happy as long as Sydney or Emmaline gave him work to do.

And there's plenty to do, from what I can see.

But if Tristan was right and Sydney intended to head directly to the surface, that sounded like a quest I'd be interested in.

"And when I find this someone who's seen Elysium?" I let the end of the sentence hang in the air.

"Contact your mother." She stood up and pretended to dust herself off, although nothing here appeared dirty.

She put her hand on my shoulder, "I'm sure several people have already told you; I don't believe in fate or any of that mumbo-jumbo bullshit. But I'm pretty sure if you come with us down to Elysium whatever you are looking for, you'll find it there." She awkwardly patted my shoulder.

"That doesn't sound ominous," I remarked.

She smiled, "Yeah, it didn't sound the least bit ominous. Suck it up, Buttercup! Head down to the gym. My son's waiting for you. Adrian's there too. The boys want to play." She winked at me.

I waited for her to exit my quarters, then kicked over a chair, slamming it against the wall. It gave a satisfying crunch. One of the arms lay on the floor not far from the main body of the chair. I stalked over and righted the chair. The lopsided frame glared at me. There weren't many one-armed chairs. This one was now officially mine.

Prometheus wasn't like Odyssey. You couldn't just ask the ship where to go. I wandered away from the bridge.

At some point, I should find the gym.

Where ever that was.

CHAPTER 3

PERSEUS

"Shifting you now!"

To say that the Phaedran ship was a rust bucket would've been kind. I'd seen Greek wood warships that were more stable than this pile of scrap metal.

Judging from modern human history, Elysium may have been a space-faring race, but their technology was no more than 100 or so years ahead of humanity.

"Who are you? Why are you here?" The man who confronted me had one eye sewn shut. The medical treatment was no better than in ancient Greece. The eyelid puckered at the outer edge as if the flesh was stretched too far.

A sailor would have done a better job.

The lack of proper medical care on Phaedra angered me.

The treatment of these people bordered on cruelty.

If their crimes were so great, why not kill them outright and be done with their evil?

To provide poor care for prisoners or slaves did no more than reveal the lack of honor the Judges of the Underworld had.

The man with the mangled eye held a rod in his left hand, and the smell of fear wreaked from him.

"I am Perseus, son of Hera and Zeus. The Fates sent me. I'm here to interview everyone," I replied, staring him down.

Most men and all women would have looked away. The sight of his puckered eye socket would have sickened them.

The gruesome visage strikes fear into the heart of all.

I had no such fears. I'd face death many times before I was exiled. The wounds of war didn't disturb me.

A man should never shy away from the bald realities of conflict.

The room resembled a cockpit, yet I doubted that was its use. There was no pilot seat.

Maybe some kind of research and tactical room?

I gleaned all of this from just one glance.

The one-eyed man before me was joined by six of his fellow shipmates, all carrying a menacing glare. Their hackles were up, and I was the cause.

Perhaps *interview* was not the correct word.

I should choose my words with better care.

These people were closer to humans in behavior.

Slavery evokes the worst barbarism known to the cosmos.

"You're here to spy on us," the one-eyed man stated. "Sydney said we would be left to our own devices. Unless we choose to be judged," he growled as his initial fear bled away in the presence of his cohorts, bolstering his resolve.

"And you will be. I'm not here to judge anyone. I'm not even here to find out what your names are. None of that matters. Your business is your own. Sydney promised you'd be safe." I opened my hands to reveal my lack of weapons. Not that any of the six men could have stopped me if I chose to kill every one of them.

My offer of peace should be well met. "I'm not here to interfere with your lives in any fashion. Sydney asked me to speak with the original sinners?" I posed it as a question only because the truth that came with that statement chilled me. "People who have actually been to Elysium. Those are the only people I want to converse with, and if they have no desire to speak to me, I will abide by their wishes." I bowed my head enough to show deference without letting my guard down. I didn't want to be caught unaware just because I was being polite.

"Only those who've been to Elysium?" the one-eyed man asked and stepped back. His head tilted to the side, allowing his one eye to fully take me in. Then his one remaining eye shifted left and right to his compatriots.

"Yes. Anyone who's actually seen Elysium from space," I clarified.

Just passing from the planet to a ship won't be enough.

"There are some from Elysium," he whistled, "Seeing the planet from space, that is another issue..."

I repressed an unbidden smile.

Themians don't whistle. Not even the children.

The sound was a welcome respite from the tension that laced the tight quarters.

"Many of us were transported in a prison ship with no windows," he spat, and the resentment oozed from every word. The anger was deep and palpable.

Yet, he didn't seem interested in telling me why he lost his eye for all his bitter resentments.

When I was a child, it was commonplace on Earth for people to have slaves and for their children to be enslaved also. These people were enslaved for crimes. War causes people to overrun one another.

The strong prey on the weak. You want to be bitter, be bitter. If you want to live, live, these are the only choices.

The whys of the situation were irrelevant. We needed action, "If we don't find someone who's actually seen Elysium from space, we will be in space for six years." I cocked a brow at the group to emphasize my distaste, "Now, I don't know about you or how long you're going to live. But I do know that I don't want to spend the next six years on this spacecraft." I hooked my thumb at the dead console, "Your craft is even less space worthy than the one that's holding it." I didn't want to run down the chances of them surviving six years on this pile of dung. It was low.

"Come of your own free will. Tell me what you know. Better yet, show me what you know. Dig something out of this ship. It doesn't have to be a star chart for Elysium. It just needs to get us close."

The single eye narrowed at me.

"There is one person who's seen Elysium."

I whirled around to face the voice of a small sickly man. His shoulders were large, but the meat hung off of them, unable to cling to the bone.

"Take me to this person," I requested with as much control as I could muster.

I moved to follow him when a hand clasped my shoulder and yanked me around. The one-eyed man stared me down.

"Remove your hand before you lose it," I growled.

"We will bring them to you. You're not welcome to wander our ship as if it was your own. This is our home."

Any additional threats dried on my tongue, and a hot flush rushed over me. To barge into a person's home uninvited was rude.

I replied, "I was quick to jump to conclusions about your motives. I'm sorry." I nodded my head to him out of respect. "You haven't introduced yourself, although I have. Generally, when you enter someone's home, you know who they are." My manners had atrophied with the lack of use. My mind began to grope for any way to reclaim my honor in the eyes of the Phaedrans.

He stepped back and laughed dryly while scratching his chin, "We are slaves. Manners are not something that our parents focused upon."

Somehow, I thought that was a lie. There was so much more to this one-eyed man than a lack of manners.

"My name is Erik, Erik with one eye. This is our home. We would prefer you not run around snooping. We are still settling in ourselves." He shrugged as if that answer should have allayed all my questions. "Kelan will bring you this person. You are welcome to sit in any of these chairs and wait. But do not leave this room or attempt to. That will provoke us." Erik's threat was more posturing than actual poison.

I understood him. It's rude to wander around someone's house, especially when you aren't invited.

Sydney foisted me upon them with no warning.

"I am sorry to barge into your home. Sydney should've told you I was coming. I'll make sure that it doesn't happen again."

Erik tipped his head and left the room. The others followed.

There were two men stationed outside the door, watching me. They could watch all they wanted. I leaned my head back and looked up at the ceiling.

The metal plates overhead were barely fused together, if you could call it that. They'd used a type of pop rivet. There was no welding in the plating. Certain pieces of metal were butted against each other, held in place by ribbing.

The whole ship might shake apart at any moment.

The electrical grid fluctuated, causing the lights to dim and brighten. I got up and walked around, inspecting the room. There were tactical displays.

At one time, this was a gunship.

The displays were powered down. Some were cracked, others foggy with age.

They were made from a form of polymer-plastic. I ran a finger across the screen and tried to push one of the buttons. The pressure cracked the surface, and it crumbled away, exposing the circuit board underneath. I rubbed the tip of my index finger to my thumb.

This ship is literally falling apart.

Maybe that was why they left it on Astrondel. They didn't think anyone would be able to use it to get anywhere, or they would die trying.

A tap rang on the door a moment before it slid open.

"She's not been with us long," the old man murmured.

In walked a young girl, no more than 16. She was missing most of the lower half of her right arm, and she clasped it to her body as if to hide it. Her eyes darted around the room like an animal. She immediately ducked behind the sickly old man, Kelan.

"It's okay, Laza. He's not going to harm you. He only wants to talk. So, we can get you the care you need for your arm," he soothed her with a low tone.

She shook her head and backed away until her back hit the wall.

I moved opposite her and sat down.

Maybe if I wasn't so tall, I wouldn't be as imposing.

"Kelan says you've seen Elysium — from space?"

She glanced at the man, then her eyes darted back to me, and she nodded her head.

"Can you tell me how you lost your arm?" I inquired.

Tears filled her eyes. She opened her mouth to speak, and a choking sound filled the room as her throat worked to answer. She swallowed, "They took it. My family was poor, and my omare sold me to the Judges. They take girls - none of them are ever heard from again. They bought me because I was pretty." Her tears were falling like a river now, and she choked on her words.

Anger rose inside of me, "Your mother sold you?" She nodded her head, wiped her eyes with the back of her single hand, and then used her palm to wipe the other cheek.

"Yes, my omare sold me. She couldn't take care of my brothers and sisters. It was my idea, actually; it was either that, or I go live on the streets. They couldn't afford to take care of me anymore. I told her I'd be better off being sold to the Judges," she shrugged, "at least she would get something for me. So, she took me to Rhadamanthys. He purchased me for more money than she'd ever make in 10 years, and at first, it was wondrous." She stopped to swallow, her eyes darting around the room. She didn't want to meet my eyes.

"They fed me and clothed me and braided my hair. Everyone who is sold to the Judges is presented. I went and met one of the Judges. He didn't even look at me. He didn't spare a glance for any of us," she sniffled.

I wanted to ask more questions, but I held my tongue. Obviously, she wanted to tell me. If I pushed her, she might clam up, and then where would we be?

I needed to find that world.

It's the only way to kill this evil man.

"He was eating grapes. They were red. He didn't like any of us. He waved a hand and said, '*have them recycled.*'" Her voice quivered. She sniffed her nose to keep the moisture from running down her face. Kelan moved behind her and put his hands on her shoulders. He petted her hair like a father would and murmured in her ear.

Her words struck me.

Recycled? What does that mean?

"I thought he meant that we would be cleaning the garbage on one of the garbage worlds." She shook her head, and her lower lip trembled. "They rounded us all up and put us on a ship to one of the Elysium laboratories." Her whole body shook.

My jaw was locked down to keep the stream of words I was dying to release inside. I gripped the armrest on the chair, locking my muscles in position.

"We were divided into blood type groups. I was put in with the ARS. That's my type. I didn't know that." Her teeth chattered, and her hands clasped her half arm in an effort to hold it still. "We were taken out in groups. I didn't know any of the girls. I hadn't conversed with anyone on the flight. I didn't have anything to say." She swallowed, and her chest heaved with terror. "They took us out of the space bus and into one of the space stations orbiting the planet." Her eyes trailed over the console and back to the table in the middle of the room. "I thought we'd be going to a dormitory to choose our beds and get ready for the day's work."

She bit her lip and shook her head, "They didn't take us to the dormitory at all. They took us into a big room, and then they filled it with some kind of gas, and it put everyone to sleep except for me. I don't know why I didn't sleep. I had a stuffy nose." She ran the back of her hand across her nose. "Maybe, I didn't breathe enough of it in."

Now, she is making excuses for living.

I'd seen this before. Men in battle often make up reasons why they lived when others didn't.

Guilt comes with such thoughts.

"I felt a little groggy, but I didn't go to sleep. Everyone else passed out on the floor." She finally looked up at me. "*They* came in and started picking girls up and taking them away. Every time they came back, there was more blood on their uniforms. When it was my turn, I was too tired to fight them." She stared me down hard. Her entire body was as rigid as mine. "When we reached the room, they were taking everyone... that's when I saw what was really going on. There was a pile of bodies on one side of the room and a wall of refrigerated storage drawers on the other. A man picked up the girl who was on the table ahead of me and tossed her to one side. As they began to put me on the table, I realized that if I laid down, I would never get up. It struck me that everyone was dead." She moved in closer to me, and her voice rose with her movement.

Our eyes aligned.

"I fought them, and I kicked them, and one of the doctors cut off my right arm. And blood squirted out everywhere, but I managed to get a hold of the saw, and I swung it like a weapon. I escaped," she shook her head, "Operating room. That's what it said on the door. A lot of alarms were going off, and I was bleeding. I passed another room labeled as an *operating room*. I ducked in and found a healing spray of some kind. It said for blood. So, I sprayed it on my arm, and my arm stopped bleeding. I hid in there for a couple hours until I realized that the side of the room where they had been piling bodies in the other room was a shoot. I hit the button for it, and I slid down into an area that looked like it might be near an incinerator for trash. I climbed inside one of the trash ships that was going to Phaedra, and that's how I escaped."

She was yelling. "I thought I was gonna be free. I didn't know it was just another prison."

Every word was like hot iron, dropping in the pit of my stomach. They were killing children for body parts, and she only managed to escape because she hid with the trash.

<Perseus, what's wrong? >

<Eos, you were right. It was in our fate to come here. Prometheus is the right place for us. I know what I need to do. >

My sister didn't ask any more questions. When I looked at Laza, at her missing arm, and the way her body trembled with fear, my nostrils flared with my anger.

These judges are evil, and their rule has to come to an end somehow.

"Laza, are you willing to come with me to Odyssey to meet Sydney, my mother, and Isolde? They are the Fates!"

She wiped away some of her tears, swallowed hard, and took a deep breath. "I'm ready to meet my Fate. I know I haven't done anything wrong, so if they want to judge me, I'm sure I'll survive. I won't be like others. I didn't commit any crime. I'm not here because I was bad. Will you do anything about Rhadamanthys?" she asked, her lip trembling in fear.

"Yes, I vouch for it on my honor. If you help us get to Elysium, I will kill him. What they're doing is evil, and I will put a stop to it."

She managed a tight smile and nodded her head, "Take me to the Fates! I'm ready!"

I shook her remaining hand.

<Eos, tell Tristan that myself and this girl, Laza, are ready to be shifted. He can take us to Odyssey.>

<Yes, brother.>

In a blink of an eye, the pressure changed, and a quick pop later, we landed on the bridge of Odyssey.

I smiled to myself, "Ixis, are you now doing work for my grandson?"

Ixis didn't rise to the bait. "I do whatever is required."

Emmaline snorted, "Don't be a fool, Perseus! Ixis has been playing with your kind for thousands of years longer than you've been alive. Anyway, if you want to bait someone, I'm your Huckleberry. Now, I do believe the Fates are waiting in the adjoining room for you and whatever information you brought back," she smirked and took in the pretty girl next to me.

"You must be Laza. I'm Emmaline. You'll be safe here."

Laza stepped behind me. It was a different world, certainly than the one she'd been born into.

"Let's get this done! The sooner you give the fates what they want, the sooner Rhadamanthy can get what he deserves." I indicated an archway.

She swallowed and bobbed her head.

CHAPTER 4

SYDNEY

Perseus found it, them, her. My focus was so tight I forgot that people were actual beings. Laza had not only seen Elysium from space, but she even knew the coordinates for it on an Elysium chart. I was impressed with her fortitude.

I only wished we could do more for her.

It burned me up inside.

Using people for spare parts is disgusting.

Rhadamanthy would pay for this. I didn't know if all the judges were in on it, but it didn't really matter. Nothing I had heard about them gave me any hope that the others were better.

I went on and sent a mass message, <I wanted everyone to know we were about to shift to Elysium.>

I had no idea what would happen once we got there, yet my gut told me it wasn't going to be the panacea we were all looking for.

"We are all exiles, and we're all family and friends. In the end, we all want the same thing - freedom, home, safety. We're about to make the final jump. The reason we can do this now is because we found someone who had the coordinates for Elysium. You might've heard a lot of things about Elysium. Some good, some bad, I'm here to tell you that no matter what happens, we are together in this, and we will keep each other safe. We are not at war. We're looking for friendship and alliances. To our friends from Phaedra, thank you for joining us. We're happy to have been able to help you. Freedom is more important than anything. Freedom is the choice to choose. You chose to come with us. To my fellow hybrids, I know we didn't have the choice to stay not without changing who we were on the most basic fundamental level. However, we are here, and every choice we've made since we left Earth has brought us to this one final place - to our origins, to where it all started, where our true ancestors come from. So, without further ado, Tristan, Ixis, take us home!"

Emmaline's hand slipped over my shoulder. Our ship slipped into subspace, warping the stars in the window as we moved through the cosmos. One moment we were staring at Dido and her rejected lover with Phaedra nearby. The next moment, we were floating next to a blue gas giant. It was indescribably beautiful. A single planet blotted out some of the giant light as it moved through the system.

I waited for the pregnant moment to burst and the next problem to descend upon us. Instead, a gorgeous golden star moved out from behind the gas giant to reveal itself and its two sisters. I gasped.

The golden fields of Elysium... It looks like the sun can never go down.

<Mom, I think you need to get over here. > Tristan called.

I looked from Isolde to Adrian and the world blurred as Adrian shifted us. A moment later, I was standing on the bridge of Prometheus.

"What?"

He didn't say anything, instead, he pointed to the missing wall panel. There, sitting on a double-wide ivory throne, were a man and a woman with glassy eyes.

His hair was jet black, and his beard ran down his chest. He was handsome and chiseled, yet something about him looked remotely familiar.

The woman was beautiful in the classic sense. She was how I imagined a Greek Goddesses would look. She wore a white A-line tunic   draped down her body in folds. She had large earrings which dangled from her lobs, tickling her shoulders. Her hair was braided, twisted, and thrown up into chignon with curls dripping down the back.

They were holding hands.

The image of them took my breath away, "who are they?"

"They are whoever Pythia put inside the wall to wait."

"Prometheus, who are the people on the throne?"

"Hades and Persephone, son and daughter-in-law of Pythia, the Oracle, brother to Poseidon, the new leader to the underworld."

My head tilted back on my neck as my eyebrows pulled down, creating a crease between my eyes.

"What the fuck is he talking about, mom?"

"I don't know, Issy, but we don't need to say *fuck* so often, do we?"

"Sydney, you do say it rather often," Adrian remarked.

"I have waited a long time to be here to meet my fate." My head whipped back to the black-haired man as he stood up. His right hand held the hand of his bride. In his other hand, he was cradling some kind of helmet with horns.

"Excuse me."

In my mind, I heard his voice. He didn't boom, and he wasn't demanding. He talked in a matter-of-fact kind of way.

"You are the Fates. My mother placed my bride and myself here to await you. You must be Sydney. I am your uncle Hades."

Isolde gripped my hand and whispered low into my ear, "Mom, I could touch him. I could find out everything."

I shook my head slightly, "You say that the Oracle placed you there?"

"Yes, my mother had the gift of sight before she left Elysium. She was a seer. My grandfather imprisoned her. I do not know why. However, she managed to free herself. She found Charon and his friends. Together they hatched a plan to leave. Only not everything worked out as they intended. After my brother and I were born, my mother had a vision, and she shared it with me. I trusted my mother, and I loved her more than anyone." He glanced back at the woman seated on the chair, her delicate hand clasped in his, "That was until I met Persephone. We were the first to be mated. My mother proclaimed it a miracle. It was only then that she told me of my fate - I was to meet you. She indeed said I would have to wait a long time. I couldn't be parted from my bride, so she built this chamber for us and put us to sleep. And now, I stand before you. I know you are the Fates. If you wish to judge me, you are welcome, as I have nothing to hide."

I could hear the truth of his words. There was nothing about what he had said that was a lie. Even when he called himself my uncle, he was not lying.

Just because he believes it, it doesn't make it the truth. It just means he wasn't lying.

The woman stood up, "I joined the crew of Prometheus, knowing I had no family. Yet, here I stand with a husband and surrounded by family. There is no dream more worthy than being surrounded by one's loved ones." She came and immediately hugged me and Isolde.

Issy stiffened as her ability flooded into her. Persephone had no idea what she was doing to Isolde. I couldn't thrust the woman away. She spent millions of years locked behind a wall panel, frozen, waiting for love?

<You'd do the same for me, wouldn't you, beautiful girl?>

<You know I would. I know you did for me.>

She stepped back into the grasping arms of her husband.

"She's not lying, mom. Neither of them is. Pythia put them there, and... Poseidon is your father."

I shook my head, "Sorry, but without a DNA test, I think I'm going to hold off on agreeing with anybody on being the daughter of Poseidon, God of the Sea. No offense, but I don't see how Mr. I'm wielding a big damn trident being my biological changes anything. And so far, my luck with fathers has been between suck and shitty. I will pass on this opportunity. Thanks"

"Your mother's name is Mary. Is it not?"

My head whipped around to stare Hades down. He knew it was true.

There's no way he could've known my mother's name

"Yes, so?"

"Your name is Sydney Rhiannon O'Dear. You are my niece. You are Poseidon's daughter. My mother foretold that you would come, that you'd be a Fate, and that you'd bring justice to this unjust world."

"Okay, let's get things straight. First of all, I don't believe in the Fates shit. And even if you do know my whole name, it doesn't mean anything. As for bringing justice, I have no idea what you're talking about. Unless you're talking about the Judges of Elysium, who sound like pretty big assholes. Then, yes, your people should rise up and absolutely kill them."

"It is impossible for Elysiums to rise up against a God," he replied, his eyes clear and without guile.

With a smirk, I continued, "Really? Well, I'm not Elysium. I'm half-human. We're well known for not only rising up against our Gods but also tearing down any governmental construct that we think sucks ass. So, if that's the kind of justice your people are looking for, yeah, I got a whole ship full of people probably pretty happy to make it happen for you. However, that's not what we came here for. We came to make alliances and hopefully find a Homeworld."

"You cannot come to the underworld and join Elysium without facing the Judges. Persephone and I will wait here while you attempt to enact your dream. Where is Perseus?"

I sputtered for a moment.

What the fuck? How does he know everybody's name? Of course, he knows everyone's name! If your mother's the all-knowing Oracle and can see the future, why wouldn't you know everyone's name? Duh!!

The cold hand of fate ran down my back. He knew everyone's name!

Did Poseidon know them too? Did he go to Earth on purpose?

With a dry mouth, I glanced from Isolde to Hera, to Adrian.

<All questions for another day, beautiful girl. Now, you need to focus on the task at hand. We need to go down to the planet and make a peace treaty with these Judges.>

<What? Put on a brave face and do my job? > I asked with a sour taste in my mouth.

<And you do it so well. >

I gave him a half-smile as Hera's son stepped into the cockpit, stealing all the oxygen as he did.

CHAPTER 5

PERSEUS

All mythological stories from Earth spoke of Hades, the crazy old guy living underground. They said that he tricked his wife into marrying him. Human stories were such a complete fabrication. But then again, the Themian stories from my childhood were not much different.

Hades, the Lord of the Underworld, was sitting on a white throne, with his bride, Persephone, by his side.

My mind froze when I saw him standing there, holding his helmet and her hand.

Wedged into the wall cavity was a reclining stasis chamber. Persephone was sitting up in the white capsule, looking as young and refreshed as if she'd only slept for a few hours. The clear crystalline lid disappeared into the deep recesses of the hull cavity.

Thinking about it now, the only reason to consider the stasis container to be a throne was its reclining shape.

My insides quaked. The difference was a trifle, yet the context changed my perception in the extreme. The spider web-like circuity laced the outside of the blue lite chamber.

The deep dark stories of my childhood have come to life to haunt me.

Mother was visibly trembling. She muttered something to Sydney. However, her words were lost on me.

Tristan scratched his ears. He was probably receiving an ear full from all the minds in the room.

Suddenly, the man gazed around the room and said my name. "Where is Perseus?"

We collectively gasped, and I found my feet cemented to the floor.

Pythia closed her child up in a wall for over 2 million years.

And yet, he knows my name.

I didn't care what Sydney, Isolde, or Mother thought. They were the Fates. But something brought us all here.

Eos said my fate was to be on this ship, that it was necessary.

She saw the future. Of course, only in dreams and only bits and pieces. Nevertheless, Eos was right.

And here was Hades calling my name.

My tongue worked its way around inside my dry mouth. I searched for the proper words to fill this momentous moment. I was not clever with words like Hercules or capable of war with my lips. I was the forthright son with no guile of any kind. Rather than mentally sift for a pithy response, I offered the simplest answer that came to mind.

"I am Perseus, son of Hera and Zeus!" I proclaimed. I ran my tongue around inside my maw to gather as much saliva as could be found. Readying myself for the next barrage, I pressed my lips together to further spread the moisture.

The man in front of me released the hand of his bride and placed it on my shoulder. His cheekbones rose up in a partial smile that was hidden by a heavy beard. "I have something for you." The ease of his smile was meant to take the steel from my spine, "I've waited a long time to give it to you. I made it for you." His deep cobalt blue eyes pierced me. "And you will need it in the days to come. Use it wisely, and don't lose it." His words carried a dark tone that vibrated in my bones.

He handed me the golden helmet he had under his arm.

It only appeared golden at a distance. It was really just the yellowing of the crystalline technology that was embedded in it. It gave off a sheen, and then it struck me.

Of course - Orichalcum, the metal of the gods!

The very metal that all of Themian technology was lined in.

"Thank you, Hades! What am I to do with this great gift?" I asked, perplexed, then closed my mouth to keep the feeling of awe that engulfed me at bay.

He replied swiftly. "Keep it with you always." His brow pulled down, and his features darkened, "When the time comes, you will know what to do. Also, stay close to your mother's side."

My forehead pinched.

He meant that I was to protect my mother.

Why did he say it? He did not mean it as a threat.

He released my shoulder and took back the hand of his bride. Her serene smile was infectious.

She gazed at everyone in the room, then she leaned over and squeezed my shoulder, "Good, Perseus! We have waited a long time to see you." Her words struck me as being fatalistic.

"Alright! Let's get this show on the road!" Sydney snapped, "We're here, and apparently, we've awakened the Lord of the Underworld." Her obtuse attitude raked over the situation like turning hot coals to fresh tinder. "There are three judges to go say hello to and a peace treaty to try and get out. Since everybody's had a good night's sleep and no one's tired from the shift, except Ixis, who is not joining us? Tristan, you're staying here, aren't you?" she inquired.

"Yep, I'm here if you need me," he remarked and pulled at the hair hanging over his eyes.

Tristan would listen to all of us, like the little eavesdropping half-breed he is.

I can't say that I wouldn't listen in too.

Flipping it around, I realized that kind of ability could be a blessing and a terrible burden at the same time. He winked at me just as I was thinking about it.

<It is a blessing and amusing, all at the same time. You can give me a shout-out, and I'll send in the calvary.> Tristan used a word that took me some time to decipher. In the end, the message was clear - '*I will guard your back.*'

I took comfort in that. Tristan was a young one of his word.

<Just please don't send Ares. Not unless you plan to start a planetary war.> I replied with a knowing smirk.

His mental chuckle washed over me with a deep and reverberating flash. I could almost feel it in my own chest. He understood Ares, the son of Hera you send when you don't want anyone to survive.

I think the humans referred to it as a neutron bomb.

That was the term Hercules used, and I agreed - Ares was an explosion waiting to happen.

I went and took my place next to Mother. She reached for my hand, so I moved Cytec, the helmet, under my arm. By doing so, I realized I wasn't armed. "Mother, we can't go just yet. We are not properly armed. Adrian, Hercules!"

"He's right, beautiful girl. I don't care if you do think we're going to negotiate a treaty or some kind of refugee status. Going down unarmed to a strange planet after what we've heard about the judges would be foolish," Adrian said.

A moment later, a belt rested around my waist pulled down by the weight of a sword in its scabbard. Hercules once again wore his crossed leather braces and his leather kilt.

"Thank you, son!" Adrian smirked.

A set of crossed scabbards covered Adrian's back. The handles were white and bound in heavy leather, carved to look like the heads of a serpent on the pommel.

I cocked an eyebrow at him.

A sheepish smile peeled across his face, "When I killed the Khimera, I took the horns of the goat."

I nodded in understanding.

A trophy from a hard fight is better than any metal a country could bestow. Plus, twice as useful as it will instill fear into any enemy.

He cocked his head to the side and leaned in, "If you could find a better weapon with a sharper edge, please point the way," Adrian pulled one and allowed me to inspect the edge.

It spiraled like a drill from the old world, yet it was as sharp as an old woman's tongue and twice as hard.

They truly were a thing of beauty. The heads, in fact, resembled the head of the Dragon from Khimera. I handed him his monstrous weapon back reluctantly.

"The next monster we kill, I get to keep for my own personal weapon," I chuckled.

I was hopeful there would be a next monster and found I was looking forward to not only the fight but the thrill of the battle.

He threw back his head and laughed, "You're the great and wonderful Perseus. Why would I stand in the way of you receiving your own trophies?" he demanded, and mirth colored his reply. "Mine was hard-won. I would've kept the tail, but your brother thrust into the creature's chest. There wasn't much left of it."

Adrian's tail of the battle was well known on both ships. Though the telling was done by Hercules, leaving me to wonder the truth of it.

"The tip of its tail looked like a halberd spear. It was made of some kind of lead-like metal, and it turned molten."

I glanced at Hercules. He gave me the '*I told you so*' look. I snorted at him.

He lies so easily even the truth sounds like a fable.

"We killed it from inside," Adrian finished with a little preamble.

"If you boys are done telling your big fishy war stories, can we get on with it? I've got an alliance to forge and people who want to see an ocean, and maybe some mountains, before they die," Sydney snarled as She had no time for levity.

This, I can understand.

Adrian chuckled under his breath, "Of course, beautiful girl!"

Now, it was my turn to laugh. He always called her that. I was sure that he meant it, as she was a beautiful woman.

He never said it with disdain. But every now and again, he said it to shut her up.

And she lets him.

Adrian was the only person I had ever seen that could talk her into something she didn't want to do. And the only person I'd ever seen stopping her too.

Jealousy rose up in my chest. I glanced from Hades holding his bride's hand to Hercules with his Isolde. He was carrying fate in his hands.

Envy and jealousy are wrong.

I knew that. But when I looked at them, all I could see was something I didn't and couldn't have.

It's uncharitable of me.

I pushed the feelings away, hoping they would lose their edge or I could just keep them far enough to be out of reach. Yet, the wound they cut was sharp and deep.

Mother placed her hand on my shoulder and whispered in my ear. "Remember, Perseus, everyone has their time."

I turned to her. A dark sadness clouded her eyes. My own mother hadn't found true love. My father used her.

And here I was, complaining about my lot in life.

When I should be following her example.

She'd never given up hope. She'd never turned away from the righteous and hard path. That was always the path she chose. She never backed down, no matter what it cost her.

I quirked a half-smile, then pushed my mouth to the side. "You're right, mother! Everyone has their day. Let's go find our people a home!"

Focusing on the greater issue at hand and not my petty feelings was a better use of my time.

She patted me on the shoulder and gave me one of her pressed smiles.

From the other side of the room, Sydney shot us a glance of 'shut up and let's go, we got work to do'.

CHAPTER 6

SYDNEY

I hadn't told anyone my plans, other than Adrian, of course. It was not like I could keep a secret from him anyway.

Laza's horror story shook me more than I'd have liked to admit. Going directly to the Judges of Elysium was a bad idea. Or so I thought. Spy-craft was just that - a craft.

One we need to use to our advantage.

Other than our clothing, and perhaps the fact that Perseus insisted upon bringing weapons, we wouldn't look any different than the Elysians. This way, we had a chance to blend in and get the lay of the land, see for ourselves how the people were ruled.

I didn't like taking one person's point of view on anything.

For all I know, Laza is totally whacked.

Though my heart told me that wasn't true, I had to follow my head. I was not risking everyone's safety based on a feeling.

The shifting room on Odyssey was strangely empty when Adrian shifted me over. Relief washed through me. Emmaline was the one person I *had* to talk to about anything that had to do with the ships.

"Emmaline?" I tilted my head at one of the dreamwalk couches, and she moved to join me.

In a low voice, I said, "I want to turn on the obscure-a."

"I'll have Tristan move Prometheus, so Odyssey is in between the planet and the ship," she replied. The obscure-a shield would hide both ships, making them look like the cosmos.

I heaved a sigh. Emmaline was quick. I loved that about her.

She may have a sharp tongue, but she's got a mind to go with it.

"We will shift away if necessary," she murmured.

I tipped my head down in agreement. She reached out and gave my shoulder a squeeze. "You know we don't need to do this. We could leave, go back through the gates and find a homey planet to make babies on." Her worried smile gave me a second to waver.

We could, we could go back.

But I can't. This must happen.

I swallowed back the taste of bitter resolve. Fate or not, I couldn't walk away if the Judges were tyrants. I couldn't leave anyone to live like that.

It hits too close to home in a very sore spot.

"This isn't a choice. I have to do this," I replied.

"Then, get it done fast, so we can move on." She stared deep into my eyes with her unnerving way, then quickly walked back to the center of the shifting room with her head held high, her heels clicking on the floor.

CHAPTER 7

SYDNEY

A moment later, the pressure changed as Adrian shifted us down to the planet.

It was a park. Isolde and Hercules found it while scanning the surface.

"Where have you brought us, Sydney?" Hera asked.

She never judged. She was always inquisitive.

I glared from Perseus to Hercules, and Isolde, only to settle on Hera.

"You spoke to those slaves and Laza. You heard their stories." I turned and bored into Isolde's eyes, "I'm sure your brother has repeated things he's overheard."

Issy nodded her head. As she found her feet of interest, her fingers laced into each other. Hercules grabbed her hand to still her fidgeting.

"Yes, Sydney, we've all heard the rumors. We know what she went through. But are we here to make peace or war?" Perseus inquired.

I stared them down, meeting each one's questioning eyes. "On Earth," I started, then took a deep breath. "Being raised the way I was, with all the torture Edward put me through...let's just say that I see what subjugation does to people. I understand how it feels to be nothing more than pieces on a chessboard. So, there is no way in hell or heaven, the cosmos or anywhere else, that I am ever going to make some kind of a peace agreement with monsters." Adrian and I were in complete agreement. "Nor will I allow any of our people, whether they're from Phaedra, Earth, or any other world, to set one toe on this planet. I don't give a crap how pretty it is. They're not coming here if I think for one second that their safety isn't 100% assured, at least as much as anyone can be." I waited for a reply of some kind.

"You do realize how arrogant that sounds? Sydney, did you not listen to what people were saying on Phaedra? They don't have abilities. We are already more powerful than they are. We could easily subjugate this planet if we wanted to. Nobody here wants to do that," Hercules replied.

He was right. We had mental abilities that these people lacked. But if even a speck of Laza's story was true, then their leaders were monsters.

My gut told me so, and I couldn't let that go. I couldn't stand by and do nothing, "all I want to do is find out what kind of evil lurks here."

Perseus opened his mouth to speak. I raised my hand and silenced him, "There is evil everywhere. There is no such thing as pure goodness. I know none of these people are human, but evil does lurk in the heart of man whether you're a Themian, an Elysium, a hybrid, or just a plain old Homo sapiens. There is no such thing as perfection. This is why I want to see what kind of rot is here before we make a deal. Of course, we could also leave and find another planet and not look at all."

Perseus' face contorted as if he'd sucked on a lemon. He looked away, feigning a watchful eye on the park.

"Can you turn away from the injustices done to the prisoners on Phaedra and Laza and all of their kind?" I demanded.

I tore my eyes from our crew. Standing in a park to have a fireside chat about morality was dumb.

We should have hashed this out on Prometheus.

I scanned the area furtively for trouble.

"I'm with Sydney. What was done to Laza was evil on the greatest scale. She was probably the only person to ever escape the harvesting facility," Perseus jaw ground down on an emotion I couldn't identify. He turned back to our group and glanced at Hercules before returning to his careful watch. "Don't get me wrong, brother. I have no desire to force my will upon anyone. I am not going to dominate an entire planet. I am not our father, and neither are you," Perseus finished.

He, too, began surveying the area for trouble.

"None of us are our fathers. I'm not Edward, and you're not Zeus. We didn't come here to carry on the sins of our fathers. We came here to make an alliance." Deep in my heart, I knew we came here for something else. I just didn't want to admit what that was.

Adrian grabbed my hand.

I looked at Hera, who had been suspiciously quiet, "Nothing to say?" I asked.

The trees in the park resembled ash and birch. The peeling bark with the ghostly colors lent to the crawling feeling of my skin. The level of technology on this world was well in advance of the one from Earth.

The itching hands and twitchy muscles of all men in our group, Adrian, Hercules, and Perseus, spoke of readiness for danger.

"You are always speaking of how you don't believe in fate, of how you think it's *bullshit*. Well, I believe in it. I do it because every step on my journey has brought me here. And I believe that this journey has brought you, Isolde, and everyone else here because we are right where we are needed." She stared at me while I avoided her inquiring gaze. "We have something to do. You cannot tell me that the waking of Hades and Persephone, at the very moment we reached the orbit of Elysium, was by chance? All the known stories say that Hades, the Lord of the Underworld, slept in a spaceship put there by his mother. Well, guess what? He went willingly." She tore her gaze from me.

Relief washed over me as her heated stare was no longer burning my insides. Hera had a way of making you feel shame for no reason.

I can deny who and what I am, all I want.

I did it for years. Yet, every step on this journey changed me in such a way that I couldn't hide. Not anymore. Actually, it made me realize that I never really could. Her voice cut into my soul.

"You can believe what you want, Sydney. But I believe in us. I believe in Fate. I believe that we are here for a higher reason, something we couldn't possibly understand, and yet we have a role to fulfill." She grabbed my chin and forced me to look at her and listen. "We are not Gods, and I'm not here to pretend to be one. However, if there's a great injustice going on, we are obligated as moral beings to do something about it. I will not turn away from suffering. I will stand up, and I will put a stop to it in any way I can." She looked around, "We have a job to do. And we need to do it right now! I believe our job is to simply mingle as there is something coming. I can feel it." Her fingers curled. She released my chin and moved back.

My fingers, too, tingled with what was coming. I couldn't keep pushing it to the background.

Every step on a journey leads you closer to the objective of that journey.

I squeezed Adrian's hand, "Everyone, keep in contact with Tristan. He's listening." I could feel him smirking in the back of my mind. "We have three days to find out what we can. Regroup back in this park at noon!" I ordered.

Adrian and I headed south. I didn't turn, but I knew Hera and Perseus went west while Isolde and Hercules headed east.

The suns rose a couple of hours later. I was happy to have it on my face. It felt good to walk through the grass or at least what looked like grassy moss. It wasn't quite green. Instead, it was yellow-ish, as if it was starved for iron.

Everything about Elysium carried a golden hue. It was as if it was touched with a lemony-yellow wash.

Adrian pulled my hand to his lips and kissed my fingers.

I couldn't help but smile. "Hopscotch, beautiful girl?" he asked. I smiled, and we shifted only as far as the eye could see - maybe 10 miles.

We were on a rise, looking down into a valley. Nestled in the center was a massive city, buildings reaching towards the sky with a futuristic feel.

I'd say Earth in +80 years.

It reminded me a little bit of Tomorrowland. There weren't any flying cars or jet packs, but the buildings all carried that futuristic groove. The Themian world had an ancient Greek twist, or in the case of Delphi, an ancient Egyptian one. This city was a step into the future, a vision of an Edgar Rice Burroughs story - John Carter on Mars. Only, instead of having a red glow, everything was touched with gold.

We shifted again. A second later, we were outside the base of one of the buildings. It was covered in a golden material that resembled a metal.

Or is it orichalcum?

"Did you get a good look at Perseus' helmet?" I asked.

"Yeah, it's kind of like this," Adrian said and indicated the building. "His helmet had crystalline technology threaded through it," he remarked.

Every answer always brought more questions.

In the early morning light, Elysians walked in the spaces between structures and under overhead bridges. They were dressed in varying styles, none of which matched ours.

A moment later, we were standing in front of a clothing store.

"Do you think we need to change?" I asked with a little giggle.

"Of course, beautiful girl. Anyway, when was the last time I bought you a new outfit?" a smirk hitched Adrian's mug.

I shook my head, "Never. You've never bought me clothes." I wanted to enjoy this small moment, its normalcy, and the intimate nature of Adrian wanting to buy me clothes.

Is this so wrong?

"I'm a terrible husband," he tutted. "Now is a great time to remedy that." His hand found the small of my back, urging me inside.

My heart fluttered. Adrian really was a romantic. Who could turn away from such an offer?

The Elysian in the store spoke with a perfect Themian accent. I never expected them to use English. Hell, I didn't think about language at all.

Gazing at myself in the mirror was a guilty pleasure, so I pushed that feeling away. The fabric felt like silky air that was clinging to my skin as free and easy as clouds floating in the sky.

We were sneaking around and had to blend in.

Red does not blend in.

Part of me wanted to be Jamie Lee Curtis in True Lies with her sexy black dress, while the other part of me wanted to simply wear black and bleed into the shadows.

The red of this dress isn't even a true red. It's golden.

<Shifting you now.> Tristan's voice rang in my mind like a bell.

My eyes adjusted to the blaring light of a beach. In just a blink of an eye, we were standing on the shore of an island. There, in front of me, I could quite clearly see a palace.

My head whipped from left to right. Perseus, Hercules, Isolde, and Adrian all stood close by.

Hera.

"Where the fuck is your mom?" I demanded from Perseus.

"That's why you're here," he growled back at me. His chest was covered in cuts and fast-forming bruises.

"Did anybody learn anything?" I asked, ignoring Perseus and the clear signs of a fight he'd been in.

Issy nodded her head quickly.

<You're at Rhadamanthys Palace. He's the Judge of the East. He has Hera. Somehow, he knew we were here.> Tristan supplied most of the answers I wanted, and a few I wish weren't true.

A loud piercing ring cut the air. My ears ached, making me cover them and shudder. Someone screamed. I coward on the ground, holding my hands to either side of my head.

I squeezed my eyes shut as if the act could help close out the sound scrapping the gray matter out of my head.

Moisture leaked between my fingers from my ears and ran down the side of my face. The drops falling onto the ground were as red as the dress I was wearing.

Blood.

Slowly, the ringing subsided, but my screams didn't. My throat was horse.

A hand caressed my back, "Mom! Mom, it's okay! It's over," Issy whispered with a rough voice.

I could still feel the vibrations in my ears. The sound warped my vision. My daughters' eyes were practically translucent. The only color left was the dark ring around the edge.

"What happened?" I croaked.

"Rhadamanthy is like us. I think I know what Charon did with his gene therapy," Issy shivered.

I, too, shivered at the idea. The name Zeus played over my lips.

"I pushed him back. He's a very strong mom. However, he's been living the easy, cushy life here in his palace. He's not sharp like us." Isolde offered me her hand. I took it and ripped some of the fabric from the bottom of my new dress.

I knew it wouldn't last.

Pretty is a waste of time.

I used the fabric to wipe the blood from my face and ears, then I handed it around so everyone else could wipe it off too.

"Tell your brother to shift down several vials of Primordium," I remarked with a sigh.

"That won't be necessary, beautiful girl," Adrian intervened. His blond hair was plastered to his neck and soaked with blood.

"We need to heal," I replied.

"Remember what Melinda said that *it's like water for them, but it's ambrosia for us*?" He pointed at the ocean of water behind us and smirked.

The lapping waves on the beach promised refreshment. I cupped the salty water and took a drink. The power of Primordium jetted through my system, energizing me instantly.

Elysium...Primordium, the water of life...is just plain water on this planet.

I turned back to face the palace, "How did you fend him off?"

"Remember I told you I figured out how to weave sound, fear, and pain?" Issy asked and then continued, "I used it on the Khimera."

I didn't understand but figured she knew what she was talking about.

"Well, that's what I did, and I threw it back at him. It hurt him enough to stop. I think he is willing to talk now." A satisfied smile lit her face.

Hercules whipped the blood from her neck and moved her hair out of the way to clean her ears.

"And you said you didn't have any defensive abilities... Never underestimate yourself, Isolde. You certainly surprised me often enough," I remarked and gave her my best mom-smile.

Perseus was no worse for the wear. His helmet hung from his belt while his scabbard was empty, leaving him with only a dagger. He stalked away as soon as he stopped drinking, leaving the rest of us to follow.

The beach turned into a rocky berm before we came to a set of stairs flanked by a type of tree. The branches feathered like a hapua fern, providing little shade.

"Before we go any further, can anyone hear Hera?"

Our group stopped as a whole and hung their heads.

<Mom, if I could hear her, you wouldn't be there.> Tristan said.

Perseus seemed to take my question the hardest.

The crest of the stairs stopped at the top and flattened out, revealing massive gardens below. They were some type of maze.

I am in no mood to play games.

I knew what always lies at the center of a maze - trouble or death.

"Adrian, can we just hopscotch, please?"

He quirked a half-smile, and we appeared on the other side of the maze.

A presence permeated the area. He was mentally lurking here in the background, listening, and watching us, seething disappointment floated in the air.

He'd hoped we'd enter his silly maze.

Behind all of that were fear and surprise.

Does he know what shifting is?

Adrian, Hercules, and Perseus brandished their weapons as Isolde, and I moved shoulder to shoulder. The three men kept to the outside, slowly circling as we moved forward. The outer portion of the palace was surrounded by pillars.

CHAPTER 8

HERA

Arms surrounded me from behind, and the golden light of the Elysian star faded from my sight. It was but a moment in the sun. My soul called for it, and it was gone.

I awoke to the face of a man I'd seen in a dreamwalk once. Helios and I had tiptoed through the minds of several members of the High Council when we were young. This face appeared along with a deep-seated terror.

"I don't care what you need to do. Just wake her!" The man shouted as a vein on his forehead stood out from the otherwise smooth brow as he sneered down at me.

Another person in the room raised their hand to strike me. A flush already covered one side of my face when this person angled to hit the other side.

Before the blow could land, I pulled the wind to me and forced the man into the nearest wall. His head hit with a sickening hollow thud. A moment later, I released him, and his body slumped to the floor in a lifeless puddle. For a moment, guilt stabbed me over the death.

"So, you are like me? Interesting." The name to the face rushed to my mind out of the deep recesses of the past - Rhadamanthy. "Put the cuffs on her. We can't have you using whatever powers you have against me, can we?" he chuckled, his robe clinking in time with the movement of his body.

Bans the color of orichalcum snapped over my wrists, and the dull hum of voices that feather my mind was immediately silenced. The sudden loss of the lifelong din lifted a weight I didn't know held me down. What followed was a split second of terror. I was once again cut off from my children.

I blinked to push back the overwhelming emptiness of my mind.

"Now that you are contained, tell me who made you," Rhadamanthy demanded.

My stomach turned.

Charon! He thinks Charon made me. Will we never be rid of that man and his legacy?

"Who are you?" It was better to deflect than to give my enemy ammunition he could later use against me. It also bought me time to swallow the bile that laced the back of my throat.

"I am Rhadamanthy, Judge of the Men of Asia, a onetime Lord of Elysium. You will address me with respect, little one. Now, who made you?" he growled.

I needed only to give him what he already knew to survive. "Charon, he is my originator." It was a stout reply, one seated in the truth, easy to work around and mold. Isolde and Sydney shared enough of Charon's life with me to spread that truth out like butter scraped across toast.

"Charon? Not Anu?" he scoffed at me. "Have they parted ways then?" he waved a hand at me, "No matter. Tell me where to find him so I may kill him."

"I have not seen him in many eons since he left me here." My tone was purposely weak.

"Who were the others in the park? Don't act as if you don't know whom I speak of," Rhadamanthy barked, his heavy robes scraping the floor and setting my teeth on edge.

"My friends," I replied, lowering my head, so the hair that pulled loose from my chiton covered my face, hiding my searching eyes. I took in my position in the room and the placement of the doors and furniture.

The opulence was breathtaking. Every Themian would be in awe of the balance and beauty infused into every detail. The carvings alone took several human lifetimes to create. Orichalcum lined the walls as if painted over the surface for the owner's delight. It shone with its rose gold-colored hue. The use of the alloy took up the station of regular gold on Earth. They were interchangeable.

I found this curious, to say the least.

"Friends are for fools and children. You don't strike me as a child or a fool," Rhadamanthy roared, then smoothed his hair back to control his temper. He took a deep-cleaning breath and plastered a smile on his flawless face.

"Who are these friends, and how do I find them?"

I reached for the forces again, hoping my ability was stronger than the technology locked around my wrists. Yet, the room remained still. The wind was no longer with me as my constant friend. The loss was acute.

Being without Helios was the first cut of my heart, losing my children then next, but the forces were my lifelong companion. With them gone, I was naked before my enemies. Even Poseidon wasn't able to take the forces from me, try as he might.

Left only with wit and guile, I scraped a smile across my face to hide my fear. "Don't worry, my friends will find you."

"Are they like us too? Are they immortals?" his breath caught on the questions. He was excited. "Was that man you were with your lover? Should I take you in front of him to get what I want?" he giggled and straightened his sleeve. A bulge formed below his waist. "Oh, I know." He snapped his fingers, "Strip her! I want her friends to see her as one of my many bed slaves."

He was no longer talking to me but around me. In an instance, the slaves tore my clothes from my body.

I looked around at his slaves. They were all barely dressed. The young ones were naked, while the older slaves wore only loincloths. The short glimpse I'd had of the city before being taken was of finely dressed Elysians, covered from head to toe.

Rhadamanthy doesn't understand the Themian mindset at all. He believes we are just like Elysiums.

The room wasn't cold. Yet, my body reacted to the lack of covering all the same. My nipples hardened, and the hair covering my body rose.

Rhadamanthy smiled with excitement, "Aren't you cold?" His eyes gleamed with hope as he rubbed his hands together. Color rose in his cheeks, his eyes dilated with desire.

I shrugged, "Not really." My only adornment now was the orichalcum bracelet keeping my powers at bay. The clothing on Delphi didn't cover much more than what I wore now. The make-up was better. If I'd been on Delphi, my nipples would be covered in rouge and my pubic hair removed. Delphi of all the Homeworlds was the most open with their bodies.

His lips hitched to the side. He paced around me, staring at my every curve.

He wishes to embarrass me.

It didn't work. His behavior reminded me of Zeus - childlike and predictable, with the need to dominate, holding to the forefront.

If I sigh, it will only set him off.

He was a child, and I needed to handle him like one.

"Is everything to your liking?" I asked, then added, "My lord—"

"You are lovely, for a creation of Charon and Anu, that is. I prefer the natural-born Elysian...most of the time." His little dig at the end was added to keep me off balance.

"Thank you, you are most generous in your acclaim. I hope to hold your eye." I did my best to infuse warmth into my voice. I moved my arms wide and turned in place with slow grace. Lifting my hair, I allowed him to inspect my neck and the unmarked skin that made up my body. I let my hair slip through my fingers slowly to catch the light streaming through the windows. The golden light of the Elysian star would highlight the red tones, giving my hair the overall color of orichalcum.

Many Themians remarked on my coloring and the sheer volume.

One of the slaves clapped her hands and giggled.

"Silence!" Rhadamanthy shouted. "Do not look at my new bed, slave." He moved to my side. A cruel smile crept over his face. He cradled a curl in his palm and rubbed it between his forefinger and thumb. "A most unusual color." He pulled the hair to his mouth and rubbed it against his lips. "I'll keep you whole for now. But, when your friends arrive, that may change," he whispered, then released my hair before trailing a long fingernail down my cheek to my collar bone.

I fought the response to shiver. I didn't want him to think I was scared or affected by him.

However, the truth is that I was and that scared me. Without my access to the forces, I was no stronger than any Elysian in the room or human on Earth.

I was at his mercy in every way, leaving only my mind.

CHAPTER 9

SYDNEY

The next room was cavernous, and it resembled one of the citadels from a Themian ship.

Just goes to show you can run away from your past, but you always take pieces of it with you.

I couldn't sense any other minds around me. There was no way I could judge whoever this Rhadamanthy was without Hera.

We needed her to start the process. I wasn't even sure if I was capable of dominating his mind all on my own. My job came after they were softened up.

<Stop musing, beautiful girl! Keep your head in the game and out of your own head.>

<Rodger, rodger!>

We came to two great doors, covered in that golden material, orichalcum. It seemed to be everywhere here.

Is there a connection between that and Themian tech? If so, what?

Reliefs divided the center of the two doors. The relief covering the doors formed one large carving. It was a man. He stood strong with his arms crossed. His body was sculpted with the muscle definition of a God. Each foot spanned wide to either door. Underneath the feet were humanoid creatures being crushed by a giant foot.

Typical! Why do the villains always need to subjugate everyone? Why can't they just, I don't know, fuck off?

With my mind, I slammed both doors open. The hollow relief crushed in on itself with the impact. The echo of crushing metal rang against the stone behind it, then reverberated into the rest of the room.

"How nice of you to join me. You're probably wondering how I found you?" The deep, cultured voice of Rhadamanthy invited us in, like a spider to a fly.

"No, not really. Couldn't give two shits," I retorted. I smiled back at him as his smile faded away.

He steepled his fingers between his clasped hands. "No matter. I have something you desire. So, let's discuss how it is you wish to win it back from me." He arched an eyebrow at me as if he was the cleverest of creatures.

I opened my mouth—

Perseus cut me off, "We don't negotiate with murderers. Return my mother, and I might let you live."

Rhadamanthy leaned forward and laughed. He reeked of youth and the scent of immortality. That was until you reached his eyes. They were the watery color of a 1000 lifetimes, and he was bored with every single one.

"Oh yes! The fire of youth. It's my favorite. I do enjoy killing the ones with the zest for life most. Yet, that woman couldn't possibly be your mother. She's far too young. You jest. Perhaps, she's your lover, and you don't wish for me to take her in front of you before I kill you?" he chuckled.

Ugh! He enjoys playing with his food.

"I can assure you that the woman you have in your possession is my mother. You will treat her with the respect she deserves. Do not speak your disgusting insinuations again. Now, give her back!" Perseus growled, his hands gripped his daggers, working his fingers over the hasp.

Rhadamanthy laughed, "You say she's your mother? I'll play along. If you wish to win her back, in one piece, of course, you must perform a service for me," he chuckled again, and the harmonics of the room made the sound echo back to us as if we were standing next to him.

I hate this type of shit.

"I'm not in the mood for any of your games," I replied. "What are your demands?" I needed to take control of the situation back from Perseus. His head was in the wrong place for this.

"Your women speak. How quaint. We like our women silent here on Elysium." He clapped. "What planet are you from?" Rhadamanthy asked Perseus.

My nostrils flared, "It doesn't matter what planet we're from. You've never heard of it or been to it. And you never will. As a matter of fact, I can guarantee you that when I'm done with you, you will never leave this palace again," I began moving across the room at a leisurely pace.

Rhadamanthy clapped his hands again and laughed. "Oh, she's feisty! Is she this way in bed also? I like it when they fight back."

Adrian bristled

<Don't take the bait.> I stated.

<No shit, beautiful girl. >

"You will not speak to a Fate in that fashion! You *will* return my mother to her rightful place. I will not dance to a tune for you or play your pathetic games designed to entertain!" Perseus shouted.

I groaned. *Fuck! Couldn't you have kept the Fate shit to yourself for five minutes?*

"A Fate? You say that, like I should know who they are. Your words mean nothing to me. I am the ruler here on Elysium!" He took to his feet, and the naked servants lining the walls fell to their knees. "Me and my other Judges. So, if you wish the woman returned to you, you will bring me the head of the Gorgon, Medusa."

I wasn't the only one in the room to gasp.

"She has two sisters, Euryale and Stheno. I am not interested in them. I only want her."

I immediately glanced at Perseus.

Issy murmured, "But those were just stories. They can't be true."

"If you need to discuss amongst yourselves how important this silly woman is, go right ahead. I shall retire for my noontime meal. My slaves will bring you some refreshments." He clapped his hands once more and rose.

The clinking of metal and jewels followed him. His robe must've weighed a ton. The sound of his slippers slapping on stones grew softer the further away he moved.

I rounded immediately on Perseus, "Okay, yes, it's a stupid human story. You also said that your mother told you stories about the Gorgons. What were they?" I demanded, then glanced around.

Perseus gapped at me and then searched his brother's face for answers.

Hercules ran his fingers through his hair and down the side of his face. "Mother said it was just a story. That it wasn't about you," Herc shrugged, his usual self-assured manner gone, replaced by bewilderment. "She named you after the guy in the story. Right?" he asked.

Perseus blankly nodded his head and blinked. He licked his lips before replying, "The Gorgons are three beautiful sisters. They live on an island together. They are all immortal."

Issy opened her mouth to say something, but I put my hand up.

Perseus looked at her and back to me. "I know the human version says that only one of them was mortal," he shook his head and looked away, his face pinched in anguish. "That's not how it goes. They were all immortal, perfectly normal, nothing strange— "

He's in shock.

I bit back the urge to smack him in the head. "And? There has to be something more." I raised my eyebrows, hoping he would spit out something useful.

Perseus's shoulders sagged, "According to my mother's stories. They were scientists and engineers. They created something of great value, and it altered Medusa. She hated men and would kill any of them that came within her site." He began to rush on, "Now the '*turning to stone*' part, that's… that's totally a human fallacy. That was never part of the story." He shrugged, "The hero, Perseus, kills Medusa." He turned away and stared out one of the many windows lining either side of the room. "My mother always made it sound very scary. She told us the story and said, '*be kind to women or Medusa will come and get you. She can kill you with one look.*'"

My mind raced. Of course, humanity changed the story over thousands of years.

Telephone is the worst game in the world. You can't even get it right in one room, let alone over a millennium or two. Add in a few different races and voila - crazy snake-haired-man-hating lady.

Turning someone to stone with a look was a story that would stick. Hating men needed some explaining, so some kind of rape story had covered that. They threw in a God to explain the powers.

Okay! That works.

They were called witches, and that was a smart cover.

But the snake hair, where did that come from?

That was not normal, also not something anyone would throw in for fun.

"We should accept his offer, beautiful girl."

I darted a glance at Adrian. He'd put one of his Khimera horns away, leaving one hand free.

It wasn't really up to me. "Perseus, there's no way we can do this without you. You're familiar with the story."

Hercules, the bullshit artist, stood off to the side with his arms crossed. I expected him to jump in and offer an idea or add a detail or two. Instead, he quietly waited.

I ignored him.

"I do not know the first place to go find this Medusa or how to beat her."

I watched the Clash of the Titans. It was a freaking cheesy movie made in the 70s, which I loved at the time.

But even that didn't tell the story right.

A string of servants entered the room carrying tables and chairs. None of them ever met our eyes. They didn't try to engage us in any way, and they were all naked as jaybirds.

Rage seethed through me, and the doors rattled behind us.

"Settle down, mom," Isolde soothed.

I couldn't bring the whole building down on top of us just because I didn't like what I saw. I clenched my teeth and let my eyes bore into the seat at the head of the room.

"Go tell your master we wish to speak to him!" My pronouncement echoed through the room.

One of the women bowed and quickly exited the room.

Adrian handed me a piece of bread and a cup of water.

The water will heal me, the food will sustain me.

We needed all the energy to fight.

Using my teeth, I ripped off a hunk of bread. It was dry and tasteless in my mouth. I washed it down with a swig of water and waited.

"Hey, strange creatures from another world. So, you've come to a decision," Rhadamanthy said, waving a prepubescent girl away.

"Yes. I'll kill the Gorgon for you. Tell us where to find her," Perseus replied with as little emotion as he could muster.

"Surely you jest? I do not know where to find her. She keeps me trapped here. I dare not leave." He indicated the island as a whole. "If you go north to the Graeae, they can tell you how to find her. Now you've bored me. Eat, drink, even rest if you must. But by sunset, be off my island or face my wrath." He placed a cracker with something on it in his mouth, chewed slowly, and swallowed it. "If you don't do as I say, our deal will be over. I will personally cut your mother apart piece by piece and then throw them at you, all the while making sure you hear all of her lovely screams." He smiled like the predator he was.

Perseus took a dive towards him. Yet, Hercules grabbed his belt and pulled him back. "Don't worry, brother. We will have our chance," he murmured.

Perseus raked his hands across his brother's back. The emotion bleeding off of them gagged Isolde.

I used to think that Herc was the impetuous one. Perseus appeared reserved, yet under it all, was a hidden volcano of burning fire.

Adrian laid a hand on Perseus' shoulder, "This isn't the way," He muttered.

A bag appeared on the table in front of us. <Fill up and leave now! Don't wait for sunset. Take as much food and water as you can carry.> Tristan said.

"We shouldn't bother to stay. Let's grab our supplies and go," Isolde agreed and began shoving bread and cheese into the bag while I gathered fruit.

My children and I worked as a machine in battle mode - gather supplies, organize weapons, come up with a plan.

Hercules slung a wineskin over his shoulder. For a planet that appeared to be so technologically advanced, the fact that they were still storing wine in skins was bizarre.

Adrian announced, "Shifting now!"

CHAPTER 10

SYDNEY

My vision immediately met Tristan's, who was standing on the bridge of Prometheus.

Not where I expected to land.

"Prometheus, tell us all you know of the Graeae!" I shouted and cringed at the volume in the small space.

"The Graeae, or the three sisters born of the white foam of the sea, gray-haired from birth, they share amongst themselves a single detachable eye. To find them, you must cross the stream that binds two continents and cross over the surge of the sea to the east. This leads to the Gorgons' land. The Graeae are sisters of the Gorgons."

My mouth fell open, and it felt like a blow landed right in my solar plexus. Prometheus' computers were not synced with the ones from Odyssey. The data was untainted by humanity and our version of Themian stories. Everything Prometheus knew about this was Elysium, a Pre-Themian world.

"Where is my mother?" Eos' demanded, her lip trembling in fear.

I shook my head. Professor Michelson wrapped his arm around Eos.

"Rhadamanthy has taken her. He's demanding we bring him the head of Medusa in exchange." I crossed my arms, then touched one of my fingers to my lips and tapped.

<You don't have all the answers, beautiful girl. Maybe, now would be a good time to consult Ixis. >

<No! Ixis and Emmaline can't be involved in this. It's not their destiny.> I replied and ran a hand over my eyes before covering my mouth.

Did I just say that?

Deep in the pit of my stomach, I knew that everyone on Odyssey needed to stay right where they were. Hidden. Protected.

Whatever solutions there are to be found will be right here, on Prometheus.

"Okay, work the problem, people! We have to find these old ladies," I barked.

I moved to a terminal and began flipping through data. I scanned stories, hoping to snag a detail or two that would help us.

"They're not just females. They're supposed to have the upper body of a woman and the lower body of a swan."

I stopped what I was doing to raise an eyebrow and glance at Michaelson.

He continued on, "According to Greek mythology, they live in a place that no sun has ever looked down upon during the day or a moon at night." He glanced up with a bright smile and looked around.

Hercules scowled at him.

When no one replied, he added, "It has to be a cave. It has to be somewhere deep in a cave."

"Or a moon," Tristan intervened.

Trust Tristan to come up with the most unlikely location.

"What makes you think they'd be on a moon? It says that it's a place that *no moon has ever touched.*"

"It's simple, mom. One of Elysium's moons is tidally locked, so it would never have seen another moon," he stated with a smirk.

Every so often, I wanted to smack him.

"Yeah, but if it's tidally locked to Elysium, it's going around the planet. So, at some point in time, the suns would hit both sides eventually, brainiac." Issy retorted.

I waved my hand at Isolde to stop her. Their sibling rivalry wasn't helping us.

"No, I agree with Professor Michelson. A cave makes more sense."

"Rhadamanthy said that they were in a cave North of him. This means that they must be in a cave on the other side of the continent above his island. Therefore, we cross over a river till we come to the ocean and we follow it," I remarked and went back to the data on my terminal.

"No. We must cross the stream that divides two continents. However, we have to cross it where the surge of the sea meets the stream towards the sun. In other words, the stream has to be in the East." Perseus flexed his hands open and closed.

"Prometheus, give me a three-dimensional topographical picture of Elysium. Remove any cloud cover. I only want to see continents, rivers, streams, lakes, oceans, and coastlines," Tristan took Perseus' suggestion and ran with it.

The holo filled the center of the room and everyone crowded in to investigate.

"The cave is an entrance to the underworld." Hades said.

My head whipped around as the reverberation of Hades' words flowed over me.

"According to everything we've gone through, this is the underworld," I retorted. The hint that this wasn't the end of the road grated over me.

"This is the Themian underworld. I speak of the Elysium Underworld. The original idea of an underworld did not come from my mother. It came from Elysium. The Graeae live in a cave which is considered the entrance to the underworld."

I tapped at my lips. Issy had taken to pulling on her lower lip to keep from biting it. I realized she'd picked it up from me, and now I tapped. Neither habit was a good one. Both telegraphed my motives, and I needed to curb them.

The answer to the underworld conundrum made perfect sense.

Of course, our mythologies are based on their mythologies and the mythologies of Elysian mythologies.

My head ached with the circles within circles of it all. It was fucking confusing.

Why can't these people keep the shit straight and give everything a new name?

At least the humans changed it from the Underworld to Hades.

<You're musing again, beautiful girl.> Adrian chided.

<I know. I'm just trying to get it straight in my own head. Can you imagine somebody else who wasn't involved in this crap trying to keep track of it?> I scoffed at the idea.

A picture of Dr. Glover flashed through my mind. He had a sharp mind and was willing to dig to get answers. A sad smile tickled the edges of my lips.

I didn't have time to think about Glover or anyone else on Earth. That was a life I could never return to.

"Prometheus, show me all the entrances to caves on the planet that are close to streams and oceans," I instructed.

Twelve locations lit up.

Twelve! It couldn't be eleven or six. It had to be twelve!

Internally, I groaned. The numbers never changed. It didn't matter the religion or the theological pantheon - the numbers remained the same. I wished that I understood the deeper connections.

"Prometheus, eliminate all caves in the Southern hemisphere. Rhadamanthy said it was north of his island," Adrian intervened.

I touched Rhadamanthy's island on the display and trailed my finger up from there. Prometheus drew a line around the globe. A second later, all the glowing red dots below disappeared, leaving behind only two. One was West of Rhadamanthy's island, and the other was East.

"Well, it's a 50-50 chance. Which one do we choose?" Hercules remarked.

I glanced over at him. Sometimes he really was just big and stupid.

"The one to the East, of course. Everything says it's East of Rhadamanthy's island," Issy replied with a smile and ran her hand over his arm.

"I agree with Isolde. It's to the East. If it's not there, we can simply move West," Perseus stated.

Hercules shifted from one foot to the other, "Yes, we could do that, or we could inspect all twelve. How long will it take us? After all, it's only our mother whose life is at stake. We're already in open warfare." He grumbled and crossed his arms. Issy placed a hand on his forearm as he shook his head.

My choice was made. Sending groups to each location was a waste of time and resources. "No. We're not in all-out open warfare. Rhadamanthy knows he can't afford a war. He doesn't know what kind of defenses we have—" The pressure in the room changed. Before I could get another word out, Ares cut me off.

"Tactically, we don't want to reveal our strength. He took a hostage to draw us out. It is the actions of a weak position and not of strength. Sydney is correct. Taking a hostage is an act of war, Hercules. It is also an act of someone in a poor position. He's desperate." The blue ice of Ares' eyes bored into mine.

He wants in.

"You're not coming!" I stated. "I need you here to defend the fleet."

His jaw locked down, the muscle working over the bone. His eyes narrowed as his nostrils flared, "Hercules is right. We are at war. So I should be down there with you."

"And your sisters? Should they be left unprotected? You don't know if Elysium has a fleet of warships. They're willing to cut their populace apart to feed their immortality and enslave people for all time." I moved in close to let him smell my breath as I dressed him down.

One thing I'd learned in the last few years was that there were very few people who could take me and win.

I was the water to Ares' fire, and he needed to bend to my will, or he'd never respect me.

"They're unwilling to allow any type of technological advances that don't benefit themselves. Something you probably don't know, Ares, but Rhadamanthy is immortal," I whispered, "He's like us. That makes him infinitely more dangerous. Now calculate this - we don't know how many like him there are."

Ares' fists gripped, and the blood vessels in his arms popped under the skin. "Can I redirect Hephaestus for weapons and armor now?" he growled.

It cost Ares to ask my permission. He was used to being the alpha of the demigods. It went against his nature to bow, but he understood the protection of our fleet was more important.

"Yes. Have Hephaestus stop all work on the engines' upgrades. We need weapons. Outfit every ship with armaments. Also, no one sleeps more than 6 hours at a time. I don't trust Rhadamanthy or the rest of the judges of Elysium."

Ares' eyes darted around the room. He was doing the math of war. The battle was never won in the field.

It's the logistics that will win out in the end.

We had a tactical advantage - Rhadamanthy didn't know our numbers, and we needed to keep it that way.

"No one is to fire a shot. No flights, no communications, nothing. Pull the fleet back. If we do this right, we could get Hera back with no bloodshed and earn the gratitude of Rhadamanthy." I stepped away from Ares. My point was made, and I'd given him a task to keep him busy.

Emmaline will keep him in line.

"Rhadamanthy said the Gorgon Medusa is keeping him captive on his island," Hercules offered.

"She is his daughter. He despises her," Hades remarked.

I rolled my eyes so hard it hurt. I rolled my head to take Hades in. Everything he said was in a matter-of-fact way, making him no better than Charon. They both acted as if we should know everything they were talking about.

"Medusa's his daughter? The Gorgons are Rhadamanthy's children?" Adrian asked in surprise.

I was grateful for his interjection. Handling the King of the Underworld was not a job I wanted. Adrian spent enough time with the Themians on Alethea to understand their cold, calculated bullshit.

"My mother was one of them."

Adrian's fingers reached up and pinched the bridge of his nose. I crossed my arms, my eyes boring into Hades'.

"A Gorgon or his kid?" Adrian took the bait.

"Both," Hades replied, making his wife bite her lip.

The room groaned, "Is there anything else you want to tell us that could be helpful? Maybe about the Judges or the planet?" I tipped my head left and right. "I mean, that evil son of a bitch of Rhadamanthy's your grandfather. Anything I should know about Medusa? Maybe you could tell Perseus at least. After all, he's the one who's supposed to kill her. Was that a prophecy or a human mix-up?"

"The Gorgons and the Graeae are monsters. My mother and her sisters are the only children of the Judges that were created normal." He covered his lover's hand with his own.

His dark coloring was a stark contrast to her bright eyes and blond hair. They truly were the picture of the mythological couple I'd read about. My brain stuttered over that truth.

I swallowed, working my throat to find moisture for the next volley.

"You don't believe the Judges became immortal using genetic manipulation on the first try, do you?" Hades pointed out the obvious, and that made me feel stupid.

"Of course not," I remarked more to myself than him or anyone in the room.

Of course, they would've tested manipulations on someone.

"He used his own children?" I gulped back the vitriol and bitter taste of evil.

Unbidden, my hand smoothed over my belly. The idea of using my kids to live forever turned my stomach. I charged from the cockpit and burst into my cabin before the contents of my digestive tract emerged.

In the background, I overheard Professor Michelson exclaim. "He used his children as test subjects?" disbelief colored his words as he echoed my remarks.

Hades didn't stop with the narrative. "They tested them in batches of three. My mother and her sisters were the youngest subjects. They were given the perfect strain before the Judges imprisoned them."

I rinsed my mouth out and tried to ease the rolling in my belly, then moved back into the companionway.

Hades never let up. His tone of voice was the recall of a long-remembered story told over and over again.

Like the oral histories from Earth's past.

"My mother escaped. The first children were born triplets. The nymphs created them that way - one child for each Judge to claim as his own. Though, they were a complete genetic mix," Hades droned.

Persephone remained at her lover's side. Yet, her bright coloring dimmed as the story progressed.

"The Graeae were born with one eye and one tooth. It was one of their many defects. On the other hand, the Gorgons, Medusa, and her sisters were born with snake-like hair. There were others born with such defects." He swallowed, and a shadow fell over his face as ghosts danced behind his eyes.

For a man that was supposed to punish and torture others, he seemed more haunted than anyone else on the ship. "I'm sure you will meet some of the others along the way. There might even be more than my mother knew." He shook his head as if that would get rid of the idea of more siblings. "When they finally reached my mother and her sisters' gestation time and used the treatment, the births turned out normal. They took that as a good sign. I do not know if the testing stopped after that. She couldn't tell us. She had a vision and escaped the planet with Charon and his cohorts."

<This is what happens when people play God. It makes me want to kill them all.> I snarled.

<Not all those who were forced to be Gods are evil Sydney. Hera never claimed to be a God, and she's not evil. Neither is Apollo or Athena.> Adrian always argued the other side of every situation.

Devil's advocate is a sucky job.

<I realize not everybody called a God claimed to be one. However, so many have. Don't you want to kill them all? > I demanded. The rage roaring through me needed to cool before I could hear reason.

<Before they breed? You wouldn't be here if they didn't. > He retorted.

Suddenly my fire had burned out. <Would the world be a better place? > I asked.

<We're not just talking about the world anymore, Sydney. This is the cosmos. It's everything, everywhere. Elysium Judges have the ability to enslave an entire cosmos. They haven't enslaved the underworld only because they didn't know how to get out of it. >

<Bigger problems for another day.> The heat rushing through me was gone, and my head cleared. <Let's go save Hera. She certainly deserves it. >

"Ares, get back to Odyssey and prepare our ships," I instructed.

He nodded, and Tristan shifted him out of the room.

I turned to Michelson. "Scour Prometheus' data-banks. We need to know everything there is to possibly know about the Graeae, the Gorgons, and any other potential children of the Judges." I moved on to Tristan. "The Prometheus suits, the spacesuits - I want mine. I don't need the helmet or anything else. Only the suit, with the gun attachments." I glanced at Issy and her gun harness. She cocked an eyebrow at me with a knowing smile.

My red dress had to go.

It was fun for a moment.

Tristan nodded gravely, and a minute later, a suit laid across a chair across the room.

Next was Hades, "Mr. Helpful, I realize you're probably not holding back on what you know from, the Oracle. She only told you as much as you needed to know or some such bullshit like that. All that fatalistic crap that you people who believe in destiny and prophecy would say. I don't give a crap about any of that. Now, do me a favor and help Michelson. We need to weed out what's true in the databases. I need as much information as possible about Elysium, your aunts, and the Judges. We know almost nothing."

Persephone immediately sat down at one of the terminals and began manipulating the boards.

My eyes lit upon Perseus, "Themians don't place a lot of stock in projectile weapons. Ares apparently finds them fascinating. I think I'd like one of those spacesuits." He tilted his head towards Tristan.

With a half-cocked smile, Tristan smirked, "You need one too, hu?".

"Yes," he groused.

Exhaustion was creeping up on me. Now was the time to take a nap. "Issy, head down to the infirmary and see if you can find some stimulants. I don't want to fall asleep while looking for Hera," I murmured.

"Everybody, go take care of your business. You got 30 minutes. Meet me back here. Tristan, I don't give a crap where we are in 30 minutes, but everyone is shifted down to the planet. Be ready or get caught with your pants down. We're not going down with your dick in the dark here." I turned to leave the cockpit, picking up my suit on the way. Adrian was close on my heels, and that gave me confidence.

CHAPTER 11

PERSEUS

Sydney's made it clear she's in charge. Yet, when the fight begins, the best person for the job takes over. Ares wasn't there to bludgeon his way into that slot, while Hercules was more of a berserker than a leader.

Adrian could and would do the job.

I could follow or lead based upon the circumstances.

Glory seeking is not how you achieve your objective.

*****

The shift, like all shifts, was quick and surprisingly painless. Tristan made it as easy as slipping into a warm bath.

There we were, staring at the rocky edifice of a cliff. The sky was nothing more than a gray dome hovering over us. The golden light of the lower latitudes was gone along with the warmth.

The gurgling of a stream barely usurped the distant waves, beating against the shore. Every crash slowly ate away at the nearby rocky cliff, leaving the beach narrow and littered with debris.

When mother said the Graeae were gray, I believed it was the color of their hair. I never dreamed everything around them would have that dull, flat grayscale also. It was as if the warmth and happiness in the world had evaporated and what was left was a mix of ash from a fire, creating this soupy nothingness.

"Come, brother," Hercules said, his shoulders barely fitting inside the suit he'd been provided with. Mine pulled slightly over the shoulders also. Yet, my brother assured me that wearing this protection in a fight would be good.

The only thing I was unsure about was the projectile weapon connected to my thigh. Sydney and Isolde both already had their guns out.

I don't have mental powers remotely close to theirs.

I was, however, a Demigod with the ability to control the forces.

But then again, it might not be all I'll need.

I unclipped the weapon from its harness. The grip was not unfamiliar, and like all weapons, I instantly understood it. The information filled my mind like a never-ending well I could drink from whenever the need arose.

The knowledge became a skin I could wear. My one true ability - an unworldly use of objects as weapons. In my hands, no matter what it was, it became a weapon. The simple touch to the side of a drinking vessel and the knowledge poured in. The knowledge I accessed made me capable of becoming a killer with only the object I held.

I was unstoppable. Unlike my descendants, Adrian and Tristan, I never lost a fight. The projectile weapon in my hand only ensured that the death of my enemies would come faster and with more ease.

I closed my eyes for a moment to press my anxiety away. My ability was a curse. A burden I've been carrying.

I didn't want to fight. If I fought, others died, and I had to carry the weight of their deaths with me, along with the color of their eyes, as the life I stole from them slipped away.

These thoughts ran a marathon in my mind every time I moved into dangerous territory. Like all warriors, I let the emotions flow through me, using that energy as fuel for the coming fight.

Because there is always someone to fight.

The rocky cliff was dotted with shadowy pits. Overhanging rock shelves lined the edifice, and only one covered the onyx-colored opening of the Greaea.

Mother said all entrances to the underworld began with a cave.

I was now aware that she was only repeating stories she had heard. My life has taught me one thing - just because it's a story doesn't mean it's not true.

The truth is there if you look.

There was no carving to announce what lay within. The rock on the beach gave clues to the caves' formation. Along with the black and gray rock that was leftover from volcanic activity, there was pumice stone lining the beach.

Perhaps it was an escape tunnel for gas and superheated air?

The question of its formation was a distraction. However, the terrain on the interior might be ascertained with such knowledge.

The inner walls were smooth as if a potter washed them over with a wet hand. Small smooth stones littered the ground like those found in a river or stream. The small stone only provided a thin covering to hide the rough base below.

This is not good for a fight.

The loose rocks would contribute to uneven footing and loss of balance.

Running down the list of weapons on my person, I left the gun in my hand.

It will do far more damage, even if I fall.

Hercules moved to my right, and Adrian took a position to my left, with the two Fates behind us.

Up ahead, the familiar flickering of firelight licked the walls and cut the darkness.

The light came with a murmuring, "They come, sisters. They come. Fate has arrived." a low-throated maniacal laughing followed.

Living in a cave on the edge of the ocean appeared as complete madness in my mind. Further proof was added by high-pitched squeals of misplaced joy.

Adrian formed a fireball to help guide our way, while Hercules had a light on his shoulder that issued from the suit's harness. I found mine and turned it on.

The smell of smoke drifted out over our heads. The ground was damp, with driftwood scattered over the surface.

"Why is the floor covered with sticks?" Issy breathed.

Laughter rippled up ahead, bouncing off the walls, "As if we would litter our beautiful cave with sticks of driftwood? Silly girl! And you call yourself a Fate…," one of the old women snickered.

"They are not driftwood, Isolde. They're bones," Hercules supplied in a grim tone.

A human-type skull laughed at me from the outer reaches of my circle of light. The bottom portion of its jaw was gone, as were its teeth. It was cracked as if it'd been pried open.

I turned away and refocused on the glowing embers further down the tunnel so as not to be blinded by the light.

"Maybe, that part of the story was true. They really do eat people?" Sydney hissed with dismay.

Dread filled my belly.

If we are not careful, not all of us will leave this cave.

And I was the only one they could spare.

"Awe, sisters! Look! The Fates *have* arrived. But not all of them. Where's the other one?" One of them groaned with distaste, then shook her body.

Before Sydney could speak, I belted out, "She will be here soon." My deep voice reverberated off the semi-smooth walls and echoed around the space. The acoustics were terrible. Sounds seemed to never end as they hit one wall only to ricochet to another one. Over and over again.

"We've waited for our sisters, Fates, for a long time. We can wait a little while longer." She waffled her head back and forth. "Why have you come?" The darkness faded with every step, turning a blackened outline of a body to gray.

"We come to find the Gorgon, Medusa. We want to fight her. Do you know how?" Sydney's voice rang with the higher pitch of a woman and the force of a man.

"We won't speak to you, Fate! You're not all here, so we have nothing to say to you." This Graeae spit on the cave floor before turning her toothless maw into a grotesque smirk in my direction, then quickly turning away. "You have three tender men. Which one of them speaks for you?" three chuckles came from lumps sitting in front of the fire.

"Why do you hide?" I couldn't see any of them clearly. Only the fire outlined their form. But with closer inspection, their long gray stringy hair trailed down their backs, brushing the floor with every move and turning the tips black with grim.

The cave was choked with menace, so I dared not take my eyes from the three figures by the fire. Each step became a test of my luck.

Will the ground be even, or will a pebble throw me off balance?

I waved a hand behind me, urging the Fates to hang back.

"Show yourselves! I don't negotiate with shadows and smoke!" I called into the darkness.

A nasal laugh, creaking like an old woman's chair, filled the tunnel, reverberating off the walls. In unison, all three took to their feet, turned, and stepped into the light. Their skin was gray and scaled as if it belonged to a sickly bird with no feathers.

The place where their eye sockets and lids should reside laid flat, devoid of shape. Their bone structure was not misshapen or ghoulish.

All about them was a gray parlor from their toenails to their crown. They carried not a speck of color. It was like a temple in the early light of dawn before the sun crests the hills, illuminating the walls when the world still drowns in shadows.

One held a device and spoke, "Now, you have seen us. You see, we are not unattractive." Her tongue darted out to run over her teeth, touching her lips and wiggling.

"No. You just don't have eyes and color," Hercules remarked, making me want to smack him in the head.

Instead, I scowled at him.

If you bait them, they won't give us what we want.

"We're not here to debate whether you are pleasing to the eye or not. We are here to find out where Medusa resides, and you're going to help us." I snapped and snuck a glance at Sydney. The last thing we needed was her approval or her push back.

She twirled a finger in a circle to urge me on, then pushed her bangs out of her eyes.

"Did our father send you here? Does he send his regards?" The creature released a dry laugh, "Did he tell you how much he missed us or even that we were his children?"

I tilted my head to the side. "You know Rhadamanthy said none of those things. He's a selfish, arrogant creature." My teeth ground down to hold back all the emotions I carried.

No need to give them too much.

"Are you like Pythia? She told us you would come. Not you specifically, but she told us the Fates would come, and judgment would come with them," the voice quivered as if the answer to the question mattered a great deal.

But mother was not there, and judgment couldn't be met out without her to begin the process.

"Pythia's dead. Pythia never told us anything. We came here looking for Elysium, the home of our forebears and peace. Truthfully, all the stories of you have been forgotten in time." I didn't wish to discuss the words of Pythia and the judgment she may have promised them. I wanted my mother.

They raised their hands at the same time and wagged their index fingers at me, tsking as they did so. "Now, Perseus, we are all the same. You are like us—"

A different woman cut in, "You cannot lie to us. We know the truth, as do your Fates." They sniffed the air, turning their heads like animals to find the scent of something.

The first woman began again, "The spinner isn't here, but the one that measures is. She's the young one." The gray face licked her lips and smiled, revealing a row of blue-gray teeth.

Another cut in, "Very tender, yes. She smells delicious." She moved one hand over the other.

"The inflexible one came too. Have you come to cut our thread? To end our time?" the woman demanded.

Sydney snorted, "If you don't give me what I need, I will end your time in this world without a backward glance." The rocks around her tapped in time with each syllable.

"She cannot cut our thread. Her sister is not here, and without the spinner, she has no hope of completing her job as Fates."

The three of them spaced themselves around the fire. I found my feet mirroring them.

The woman who spoke first held up a device, angling it at one of us as we spoke. It had a handle in the back, while the front was a round, flat disc that glowed with the golden hue covering everything here.

Orichalcum.

If the stories from Earth were to be believed even in part, that was *the eye*.

"One of you is Enyo, the other Denio, and finally Pemphredo," I stated for the benefit of all.

They twittered in the background.

"We know your father performed genetic testing on you," I said, "When you became less than pleasing, he threw you out." I was grasping for information, something to draw them out.

The second hag snatched the eye from her sister, "Oh, silly boy, you think you can win us over with your stories? You know nothing. We were never beautiful. We never knew life as anything other than what we are. The genetic testing you speak of was performed on our mother, and she gave birth to us." The three of them snickered, "Could you imagine giving birth to three such as us?"

The third crone took her turn, "Blind and yet able to understand all that a child ought not. Add in the gray and unattractiveness, and you can very well understand why she couldn't stand the sight of us. She cast us away. Our fathers realized we did have some use, so they created the eye." She held it up.

It was some kind of technology they used for seeing.

It must have some way of conveying the site through the module when held.

Perhaps the knowledge was passed through the hand.

"But he only made one. He did not trust us enough to give each of us our own *Eye*." The hag shook her head in disgust.

"Denio, you have had *the eye* long enough! I wish to see what they look like." She raised her nose and sniffled at the air in my direction. "Which one should we eat first? I can smell one of the males close to me. He's plump and ready."

Hercules took a step back, and Adrian kept a ball of fire firmly between himself and the three of them. Sydney didn't flinch. I couldn't help but admire her backbone. Isolde picked her way back to the mouth of the tunnel.

"What makes you think that we can't just dominate your minds and take what we want?" Sydney demanded, and the rocks around her feet tapped against each other, barely holding her ability in check.

Pemphredo raised her hand and knocked one finger back and forth, "No, no, no! You cannot dominate our minds. That's why we've been cast out. Father Aeakus refused to kill us. He still thinks we might have genetic material he can use, at a later date," she cackled at the idea.

"They couldn't control us, so they threw us in this cave. Every now and again, someone comes asking for favors, and they send them our way. I think they like to feed us," Denio snickered.

A shiver ran down my spine.

And I thought my family was a twisted mess.

At least, we never fed people to each other.

Denio stepped closer to me, as did Pemphredo, "Give me *the eye*, Denio."

Just as Denio stretched to throw it to her sister, I made my move. I leaped to snatch it out of the air. The tip of my finger connected, and it glanced away, throwing the trajectory off. It clattered to the ground rolling over and away from the fire.

A scream rose up. "You, you...have *the eye*! Give it back to us. It's not yours! Father made it for us!" The third one, Enyo, wailed.

"They don't have it! Find it, sisters," Denio screeched.

The fire exploded, casting flames around the cavern. I jumped, dodging the blast. The scent of burning hair filled the air around me.

"Perseus!" Isolde screamed a moment before a wall of water engulfed me.

I tumbled over as if the wash of a wave pushed my body with the power of an ocean. The taste of salt flooded my system, burning my eyes. My shoulder crashed to the ground, and the water disappeared as quickly as it had arrived.

"Get up!" Sydney shouted.

The three hags scrambled over the ground, groping for *the eye* or me. Adrian shifted me away from the fire along with everyone else. Yet, Enyo managed to lift her hand and slam Adrian into a wall. His head lolled to the side in a daze.

"Oh no, you didn't!" Sydney grabbed rocks from the floor and hurled them at all three women.

"They attack, sisters!" Pemphredo called into the darkness. Sydney coughed and gripped her chest, sliding to the floor. "Stop them!" she wheezed.

Hercules tipped his head to me as he raised his sword in readiness. I rolled to avoid a set of hands searching the floor for *the eye*. The claws on the tips of the fingers scratched at the ground, picking up bones and tossing them over their shoulders.

A glint of golden light flashed from the disk on the other side of the fire. Pulling my feet under me, I leaped over one of the hags. There was nothing wrong with her hearing, and quick as a whip, she grabbed my ankle, pulling me out of my arc.

I slammed on the ground a few feet from the disk. The claws of the hag pulled at me as she climbed over my form. A moment later, her weight disappeared.

Adrian's chuckle echoed around the space.

I crawled the final few feet and closed my palm around the coveted *eye*. Enyo stood over me, her lips pulled back into a cruel smile.

"None shall take *the eye*, fool!" She raised her hand and began curling it into a fist.

A pressure grew around my heart as if her fingers were buried in my chest, gripping the life-giving muscle. My vision dimmed as I caught sight of Hercules with his sword on the downward swing of a killing blow.

"No! Don't kill them!" I coughed as the last of my air left my chest.

My words came out too late, and the blade buried deep in her side. Blood sprayed my face. She crumpled to the floor next to me. Her blood gushed from the mortal wound, wetting the side of my face. The warm viscosity of it touched my lips a moment before the crushing pressure in my chest ceased, and I was finally able to breathe. Blood rushed back to my starving body.

I rolled over, gulping air and coughing over my renewed chance at life.

"Enyo!" The two others cried.

Denio turned her head to Hercules, "How could you? Are we so different as to not warrant life?" they whimpered. One cradled her head while the other held her hand to her cheek. They shed no tears, only sniffled and choked on their cries.

There was only a moment to spare, "Tell us how to defeat Medusa. What do we need to do?" I barked.

The Contact with the handle of *the eye* filtered a vision into my mind, filling a place that only moments ago was blind to the world with the lack of oxygen and blood. It was more of a shadowy outline versus a vivid picture. It gave a little more detail than one could perceive from a lit candle covered by a basket.

Theirs was a colorless gray world to match their skin.

The technology was so rudimentary that one could even consider it to be laughable. Yet, all three faces turned to me with their hands outstretched.

"You will give us back *the eye*?" Enyo asked and coughed. Her wound was healing fast. What would have killed any normal human only slowed the Greaea down.

"Yes, I might even give you each an eye of your own at some point. If we succeed, you wouldn't have to live in this cave, eating people. You could go and live amongst the others if you wish."

They leaned in and whispered to each other. "You will heal our sister and give us back *the eye? And if you succeed, you'll give us our own eyes, yes?" Denio was the bargainer. Her hair soaked up the bloody pool on the floor, as did her grimy dress.

"Yes, and I will provide transportation to take you away from this evil place." I waved my arms to indicate the cave. They couldn't see me, but my irritation found release in the motion.

"And you will not let the Fates judge us?" Pemphredo inquired. She held her shoulders stiff, unwilling to bend even in her weakened position. She turned her face this way and that, sniffing the air as if she could sniff out the Fates.

I wanted to look at Sydney., but that meant taking my eyes off the three hags.

"I cannot promise something I have no control over. No one can control the Fates. However, I can say this - if you stay away from them, they can't judge you. If I were you, I would leave this place and never come back. And I would never do anything to draw their attention." I chanced a glance at Sydney, who cocked an eyebrow but held her tongue.

I hadn't promised she wouldn't kill them, but I had promised them that as long as they did not commit any further crimes to be left alone.

They huddled over Enyo's weak body and exchanged a few words. Pemphredo lifted her head, "We accept. Give us *the eye!*" She extended a hand, shaped more like the claws of a bird of prey than a human.

"Tell me what I want to know first. Only then I'll give you *the eye,*" I replied. This was not my first negotiation. I would not part with my bargaining chip on the promise of a cannibal. Even though the pain in my chest receded with each breath, it had weakened me. So, I mustered my strength for the next verbal volley.

Her nostrils flared with each breath, and if she'd had eyes, they would have glared at me. She licked her lips and came to some resolve. Finally, the hag leaned forward, "You must first go North to the Nymphs. They are brilliant and completely under my father's control."

Denio waved her hand in the air, "They have something special, a type of fabric that is impervious to everything - acid, oil, fire, water. Basically, anything that might tear or burn cannot harm this fabric." She clutched at the rags hanging from her body and began to worry them.

"You will need it!" Enyo added knowingly. She tried to nod her head but winced in pain instead. "Medusa's blood is like acid. If it drops on you it will burn you right through, never stopping. It will find its way through the crust of this planet down into the molten core and then out the other side. The only way to stop her blood is with orichalcum laced stone," she giggled as if it was a clever trick.

"The body is not like a planet. It won't heal as the blood passes through. The cloth is the only way you will be able to transport her head once you've cut it off." She shook her head back and forth then tested the air.

Besides being strange, she reminded me of a hungry dog.

Denio carried on, "When I had *the eye,* I spied the helmet of Hades. Pythia started building that before she left. It's a clever piece of machinery. She poured all her knowledge into it. Unfortunately, she couldn't finish it. She said it would be for her firstborn son — Hades. If he's given it to you, then you must know what it does." Her dry lips allowed a laugh to escape, which was a little more than a cough, then her gray tongue found its way over her lips.

"I don't. I haven't even put it on," I remarked and kicked myself for giving them more information than needed. I rubbed my hand over my breast bone to push the last remnants of Enyo's attack away.

She clapped her hands together, "Give me *the eye!* I want to see you put it on."

Her claw-like hands reached toward me, but there wasn't a chance in Tartarus or the underworld I would give her *the eye*.

I pulled the helmet off of my back and slipped it over my head. As soon it touched my crown, the humming of other minds that always filled my life in the background ceased. There was nothing but blessed quiet. I couldn't even hear my sister. The heavy fog that plagued my mind pulled back to reveal a hyper-focus I had never experienced before.

A squeak of shock echoed around the cave. Isolde covered her mouth.

My eyes searched out Hercules. His face carried a knowing half-smile. "That'll do Perseus, that will do."

I slipped the helmet off and hung it back on my waistband. "What?"

"What do you think it did, silly boy?" Denio retorted, "It made you invisible! That is what it was designed for. Pythia knew that if someone was going to be able to kill her father, they would have to be twice as willey as he is. Invisibility is a great gift."

"You don't think it's a gift from the Gods?" Enyo remarked, and her site   less face turned toward Sydney.

"Of course not. There are no Gods, only disturbed people who believe themselves to be gods and, well, the Judges," Sydney remarked with a snarl.

"What else do I need to kill Medusa?" I intervened since my patience was beginning to wear thin.

Pemphredo sat up straight, placing her hands lightly on her knees. If she had had eyes, I was sure she would be trained on me.

"First, you must go to the Isle of the Court. It is directly North of my father's island. There, you will find the three Gorgons - Medusa and her two sisters —"

Denio cut in, "Her sisters aren't relevant. They don't care that Medusa is the one my father wants killed."

"She's the one who keeps him a prisoner," Pemphredo retorted to her sister, then sighed and turned back to me, "She will most likely be in her palace. It is a twisted disturbed place. You will need a weapon, something not of our world. Something that was fashioned elsewhere of minerals that do not exist on our planet. Do you have such a weapon? You are from another world. You must have possession of a weapon that was not forged on Elysium."

Sydney gave an imperceptible shake while Adrian mouthed a *no*. Beside them, Hercules displayed a wide smile, "Don't worry, brother. We have what they speak of. "

"If you have all of those things, then you may be able to kill her. Although, you will take no joy in it and nor should you," Enyo chided.

The hair on my flesh rose as I understood a pronouncement when I heard it. "We are going to walk out of here, and you're not gonna follow us," I stated.

"*The eye*...you promise that and more. Don't leave us here in the dark! You have no understanding of what lurks in the darkness," Pemphredo pleaded.

Hercules shook his head. He had no desire to give them back their electronic device. But *the eye* was so rudimentary and crude as to be laughable. It seemed cruel not to give them their toy. The infrared from Prometheus was more advanced than this thing.

I skirted around the fire, passing far enough away so they couldn't grab me. As I exited the firelight, I turned and yelled, "Catch," throwing it back at them.

It tumbled on the ground, and they dove towards the sound, scrambling and scraping themselves with lots of cackling and then arguing, "Why did you have to throw it?"

"We could teach him a lesson," one giggled and coughed as a few rocks made a cracking sound, hitting the cavern wall.

"We could trap them here and eat them all," another intervened.

"No! You must heal, and I'm certain we must wait for the Fates to do their work," the last one added.

Their voices were so similar I couldn't make out who was saying what.

"Don't be silly! We would never be able to eat them all. They would kill us while trying."

"Yes, but if the Fates return, we're all dead anyway."

"You heard him. He said as long as we mind our own business and don't eat anybody else, the Fates will leave us alone."

"And you believe him?" one of the hags snorted.

"Yes, he is one of the sons of Pythia. Why shouldn't I believe him?"

"He's not one of the sons of Pythia. It's the girl! Didn't you smell it on her? She is of Pythia's line."

"But she is a Fate!"

"Course she's a Fate. Pythia would only give a prophecy about her own. She'd never help out someone else," The crone grumbled.

"That's not true. She promised to free us all," the other rebuffed.

"You know as well as I do that Pythia never did anything but what was best for her. Deino, you can be so gullible sometimes. Just because we are sisters with Pythia, it doesn't mean that she cared a lick for us."

"Not true!"

Their bickering voices faded into the background.

"So, should we head North to the Nymphs?" Hercules was the first one to talk.

"That's what they said. I guess we're gonna need whatever this fabric is to carry around Medusa's head. That's if we can get it off of her shoulders," Sydney remarked.

A large hand slapped me on the shoulder, "You know what, brother? The longer I live, the more I believe in fate. Maybe all those stories people told about us did have some truth. Who knows? Earth had their own Oracles," Herc shrugged.

I shook my head. Hercules loved a good story and was more than willing to retell any story that was to his advantage. He once spoke of me fighting massive insect-type monsters.

Sydney shot Hercules an ice-cold stare, "Destiny is not preordained, Hercules! We still have freedom of choice, and I intend to make all those choices myself." She pushed past him, making me smile within.

A glacier carries more warmth than her.

He hunched his shoulders, working them up and down, "Sorry, mom!"

"He didn't mean to make you mad," Isolde spouted, then smacked him on the chest. "You know she doesn't like that," she muttered under her breath.

My brother smirked as Sydney's back stiffened, storming away.

"Why doesn't she want Herc to call her *mom*?" I inquired.

"She thinks he's a dirty old man, that's why," Isolde snorted and ran a hand down his chest.

Even Adrian was laughing, so I joined in. I couldn't help it. Hercules indeed was *the* dirty old man.

CHAPTER 12

ISOLDE

"How are we supposed to find the Nymphs in the North?" I remarked.

This had all taken a turn for the strange after Hades and Persephone came out of the closet.

"I'm not sure," mom murmured and squinted at the cloudy sky.

<Perhaps, I can send you guys some help? > Tristan offered.

<Sure. What did you have in mind?> I replied before my mom could say no.

Tristan snickered in my mind. <Shifting now.>

Six people appeared on the rocky shore in front of us. Suspiciously, one of them was wearing an eye patch.

"What? You finally decided that our fight is your fight?" Mom shouted over the crash of the waves.

Sea-spray misted our clothes and hair, plastering mom's fly-aways to her neck and face.

"No, Tristan said you needed a guide. He also said that you were going to overthrow the Elysium Judges. That is a task I wish to be part of. I said I hadn't seen Elysium from space. I didn't say I'd never been to Elysium," Erik-the-one-eye replied. He, too, took in the gray sky overhead and then refocused his one good eye on my mother.

Herc smacked him on the shoulder, and the poor man lurched forward from the impact. "So, what exactly did you do to get put at the ass-end of your universe?"

I rolled my eyes.

Trust Herc to ask the question on everyone's mind.

He really had no filter.

"Are you entering the cave or leaving?" Erik, the one-eye, asked. He adjusted his clothes and smoothed them.

"Leaving!" Mom barked.

"I am happy you made it out of the Graeae's cave in one piece. As you can see, I did not." His finger tapped his eye patch, and my stomach rolled.

They plucked out his eye. Harsh!

"They damaged my eye enough to blind me. Without proper care… I was forced to don a patch. The girls don't seem to mind." He gave a dry chuckle. Herc joined him, so I threw him the stink-eye.

He was just trying to make light of the fact that those evil witches attacked him.

If he hadn't gotten out when he did, he'd have lost more than an eye.

I shivered at the thought.

This entire planet is like a travesty of bad parents and crazy.

"I went there because I'm a Nymph," Erik stated, and a broad smile stretched across his face, revealing straight white teeth.

I pressed my hand over my mouth to smother a giggle.

I shouldn't laugh.

I pictured Nymphs as semi-naked women, roaming the forest with strategically placed leaves all over them, petting unicorns, and waiting for men to come to have their way with them.

"The term *Naiad* or *Nymph* is a title. We study the sciences. On Elysium, it's the name given to scientists." Erik's matter-of-fact statement reminded me of Hera or Ixis. They offered information in the same tone.

I glanced at mom, and her ears turned pink, trying to hold back the laugh that was threatening to explode from her lips at any moment. However, I was not as strong as she was, so very soon, I lost my battle and burst out laughing.

"Then, you know where the Nymphs' research laboratory is?" Adrian said over the laughter.

That was his attempt at diplomacy.

"Here, on Elysium, you don't have a choice over what you do with your life. You are trained from birth to be what the Judges want you to be. I was born a Naiad. Therefore, I was expected to spend all of my existence researching science." His brows pulled down, and his face darkened, "They leave out the part about your scientific discoveries amounting to nothing and never being used, recognized, or implemented."

I really hated it when people told these kinds of stories. I was not a scientifically minded person, and I definitely was not into math. I did, however, think technology was cool. And even though I liked art and music, reading history was a true passion of mine.

When you're living on a boat, it's pretty easy to figure out whether you're headed in the right direction or not.

If you're heading East, the sunsets behind you. If it's in front of you, well, you know you're going the wrong way.

"So, what did you go and see the old ladies for?" I asked.

The mirth from a moment ago turned to shivers. The sight of the clammy gray-skinned bone munchers turned my blood to ice.

"My mother and I invented a medicine that helped limbs regrow. The Judges gave me a task," he said and tapped his eyepatch.

The irony of his words hit me at my core.

"I lost my eye, and the next thing I knew, I was shipped off to Phaedra. If I told you I don't want revenge, I would be lying. I want the Judges to pay. They maimed me and thousands of other Elysiums who now live permanently damaged." His jaw ground down. "They steal body parts from children rather than allow us to create new ones, simply by implementing science and technology."

"Why do they even have you studying anything if you aren't allowed to use it?" Herc spat. His muscles flexed with agitation.

Perseus was as quiet as a mouse. I peeked around Herc at him only to find my brother-in-law in what I called the DemiGod battle stance. Herc had the same pose when he was ready to kill someone. Perseus stood as still as the bronze statues made in his honor.

"We are play   things, nothing more. Overturning their rule is the only thing that can save my people. Yes, I am here for revenge and not to get my eye back. Losing one eye opened both of them."

Hercules and Perseus chuckled at the turn of phrase.

"Nothing like good old-fashioned pain to help you see the truth of the situation," mom said, gazing over each member that recently joined our group.

"I want my mother and all of my people to have a chance to be recognized for what they do. I don't want their hard work and knowledge to be a futile waste of time," the man added.

"Well, who are the rest of these brave fools?" Mom barked, her feet shifting on the beach along with a few rocks.

She was getting antsy, which meant that shit was going to fly soon if we didn't.

"I wasn't sure if you'd already gone into the Graeae's cave. I brought them as backup. Seeing as you survived, we might need them somewhere else." He shrugged.

"Do you know what the Judge asked us to bring him?" Mom inquired.

Erik-the-one-eye paled, then swallowed. "He's asked for the head of Medusa."

Three of his men stepped back and shook their heads.

"Then we shall all die!" the closest man stated in a flat-lifeless voice.

"Say what?" Herc asked as if he didn't understand.

<Hey, don't be a dick! They aren't the great and powerful Hercules.> I chided.

<They should be grateful I'm here, not weeping and tearing their shirts like women in a death wail.> He scoffed.

"Medusa is old and powerful. She's a vengeful, angry woman if you can call her that. She's a Gorgon. They hate men, all men. But they hate women even more," Erik-the-one-eye informed us.

"They can hate us all they want. As long as we're able to cut off Medusa's head, I don't care about their feelings," Mom barked, itching to get on with it.

"And return it to Rhadamanthy for my mother," Perseus clearly stated, as if we could or would forget.

Jeez!

Information is power. Mom was always chanting that mantra.

It makes you strong.

We were raised with the strong belief that the only way to conquer the trials and tribulations of life was through information.

Otherwise, you might as well run around saying 'woe is me' killing everything in sight.

"Let's go kill her and be done with it!" Herc threw it out as if no one had thought of it before. I had to smother a laugh.

"You know, Hercules, it might do you good to listen before you decide to jump up and down, saying *I'm gonna kill everything*. Scorched-earth doesn't always work. You can't just charge in headlong," Perseus rebuked him.

"We need information and a plan of action," mom stated with clipped words as the wind whipped around her head, pulling the hair from its braid.

"Sydney is correct. You do need information, and I will take you to the place where you will get it," Erik said.

"Can you give Adrian a visual?" Mom asked and offered the holographic map that popped up from her bracelet.

"I did something even better." He winked his one eye. "I told Tristan where we needed to go, so he will shift us as soon as you tell him to."

Nice plan.

I liked this Nymph, err Naiad.

<Tristan?> Mom called.

I stuck my finger in my ear and shook it.

God, she's loud!

<Shifting you now, mom.>

The pressure around us changed with a pop at the end.

I think Tristan has lost his touch, moving people through a fixed planetary atmosphere.

<Heard that! I didn't lose my touch. I just got lazy.> Tristan remarked.

<All right! Remember - death is in the details.> Mom chided.

"It's *the devils in the details*, mom," I intervened.

"No, I said exactly what I meant - *death is in the details*. We are dealing with life and death here. All the fiddling around and not doing it right can have only one resolution -- someone will die. That's in the details." She smirked, in her smug fashion, still thinking I was wrong.

I really didn't give two shits. I'd learned long ago to let mom have her little wins.

The side of the building in front of me was fashioned entirely of trees and branches. They were woven and bent. If I believed in magic, this would be all the proof I needed.

Which I don't.

Too much of my mother's cynicism had rubbed off on me. Fairy tales and mythology were nothing more than lies mixed in the blender of time, while the color of truth was muted and watered down, and the masses drank it.

The building was natural, flowing, and beautiful, all at the same time. The wood from the trees contorted into cross beams and support posts. Their crowns towered overhead, and the canopy became the roof. Vines wove tight to one another, creating walls and framing windows and doors. Leaves melded like the scales of a fish coloring the walls. It was earthen warmth and naturally crisp and alive.

Architecture at its finest.

"Well, I guess this part of the stories is true. Nymphs are lovers of nature?" I asked.

One-eye opened his arms, "Nymphs do love nature. We love to manipulate it, study it, and contort it to our vision. What you are looking at is a building created using technology. Every building on Elysium could be built this way, incorporating life and art into the structure." He crossed his arms with satisfaction and pride. "But the Judges of Elysium don't allow it, so this is the only building of its kind." The bitterness that lined the back of his throat was palpable; you could almost choke on the acidity.

My hand found its way to One-eye's shoulder, "Maybe, this is the first step in changing that. It is a beautiful building," I murmured.

His emotions ran higher the closer we got to the structure. Finally, he shook his head and turned away.

An opening formed out of the intricately woven wood, and a woman exited with arms open wide to greet us. "Erik, the Judges have returned you to me!" Her face was covered in tears.

"Yes, mother! Though, I cannot believe you even recognize me." His visage changed, illuminating his face, as he opened his arms to embrace the woman hurrying toward us.

"Where once stood a child, I now see a hardened man. Your presence makes the air feel fresher" She pulled him in and wrapped her arms around his waist, resting her head against his chest.

Her speech, the buildings, even One-eye's behavior was an interesting mix of weird mythology/technology.

How is it that humanity got it so wrong?

<The Themian aren't any better.> Hercules smirked.

How can there be so many weird ideas about who and what these people really are? How could they not know their own people, their own origins?

"We shall go inside. There will be refreshments," the woman waved us at the doors with an arm wrapped around One-eye's waist.

"Mother, they are here to free us," Erik the-one-eye supplied.

She stopped dead in her tracks, "You left to get us permission, and you come back with a war party?" she pulled her arm from him and stepped away. Fear hung about her like a cloak.

"No, I was enslaved. They sent me to Phaedra, to the mines. These people freed me."

Her outrage melted into deep concern. She petted his jaw while searching his face.

The desire to hold one's child close, to keep them safe, that was something I understood. I saw it enough times in the memories of the people I judged. My mother gave me that hungry look more times than I could count.

So, I hung back, giving them the space they needed.

"The Graeae said you would have something, some fabric that we could use. Something to help us kill Medusa?" Erik cupped her chin and searched her eyes.

The color from the Nymph's face drained away, "If you wish to kill Medusa, you are agreeing to your own death. You will all lose your lives. Medusa is impossible to kill. She has an evil heart and a warped mind to accompany it." Goose flesh swept over the woman, and she trembled. "She will never let any of you leave her islands alive. Especially after you've shown that you are in league with her father. You may as well offer your flesh up for science testing or harvesting for everyone in your group. For that will be all that will be left of you," she choked, tears working their way down her face.

Erik-the-one-eye shook his head, "Mother, they are *like* Medusa. They've already seen the Graeae and survived unscathed. I didn't — so my punishment for my failure was life on Phaedra for me and any offspring I might have." He hunched down to meet her eye to eye. "They can move people with their minds. They talk to each other over long distances without a device."

She pressed her lips flat, then turned from her son to take us in. It didn't matter what her son said. The cloak of fear would never be forgotten.

"My name is Daphne. Please come inside our facility. We would like to help you. The longer we stand here… someone will take notice of your presence," she finished.

<What do you think, Adrian? > Mom asked, broadcasting for everyone's benefit because she couldn't help herself.

<I can't find any deception. It's mostly fear. Not of us, but for her people. She's afraid someone will come and punish them. >

<Rhadamanthy?> I asked.

<Not him precisely.>

CHAPTER 13

PERSEUS

Sydney's face was filled with wonder, as was Hercules' and Isolde's. They marveled at everything the Nymphs built here. They were both like children.

I saw something very different - a bunch of people milling around trying to figure out what to do. It made me angry. My mother was stuck with Rhadamanthy, and we had no idea what he was doing to her.

Is she being well treated or not?

His threat to cut her apart, piece by piece to listen, to her *sweet cries* still filled my ears. Rage built in me even now.

I wanted to wrap my fingers around my hilt and start chopping things apart.

Anything.

Those crazy old blind ladies said we needed something from these people.

I used up the last of my patience. That well ran dry the moment my mother pulled us off Homeworld 10. Now, all I wanted was to live, and it seemed that all we did was react.

Even now, I'm reacting.

The need to cut anybody in my way down was just another reaction.

One my father would have acted upon.

I pushed that need away. I rejected the thought that death was the best choice.

There is always another way.

I must find it.

The leader of the Nymphs was Daphne. She was beautiful, young, and nimble, just as mother described them.

"The Graeae sent you here. I'm assuming for weapons, yes?"

"Yes, they said something about you having a fabric that was impervious. The kibsis?" Sydney lacked the finesse of diplomacy. Just like Ares, she didn't dance around an issue. She went in for the cutting blow, removing all that stood in the way of moving forward.

"We've created an amazing polymer material that is impervious to everything — so far. We haven't found anything that can damage it, or even remove its luster," the woman explained, and swelled with pride, then continued, "There is a drawback. We cannot seem to make more than a few yards at a time. It requires a great deal of resources. And the Judges will not allow us to have enough for everyone. If we could reproduce this material on a massive scale, it could replace almost anything. It's practically indestructible and doesn't deteriorate. Entire industries would disappear overnight. Your favorite clothing would last forever, your shoes too. Interplanetary ships would never need new hulls. Personal transports wouldn't have to worry about collisions, as there would be no damage. If your child fell, their clothes would protect them from most harm." She sparkled with all the possibilities.

Her passion shines.

"It would free up our populace from being indentured servants, making standard fabrics or flexible materials. They'd be freed to explore more science, moving our people forward in different avenues instead of being stuck in the past like a hill that never erodes," Daphne finished.

Everyone nodded in agreement, especially Sydney. *That woman's mind was always working.*

"Do you have enough of it to make a bag? We need a bag to carry Medusa's head when I cut it from her shoulders," Sydney announced.

Daphne opened and closed her mouth, faltering. "Perhaps there's something you do not understand about the Gorgons or the Graeae. This facility has stood for many generations. The Nymphs have always been scientists, studying nature, trying to emulate it, cultivate, and recreate it. The Judges instructed us many thousands of years ago to make them immortal," she stopped and gulped.

There was weight to her words, and she carried every bit of it.

"We needed to create something that would allow them to live well beyond a regular Elysium lifespan. We were able to create serums that extended life. Life, not youth. We created treatments and cures for various illnesses. We discovered that transplanting organs from one person to another would extend life greatly. Yet, none of them brought youth. So, the Judges grew angry." The longer she spoke, the heavier the air grew. Sydney was not happy, and the pressure in the room reflected that.

"That was until a young, brilliant scientist presented himself. He took us in a completely new direction - genetic engineering. Before him, we were just creating serums to slow aging. He altered cells at the molecular level, down where the information was first gained, created, and re-created."

This was important information.

Who was that man?

"He discovered a way to turn off the aging mechanism within the cells itself. However, it required testing. We explained everything to the Judges of Elysium we needed to test the treatment. They instantly realized that if we were successful in our trials, our test subjects would become immortal. They decided to use children."

"The Graeae said that Rhadamanthy was their father."

"He is. And so is Minos and Aeakus."

Isolde scoffed at this, "They can't all be their fathers." Hercules squeezed her shoulder

Daphne smiled, "They are a genetic blend of all three. No one Judge of Elysium could claim sole parental rights over any of the triplets."

"What do you mean *'triplets'*? Why are you using plurals? You're talking in riddles, so spit it out!"

Impatience should be Sydney's middle name.

<My middle name is Rhiannon, and if you're going to make rude musings about me, make sure that you're not broadcasting to the entire globe. >

I went still. I didn't realize she was powerful enough to hear me or that I was broadcasting.

Guess you get what you deserve when you are not paying attention and being a horse's ass.

<Yes, try to remember not to be an asshole, Perseus. You'll find out that it's easier to make more friends and influence more people that way. >

"Gorgons, Graeae, Pythia, they're all the daughters of the Elysium Judges. Although, technically, Rhadamanthy doesn't claim Medusa. Yet, they are sisters nonetheless. So it really doesn't matter which Elysium Judge claims them."

Internally I groaned, as did everyone else.

"Which Judge claims Medusa?" The grinding began in my belly.

The Judges were crafty. They hadn't been around for thousands of years, outliving their entire population without figuring out how to pit one person against another.

The Judges would make sure that if you succeed, they'd have another reason to try to hurt you, hate you, kill you.

"Medusa is the daughter of Aeakus."

"So, by killing her, we will never make it any further in our goal of peace with the Judges?"

Daphne didn't reply. She looked down and away. She already knew the answer.

"That's great! Mutually assured self-destruction no matter what we do. They're never gonna let us negotiate with them for anything. Mom, this is a waste of time!" Isolde spat.

Isolde gave me a wineskin. I pulled the stopper and gulped a hearty amount. Primordium — the ambrosia of life wet all in this world. The wine was laced with it, and a heavy feeling of health engulfed me, washing away the last of my chest pain.

I heaved a deep breath. "It's not a waste of time." I took another draw from the skin, "Saving my mother is not a waste of time. It is the only way to save Hera, and maybe we can save everyone else in the process. I'm not leaving this planet without my mother. I'll not settle here, knowing that I settled for her death. Either we all save her or all die trying. Run away if you want, but I'm staying."

Hercules clasped my forearm, and I returned the motion.

"Brother, Isolde was just pointing out the futility of it. Of course, we must kill Medusa. Of course, we will rescue our mother. There is no other option. We all know this, and you would not die trying alone. I would be right by your side, killing anyone who stays in the way. I can't speak for the others, but Isolde will die alongside me because she won't leave either."

A strong hand landed on my shoulder, and I turned to meet Adrian's piercing blue eyes.

"You are not alone in your battles. We all care for Hera. She is not only your mother but mother to us all. We're not leaving her. Sydney and I wouldn't do that. We wouldn't leave anybody behind no matter what it cost us."

CHAPTER 14

SYDNEY

Adrian's words joined my own mental monologue. We wouldn't leave anyone behind no matter what it cost us.

Yet I had.

Zack, Maria, Nonna, Maria's boys, I'd left them on Earth. They were humans. I had to leave them behind. There was no other way. However, every time I thought about them, it was like a knife in my gut.

When it came to explaining Adrian, and my loss to Gabriel, things were easy. Zack, on the other hand, well, he could barely wrap his head around me crying. My emotions made him crazy.

Try explaining to Zack I'm a superhuman hybrid who has the ability to move things with her mind. Along with astral projection. Oh, and by the way, Zack, I'm also mentally connected to this really hot guy over here that I told you died years ago.

Yeah, that would not have gone over well with him. His brain wasn't big enough for that. Maria probably could've accepted anything as long as she knew that we were all alive and safe. Regardless of that, I left them all behind.

I never gave them a choice.

<You did what was best for them, *beautiful girl*. They are humans. They aren't like us. They both weep for you. Zack thought you were broken after Gabriel, and you were.> Adrian soothed.

Nothing he said could change how I felt. <Yeah, and all it took was you coming back for me to suddenly be fixed?> I snarled more to myself than him.

After Adrian, I did feel better. Whole somehow.

<*Beautiful girl*, only time will fix what happened. You may never feel any better about Gabriel or his death. But at some point, it won't pierce you to the core so deeply. >

Gabriel, Adrian...I looked at Isolde's face. It was a reflection of my own. She, too, felt the pain of the people we left behind too.

Zack wouldn't have acclimated, and Maria would've been mad because she couldn't get Locatelli cheese in space. It wouldn't have worked out.

Tears pricked my eyes. I hadn't thought too hard about the fact that I was never gonna see them again. I slammed the box holding those emotions closed. Now was definitely not the time for a pity party.

That won't save Hera. Zack and Maria are safe. Hera isn't.

So, I did what I always do - I charged ahead. "Medusa and her sisters are genetically altered. They are some kind of Super-Elysium/Themians which means they are just like us. Plus, they're all crazy. So what? Oh, not to mention that by killing them, we will be pissing off the other Judges. Can you give me an upside for this?" My mental map of pitfalls became more of a field of landmines.

One-eye shifted uncomfortably on his feet. "By killing Medusa, you save thousands from a fate worse than death? I never made it to Medusa, and I'm grateful for that. I would not have survived. No one does." His counterpoint was valid yet, distasteful.

"Why? Does she turn people to stone by looking at them?" I laughed at my joke.

Please don't let that part be true.

The Nymphs in the room shifted uncomfortably. They obviously didn't find my flippant statement humorous. Even Isolde twitched.

"Oh, come on! Really?" I groaned, "You're going to tell me that the turning to stone thing is real?" I scoffed and crossed my arms. "Agh! How in the fuck is that even possible?"

Every Nymph in the room got twitchy. Daphne clasped her right elbow with her left hand. Finally, she let both arms drop.

"She turns anyone she gazes upon to stone." She nodded for emphasis. "She went to the Graeae for help with their fathers. They plucked out both her eyes," she shivered then continued, "the Graeae said they couldn't eat their own and pushed her out of the cave." Daphne's attention trailed around the room, "She came here looking for help. We took her in. We tried to create replacements," she opened her hands as a show. She wasn't hiding their culpability, "due to her genetic makeup, nothing was successful. We weren't able to replicate viable replacements."

I wondered how long they tried.

Ten years? A Hundred? A Thousand?

The lingering traces of guilt hung in the air. Each scientist was unable to meet my inquiring gaze. They did something to Medusa, and they didn't want to admit it.

Nymphs were supposed to be nature lovers. They blended with trees and rivers, things like that. Upon closer inspection, the little differences I expected became apparent. A speckling around the eyes here, an iridescent hue of the skin there. One of the women had a green cast to her hair and hazel eyes with a green star in the center.

They've all been altered!

"Medusa is immortal. The Gorgons were our second attempt. Graeae, our first. She was created in a dish. We whipped her and her sisters together. We couldn't recreate her eyes," one of the other Nymphs hurriedly supplied.

The green-haired Nymph broke in. "We used Basilisk eyes. We transplanted them. They were the best match, blending perfectly with her genetic mix." It came out in a rush with a sigh at the end, as if just getting the words out made her feel better.

This just kept getting better and better.

I pressed my eyes closed, hoping whatever they said next was better than my imagination. "What mix?" I asked breathlessly.

A male with iridescent skin replied, "Elysian, basilisk, and reptilian. That's all we know for sure. However, we suspect more than one reptile sample was implemented."

"After being rejected by her father and having her sisters pluck out her eyes, it fractured her mind. We had to label her genetically unstable. There is some kind of connection between the three women. Her sisters, Euryale and Stheno, exhibited the same psychological tendencies. We had to mark them too." Daphne shook her head over the problem. "Emotionally, they're all devoid of something. Almost as if we'd accidentally plucked it out of their very programming." She looked from Isolde to me and back.

She knows we are from Pythia.

"Eons ago, I would've tried to right it as soon as it was identified. But none of us live long enough. We didn't create the problem. The real genetic changes were invented by someone else, Anu. He was brilliant, but he's gone now. He challenged the Judges and disappeared," she replied in a lackluster fashion.

I threw up my arms in exasperation.

Charon and his happy band of genetic blenders.

This was just another fuck-up to add to the pile. They made this mess, then ran off to start their utopia, only to create another fucking Dystopia.

When will anyone learn you can't play God?

The walls groaned with my anger. I was mentally pulling at them, like a child plucking a string hanging from my shirt. I slowly pulled a calming breath in through my nose and held it before releasing it from my mouth while I released my pull on the walls.

I can't pull down the building just because I'm surrounded by people too stupid to see that what they've done is wrong or how continuing to meddle only makes it worse.

"Let me show you our polymer. It's fantastic! I think it will fill your needs precisely," Daphne offered and indicated we should follow her through a door. "Our pieces aren't very large, but I'm sure there's more than enough to create some kind of a bag or even a suit to protect one person." she finished with a tight smile.

The tension in the room was thick, and I was the real cause. I had to ease up. Issy winced every few minutes. So, I did another breathing exercise.

"All we need is a bag. Perseus can carry it," I said.

My hair was still slimy with salt spray from the beach. It itched as it dried, and I absently raked my nails across the back of my neck. My nails came away filled with grim and the salty residue you can only gain from hours by the sea.

Perseus shot me a glare. I couldn't tell if it was anger or if he was surprised. Frankly, I didn't care. The longer this quest wore on, the more it sounded like his fucked up Greek mythology story.

Might as well leave him holding the bag.

How did humanity get it so right, yet so wrong to begin with?

CHAPTER 15

PERSEUS

"You have the weapon covered?" I asked in a low voice.

Hercules reached over his shoulder and pulled out his sword. It flashed with the cutting beams of refracted light. I'd not seen light cut in such a fashion in eons. The underlying metallic color resembled orichalcum in its yellowish glow.

This was not the sword he carried while we were living on Earth.

"She said '*a sword, not of this world.*'" Mirth bubbled from his very skin. "She also said that it had to be a sword made of a material Elysium didn't possess," he continued.

"This sword is made of diamonds and a material I can't identify. I won it from Hermes." He turned it this way and that, admiring the flecks of light that shot from the blade's edge. "He was begrudging about the whole thing. I guess when you're bested by someone you view as a lower being, it's hard to swallow," Hercules joshed about his prize with gusto.

"You bested Hermes for that?" I puffed up with pride at my brother's feat.

I wish I'd seen the battle.

Hermes was always a little too self-assured. Being a messenger of the High Council didn't really mean much. They simply had him carry messages on their behalf because he was capable of transporting himself from one world to another. Truth was that he couldn't transport anything else, but that little fact got left out of the stories.

My memory of his scoffing at Pythia and her Fates still burned me. He had little respect for the words of Pythia.

I stood there, on the verge of another Pythian prophecy, and wondered what was to come next.

What else did she warn us about and the High Council didn't share?

"So, there he was, having one of his braggart sessions, running around, talking about what a great fighter he was and how fabulous his new sword was." Hercules couldn't miss the chance to tell the story. "I moved in to listen, and he decided to show off to his friends, saying, 'I bet that I best that Demigod over there with one hand tied behind my back.' They all laughed. I didn't think it was funny, but his sword was beautiful, so I accepted this challenge."

Hercules' eyes twinkled with glee. His talent flooded the room, and the Nymphs leaned in for the next tidbit. "I said I would fight him, but with one condition - the winner takes home his sword." Hercules thrust the sword out so everyone in the room could admire the oddity. He even handed it around. The artificial light gave it an otherworldly glow. "He figured that since I was part human, I didn't represent a challenge at all." Finally, my brother handed the sword to me to inspect and turned his attention back to the hungry crowd.

Isolde snorted. Her eyes gleamed with Hercules' antics.

"He agreed. So, while he was still smirking to his friends, I disarmed him." Chuckles blanketed us.

"Well, he grew angry. I put my sword down. I had no desire to fight an unarmed man. We went at each other head-to-head and hand-to-hand. I rolled with him across the ground. We parted, and I took my feet, and we tussled again. He tore at my clothes in an attempt to throw me off balance. But I pinned him to the ground, leaving him incapable of doing anything more than crying for mercy like a baby at its mother's breasts." Hercules' smooth smile raced over the rapt crowd, "He conceded, and I took possession of the sword." He crossed his arms and lifted his shoulders as if it was no big deal that he bested a minister of the High Council.

Even though he was bragging, I had to admit that I was rather impressed.

"I noticed that Hermes stopped baiting us. I wondered why. Why didn't you mention you fought him and took his sword earlier?" I asked while slapping my brother on the back.

Hercules shrugged, then looked down and away, "It was too easy, barely even a challenge. I felt bad. I wanted him to pay for putting us down and talking about us as if we were lesser creatures," he sobered. "We weren't Themian enough for him. He always referred to us as Demigods when he knew the humans referred to Themians as full-blooded Gods. Once I took his prize, he was under no illusions." He dusted his hands, then finished his speech, "I'm glad. We obviously have need of it. I know Sydney doesn't believe in fate, but where would we be now if I didn't have it? Everything happens for a reason, and I believe that. I have to believe that."

I mentally groaned. Sydney's voice tore through the air.

The woman just won't accept her own fate.

"What would you do if you didn't believe in fate? You would make all your own choices. You wouldn't leave it to the wind. Thinking that everything has to happen for a reason, that is a weak-minded person's argument. Everything happens for a reason? Bullshit! Instead of that, why not decide the reason for yourself and make it happen. Hercules, you're with my daughter, and you make her happy. Therefore, I'm happy for that. But that doesn't mean that I have to stand around and listen to your *'everything happens for a reason'* shit," she was shouting, so I moved to her side and laid my hand on her arm, hoping to calm her.

It had no effect.

"I think reason makes things happen. You make a choice and live with that choice. No matter how good or bad, your choice is what determines what happens. Not some unforeseen creature determining your fate long before you ever had a chance to make a choice. I still think that's bullshit and have seen nothing to the contrary."

I could agree with her in some instances.

Yes, you do make a choice, then live with your choices. And those choices help determine your fate.

But I also believed that some instances were preordained, and there was nothing you could do to change them.

They unfold exactly as intended.

<Broadcasting a little loud again, aren't you?> Adrian's voice filled the empty cracks in my mind, reminding me I wasn't alone.

<Yes, sometimes I broadcast a little loud.>

<Believe it or not, I appreciate your advice. It's always good to have a new perspective on life, one that you couldn't possibly achieve on your own.>

I opened my eyes to a visage so much like my own, standing before me.

"Good job, old man," Isolde remarked with a smirk to Hercules and his overblown story.

Adrian patted me on the shoulder, "We've got the weapon and the bag. We know where she's at. All we need now is to complete the deed."

"Are we supposed to have some wing shoes or something?" Sydney asked in a snide tone.

"I think you're thinking of the human version, Sydney," I remarked, volleying her sarcastic banter.

"Then, we should have Tristan move this shit-show along," she drolled.

"Yeah, I think we got everything we need. Let's go cut the snakes off her head," Hercules chuckled at his turn of phrase.

"Snakes for hair? That's got to be another human construct?" Isolde scoffed and ran a hand over Hercules' arm.

She was petting him. A heavy dose of longing welled up inside me.

I caught Sydney's eye. Her brow was raised in curiosity. I waited for her inquisitive mind to take over and ask questions. Instead, she patted me on the shoulder, giving me a little squeeze.

"The snake hair and wings. Were the real reasons the Gorgons weren't considered a success." a Nymph with glossy black hair and obsidian eyes informed us.

We all turned and looked at him.

"What? I thought you knew," he replied and shrugged away his discomfort.

I stared him down with hard eyes, hoping there were no new revelations to be had. He gave me a weak smile and released a dry laugh that died when I bared my teeth.

One-eye tossed shields at each of us. "You can use it to block her arrows and nets."

Sydney huffed. My feelings were in line with hers. I didn't want to hear about one more thing, yet I waited to see if there was more.

Just in case.

CHAPTER 16

PERSEUS

I went into my inner sanctum. It resembled the interior of the citadels. Thousands of bench seats filled the space. Some were occupied, but most were not. I stood on the dais, taking in the crowd in my room. My mind was muddled. Too many voices floated around, all pulling me in different directions. I needed focus, and for that, I needed peace. With the loudest internal voice I could muster, I boomed, "GET OUT!" Every one of those voices vanished in a flash.

I was alone.

I'd never heard them in the background, but they were gone, all of them, and blessed silence was left behind.

My feet found their way back to the entrance of my private citadel. Stepping over the threshold, I stopped, turned, and mentally bricked it closed.

This place will never be open again.

In our world, having anyone listen in is dangerous. I'd always expected to lose my sister and my ability to contact her this way.

Now, if someone wanted to listen in on what I was thinking, they were going to have to break in, and I would put up a fight.

There were too many of *us*, those with genetic changes. It's no longer safe to keep an open mind.

"Is Medusa immortal like us?" Isolde asked and bit her lip, then pulled the lower lip from between her teeth.

"Yes. But does she have any special abilities? That's the real question," Hercules' mind mirrored his mates. Why they didn't carry on their mental chatter in the privacy of their minds, I couldn't understand.

"Have you not been listening to anything Daphne said? She has the ability to turn people to stone with her evil eyes! Or you don't consider that a special power?" Sydney returned. She was also biting her lip.

"It is not the only one. We have the ability to communicate with our minds and the use of the forces," I reminded them.

Isolde burst in, "I'm sorry, but why exactly do we call it '*the forces*' again?"

"Because *it* refers to the forces of nature, Issy." Sydney cocked an eyebrow at her. Clearly, she wasn't enamored with the title either, yet there wasn't any other way to describe it.

"Wind, fire, earth, water, what else should we call them, resources?" Sydney scoffed. She had no time for these kinds of discussions. To her, everything was what it was, and there was no reason to worry over it. She took the world as it came to her. She only made changes when it chafed against her personal honor code.

A deep husky chuckle filled my mind. It was thickly laced with amusement, the kind you have for a small, petulant child who said something to amuse you.

<Oh, yes, small, petulant children, that is an apt description.> The voice remarked.

My marrow froze with the realization my thoughts were not protected. She heard me.

<Are you all planning to come, kill me, by taking my pretty head? Don't worry! It'll be here waiting for you. As for powers? Ooops! I guess I just gave one away. I wanted to give you something to think about on your little trip all the way to my island.> She chuckled and snorted. <Just because Rhadamanthy sent you, it doesn't mean you'll succeed. Oh, I know that you've seen my sisters. You think that they decided to help you. Guess again! They are only helping themselves.>

A new voice joined the smooth chocolaty velvet, mocking us.

<One thing you should know about our family if you haven't already realized it.>

The third Gorgon took over, <We will do whatever is best for ourselves and no one else. But we can't wait to meet you all.> Three minds laughed at us, each in her special way.

A wrenching pain seized my brain. The pressure in my cranium caused every vein to rise and pulse. Clasping my hands to either side of my head, I fell to the ground. She was like Rhadamanthy. She had a mind strong enough to cause pain, from which she took pleasure.

"What the hell is wrong with all of you? Adrian!" The shrill laughter inside my mind slowly subsided, only to see Sydney leaning over Adrian. He was in the same fetal position I was.

I pushed the residual pain back and rolled over to him, "Push it out, Adrian! Push them out!" I shouted, giving him another sound to focus on.

"Where the hell did you all go?" Sydney demanded, "Your minds disappeared." She patted Adrian's cheek, who rolled onto his back, breathing heavily.

One-eye twitched. Two men from his group's eyes were fixed, staring at the sky. I searched the rest of our band, looking for my brother. His face was dark with anger. "What in Hades and the Underworld just happened?"

The laughter started in my mind again, only I wasn't frozen this time.

"Hercules! Do you hear it?" I asked.

He shook his head.

<Oh, silly Perseus, you seem to be the only one who has the heart for it. Everyone else is just barely holding on. Don't worry, Perseus, I won't kill any of your other companions. Yet— > Then she was gone.

"You were talking to her. What the hell did she say to you?" Sydney was on her feet in a flash, demanding answers.

"She has the ability to break through a closed mind," I replied. The full ramifications of this problem weighed more than the world on Atlas' shoulders.

"What does that mean?" Hercules asked. He ran his fingers through his hair. Isolde moved behind him, and he knelt. She began braiding the nest of hair he wore back. My brother always bound his hair before a battle.

Sydney shook her head, "What do you think it means, brainiac? It means she's strong. It means that she knows we're coming, and apparently, she's got a hard-on for Percy over there." She hooked her thumb at me.

I bristled and crossed my arms, "My name is Perseus. Not Percy."

Sydney scoffed, then laughed at me. "What difference does it make what I call you? Percy, Perseus, the big P? Who cares? Medusa wants to kill you. She's picked you out extra special. So once again, what the fuck did she say? Because we certainly didn't hear it." The room around us moved. The walls flexed in and out as if breathing along with Sydney and her temper.

I hate it when Sydney's right. But why me?

"She's taunting us, beautiful girl. She wants to strike fear into us or test us," Adrian offered to calm her. An angry Sydney was a dangerous one.

"She was testing us all right. Adrian, she was looking for weak spots. Apparently, those two dead guys over there are a few of them." She waved her index finger at them, then bit her lip, pulling the flesh slowly from between her white teeth.

"One-eye, are you okay?" I asked. After encountering him and his people on their ship, I'd come to feel responsible for them. He only joined us to end the Judges' control.

I believe that, like myself, he wants to be here.

One-eye pulled his hands away from his ears and nodded his head. His brows were drawn together in a tight line. Fear scented the air, seeping from his pores. He took to his feet and clenched his jaw in resolve.

"I am whole. Although, I fear going into her temple. I may never come out." Blood trickled from his ears and leaked down his neck, disappearing into the collar of his shirt.

If there was blood in his ears, it must have been on everyone else's.

Elysian's weren't meant to be treated this way.

"She killed them just by talking to them." Isolde's lips curled in disgust. Hercules put his hands on her shoulders and whispered something indistinguishable in her ear. She buried her face in his chest for a moment. Whatever he said was just enough to pacify her. However, it wasn't going to make it all go away.

You can't make this kind of horror disappear.

"One-eye, if you and your men want to go back to Odyssey, no one would think less of you. We can go on without you. You've helped enough already," I offered a way out, allowing them to save face.

He won't take it, yet the others might.

One-eye turned his head and glanced around his group. The faces of all were set in grim lines and tight jaws. "Thank you, Perseus, but we shall continue on to the end. Every one of our people deserves revenge. If I die in Medusa's Temple, then so be it. However, if even one of us lives to finish the Judges of Elysium, it will be worth it."

I took in the rest of his men. They were unflinching.

I guess if you're going into battle against a crazy snake-haired woman, being surrounded by a bunch of guys hell-bent on revenge isn't a bad war party.

Her laughter still echoed in the back of my mind. The cackling was like an old woman with a big wooden spoon and a bubbling cauldron, stirring up trouble.

My mother's face took shape in my mind.

I will free my mother or die trying. The Judges will pay! All of them!

Power was never meant to be used in such a fashion.

CHAPTER 17

SYDNEY

Even if I die today, at least both my children won't.

Don't get me wrong. I didn't want to die. I certainly didn't want Issy to die, and I generally didn't want Hercules to die.

That goes without saying.

Tristan would find a way to live on.

It sounded fatalistic, and I knew it. But the more I thought about it, the more I agreed with Adrian. - *we can't all die.*

Ixis couldn't shift every ship in our fleet. They needed Tristan. So, he had to stay. Our people didn't need Issy. They didn't even really need Hercules. And they didn't *need* me.

Emmaline would lead everyone to a safe planet because Ixis would find the perfect place for them. The fleet didn't need the Fates.

I didn't know how or why we became the driving force. They didn't really need us for anything other than finding a home. And Emmaline was right. We could've picked any planet. Sure, the Themians would eventually know where we were, but hopefully, by then, they may not care.

<Stop musing, beautiful girl. We have things to do and people to kill.>

Of course.

It seemed to be our lot in life these days.

<Where on the planet do we need to go?>

Being an Elysian wasn't much different than being a regular human. They didn't have any powers. Yes, their life span was a little longer than the human lifespan, but only by about 50 years. They weren't like us — immortal.

Adrian pulled up a holographic image of the planet with his bracelet.

He manipulated the hologram, making it big enough to pinpoint a small island. It was actually funny as it wasn't even that far away from Rhadamanthy's.

He could have said, '*hey, the island's just over there.*'

Maybe he really didn't want us to succeed.

Medusa said that nobody in her family did anything that didn't benefit themselves.

The Graeae weren't helping us. They were helping themselves. It was pretty obvious. They were sad, pathetic individuals.

I desperately wanted to touch Rhadamanthy. I wanted to judge him. It was now a compulsion, and I couldn't deny it. Even in the Graeae's cave, along with those three evil witches, the pressing need to reach out and let fate judge was there.

My desire to make them face their crimes was palpable at the tip of my finger. It was like that tang of copper you get when you put your tongue on a 9V battery. I could still taste it even now, making the desire to go back and fulfill my purpose was insatiable.

I swallowed the coppery flavor back, letting it slide down my throat, coating my senses.

"I've got it, beautiful girl. Let's go!" Adrian's warm deep voice pulled me back from the edge of that abyss. I blinked to take in my reality.

The force of fate isn't in charge here. I am!

"Shift us!" I ordered.

"Shifting now."

The subtle nuances of the change were a calling card. You could always tell who was doing the shifting, like the driver of a car.

Tristan's shift was as smooth as warm butter being spread over a piece of hot toast. He managed to ease out the ridges and crannies melting in for the ride. There was no pop or ozone change along the way. You were just there.

Adrian's was similar with a little pop at the end, and Ixis', well, although he was the strongest, he had none of the finesse. For him, it was as if comfort was irrelevant. He could have been running a dredging machine in a river, pulling up slits, and it wouldn't make a difference.

Everything about the island reminded me of my dreams of Alethea. The waving palm trees with the balmy gentle breeze, which I turned and greeted it. Everywhere you looked, there was heavy green and yellow foliage, hapua ferns, philodendrons, coconut palms, and trees that looked like papaya. One massive tree reminded me of a mango I'd seen in Hawaii. The tree could easily have been around 100 years old based on its size.

The feeling of the tropics refreshed me. I closed my eyes and allowed the lapping sound of the water and the scent of salt in the air to engulf me. It was calming. It silenced the need for justice, causing it to recede into the background.

We don't have time for this.

Rhadamanthy wasn't going to hurt Hera. He'd wait for news of our failure before he broke his agreement. He was too desperate to have Medusa killed. My bet was, he was really tired of being trapped on that island.

"So where on this rock is her palace? Er, temple? The building that she lives in?" I grumbled. Issy covered her mouth to hide the giggle lodged there.

"It's further inland. When we reach the gardens, we will know," One-eye offered. Being our only guide, he gave us what little he knew.

At least he knows something.

If we had any other Elysian, there would be even less since the Judges kept the populace subdued in stupidity.

One-eye's men hesitated.

I guess it's easy to be brave when you aren't standing on the precipice, yet when the battle nears, many step back rather than move toward a possible death.

It was natural to feel that way. Even so, I have never felt inclined to flinch. My natural instinct was to lean into it and move forward, facing the fight, and win.

"What are we waiting for? Medusa's not going to hand her head over?" Perseus remarked and kicked a clod of dirt.

A smirk reached my face, and I didn't try to hide my amusement. I liked Perseus. He was different from his siblings. His fire was a pure flame that burned bright. Hercules, too, was a good guy. I just didn't like him because of Isolde. Truthfully, he was a little too flippant about everything.

Of course, Hercules would follow Isolde anywhere, making him a great protector. He was willing to face whatever crossed his path. But he was no leader.

Perseus, on the other hand, needed a cause. He wouldn't go into battle just because there was a battle to be had. He needed a reason, and right now that was his mother.

Perseus led quietly, and men followed him because he demanded nothing from them. He inspired them to be more. One-eye wasn't here just to kill the Judges. He believed that they could be killed, and that was because of Perseus.

No matter what happened, the Fates needed to be together. It was a non-issue.

I needed Hera for 1000 different reasons, some of which had to do with being the Fates. Yet, everything went back to information. She had it, and I wanted it. She knew more than she let on, and the churning in my gut told me this was just another battlefront in a greater war.

I was like Perseus. I didn't fight just to fight. I needed a cause.

Not leaving someone behind was a good enough cause for me.

In most cases.

This time, it had more to do with the fact that Rhadamanthy would do anything to facilitate his existence. Basically, he was just a fucking bastard who needed to die.

Anyone willing to sacrifice their children so they could be an immortal is disgusting.

Yeah, I wanted Hera back for a thousand and one reasons, but I wanted Rhadamanthy more. What they did to those children, chopping them up for body parts, genetically experimenting on people, permanently maiming them, enslaving them, was simply too much for me to pass by.

The part of me that demanded I bring justice was so strong. I couldn't turn away from saving Hera even if I wanted to.

I pulled out of my own mind just long enough to feel the slap of the palm frond in my face.

"Sorry, mom!" Hercules called back to me.

My nose curled up at the side. I was almost sure that Hercules let that thing hit me in the face on purpose.

<Let it go, *beautiful girl.* He is just a big man child.>

<I know. But now he's calling me mom. So, apparently, he's my man-child. Should I take him out and paddle his backside?> I grumbled, though the idea of hitting the crap out of him pulled at the corners of my lips.

A honey-smooth chuckle issued from Adrian's mind, <Now, that would be interesting to watch, *beautiful girl*. Unfortunately, I'm afraid we simply don't have the time for you to reprimand Issy's man child. >

<I know.> I sighed, only to continue, <But, if everything goes according to plan, I should have plenty of time later.>

Adrian released a chuckle.

"What's so funny?" Issy mindlessly inquired. She smacked a bug on her arm and grimaced.

I smirked and lowered my eyes as I pushed some ferns out of the way. "Nothing. Adrian and I are just discussing what we're going to do after we're done taking Medusa's head."

"I think waltzing into her palace to have a Battle Royale sounds like a terrible idea. We need a better plan of action. What we need tactics because that's what wins wars," Adrian remarked.

"I'm not really the Goddess of War. As for wisdom and tactic, we left Athena back on Earth. She would be handy right now, right?" I threw that out there as a gag just for a laugh. Yet, no one appreciated my sarcasm.

"Do you have a plan of your own? Something you want to share with the rest of the class?" Issy asked her mate.

"I'm more of a jump-in and get-it-all-done type of guy," Hercules replied.

We collectively rolled our eyes.

As if we didn't know this about him already.

Perseus stopped and crossed his arms. He tilted his head to the side, moving his fingers over the stubble of the three-day-old beard. "I think we should leave someone outside to cover our retreat. Maybe you and Isolde?" He pointed at Issy and me, then continued, "Hercules and I can go in first, while Adrian brings up the rear," he stopped, waiting for an argument which didn't come. "If there's any problem, you're the only one who can shift us out." He then turned, "One-Eye, you and your men take alternate flanking positions. When we enter the temple, we should probably divide up."

"Keep her distracted?" Adrian asked.

"Yes, we don't know where her sisters are or even if they are on the island. The Graeae made it sound like they were nothing, hardly even a blip. But we can't be sure of anything they said. So, everybody, keep your head down and don't look at anyone you don't know. Especially, don't look at Medusa."

"Don't look her in the eye, isn't that what the stories say?" Hercules asked, then checked our faces to see if he was right.

One-eye was squatting on the ground, pulling leaves off of a yellow fern-like plant. He tossed the small leaves to the side and stood up, "My men and I don't have any protective clothing. Our weapons are nothing more than short knives. If we get close enough to Medusa to kill her, more than likely, she'll kill us. We're merely a distraction. We should behave like a small insect, moving around her palace, irritating her, and creating chaos." He pushed his hands under his biceps, reflecting Hercules' stance.

Judging by the stunned countenance of One-eyes companions, I assumed that none of them had counted on being fodder. They didn't have real weapons, and they weren't physically nearly as strong. Without the control of the forces, they were at a severe disadvantage.

Causing a distraction could create a window of opportunity for everyone else.

"It's a good idea. I don't expect you guys to throw down your lives for Hera or for the rest of us. So, don't do anything stupid or throw your lives away unnecessarily. If you find a weapon in her palace, use it. If you see her coming, but she hasn't seen you, hide. We want as many people as possible to leave this island alive," I said, then pointed at two of One-eye's men, Rogo and Fedar. "You two can stay out front to watch our backs."

They both visibly looked relieved. They'd been the most scared, yet neither of them pissed themselves. So, I wasn't sure about them. *The piss could happen at any moment.*

Rogo looked a little green around the gills.

"That's the best plan we're gonna get, all things considered. I can always call my brother. I'm sure Ares could come up with something much more interesting and effective," Perseus remarked.

My brow pulled down as I scowled, "Absolutely not! Ares stays with the fleet. Though having the Demigod of War down here is mighty alluring, they need him more than we do. He's the best line of defense." I shook my head. T and his girls, along with Tristan, were up there. "We all have people up there we care about more than ourselves, and Ares needs to be there to protect them."

The sparkle in Perseus' eyes when I finished my answer made me think that he only offered this alternative so I could say no. He wanted to make sure I believed in him.

And I do.

He had a helmet that made him invisible and a sword-like I'd never seen before. Even though I was still surprised, Hercules managed to win it off of Hermes.

That guy seemed like a real cock.

And most of all, Pythia said he would kill her.

I don't believe in fate, but this was just too close to the truth to be wrong.

CHAPTER 18

SYDNEY

I used my powers to push the plants out of the way. It was a thoughtless reaction. I didn't want to get smacked in the face again, so I moved everything mentally.

It was like having the entire universe bend around you. A lot of people would've been a little drunk on that kind of power. All things considered, it had been almost 3 years since Gabriel died, and I discovered my ability to move things.

Thinking back, I realized I'd had it a lot longer. I'd used it, so intuitively, it wasn't even noticeable. There were always little things such as my control of water, pushing the boat, packing a suitcase.

Gabriel commented several times we made better time when I was driving. However, at the time, I thought he was just being flippant.

An impenetrable wall of plants filled my vision, blocking any chance of surveying the field, removing any advantage we might gain.

"Great! You guys want to hack through this or walk around?" I asked and rubbed my hand down my legs to wipe the sweat from my palms.

One-eye stepped closer to Adrian, "Can't you move us to the other side with your powers?"

Adrian shook his head, "Doesn't work that way. I need a visual, and we don't know what's on the other side of this hedge or how thick it is. I have no idea what will happen." He turned and stepped away.

<Boy, do I wish it was that easy sometimes. > He remarked.

"Heads left, tails, right?" Trust Hercules to leave everything to chance. He flipped the gold coin into the air, and I grabbed it. There was no way I was leaving anything to fate.

"If you're going to let fate decide, then I'll make the choice. We're going right," I said and tossed the coin back at him.

He scrambled to catch it as a broad grin covered his face, "I love it when fate takes you by the hand."

That was it! I was going to smack that man.

How can Isolde be in love with him?

My eyes wandered down as she took his hand.

What a cheeseball!

The twinkle in Issy's eyes told me everything. She thought he was funny, he did it to annoy me, and it all worked.

I wanted to stamp my foot.

"To the right it is, *beautiful girl*," Adrian's remark was meant to distract me, and I let it work.

Adrian gave me a half-smile while stretching out a hand, inviting me to lead the way. So, I did.

We walked for an hour, finally, Issy's irritation came to a head, "I'm tired of walking around. I want to get where we're going before the sun goes down or I die of old age," she finished with a small smile and a pout.

"I can fix that." Adrian coughed, and there was a giant hole in the hedge where previously dense foliage once lived. The opening was big enough for one person to enter at a time. Perseus plunged in before a word was uttered.

One by one, we stepped into a new and orderly world. On the other side were low box hedges (at least they looked like box hedges), no more than 3 feet tall. Bushes of all kinds covered in flowers and blossoms interspersed the hedged areas. In between the hedges were paths made with slabs of a marble-like substance. It reminded me more of the Themian crystalline composite than marble. The flecks of crystal circuitry along with the golden veins of orichalcum were, however, absent.

A precursor, perhaps?

Fountains spewed water everywhere. The splendor of it put Rhadamanthy's meager garden to shame. The garden flowed from decorative and orderly to a jungle-like chaos. The fruits hung down low enough to grab, though no one did.

The edifice of the palace peeked through the trees, teasing my senses. Something was off, and I couldn't put my finger on it. Everything was moving too fast, too easy. I expected to encounter resistance well before we laid eyes on the palace.

Yet, we were almost there without even a stubbed toe. I stopped.

<Come to me said the spider to the fly.> I murmured.

<Yes, it's a trap.> Adrian replied.

Under different circumstances, the plants would have distracted me for hours. The twins and I would have filled our bellies with fruit. Instead, my body was on high alert. I barely registered the different types of leave except to categorize danger from harmless.

I batted leaves, vines, and hanging fruit out of the way, never letting my eyes rest. I tracked every movement.

<I've got our backs.> Hercules announced.

I hated it when art reflected life. I just couldn't understand why every time I turned around humanities, ancient buildings were cheap reproductions of the originals.

The temple was enormous. The outside was lined in Greek-style columns, capped with a standard pediment for the Greek style.

I guess none of it was Greek, but Elysium.

Even the Themians didn't create this building style.

In front of me stood the Parthenon, or rather the Palace of Medusa. The one in Athens was nothing more than a replica. That explained the Athena connection. The temple was never hers, but Medusa's.

How could they have replicated it? How did humanity know so much about this culture and not even realize they were emulating aliens?

The gleaming white of the pillars and the edifice was blinding after the dim light of the jungle. I could just make out the reliefs on the pediment, showing three women holding hands. Each had a head of wild hair.

From this distance, I couldn't make out how many snakes were there. Each had a foot on top of a head.

The heads of the Judges of Elysium.

If it wasn't for Rhadamanthy's demands, I wasn't sure we had an argument with the Gorgons at all.

There was nothing wrong with wanting to kill an evil regime, any which way you could.

Although, why Medusa didn't just dive in and kill Rhadamanthy with one evil stare, I can't imagine.

She could cut the supply chains and starve them out. I shrugged to myself.

The shrill laughter of a woman filled my mind. She was at it again. Our group of men clasped their heads and fell to the ground, leaving only Isolde and myself unaffected.

<You've arrived! Excellent! Let's play! > the voice was laced with amusement.

Evil people always say stupid things like, '*let's play*' or '*let the games begin*' as if it's all a big game they are destined to win.

I was not there to play. I was there to kill. This wasn't a game! This was life or death.

The laughing receded, disappearing like smoke on the wind. "I guess the element of surprise is out of the question," I drolled, then pulled Adrian to his feet.

Perseus held the sword of Hermes, knuckles whitening as he tightened and loosened his grip over and over again. "It's our fight. If it was going to be easy, Rhadamanthy would've found someone to do it long ago." He clenched his jaw and glanced back at me, "Are you staying here, Sydney?"

"Not for the world," my reply came instantly, as I'd already made up my mind.

That crazy bitch wasn't going to stand in the way of Hera's life.

I unclipped the gun from my hip, double-checking to make sure I had enough rounds, then gave my suit a once-over. Issy did the same. Both my guns were in good working order. Issy and I didn't haul around swords. It wasn't my forte.

First rule of a fight - stick to what you know.

We found our way over the paths in the garden. It was a strange type of water garden that changed to grounds of sculpted yellow grass that curved this way and that for an indirect path to the palace.

I didn't notice at first, yet there was a light pressure in the background. The pressure grew heavier the closer we came to the palace. It was like trying to pull your head off the back of your seat while on a roller coaster. My breath and steps were labored. When we finally reached the base of the steps to the palace, I couldn't take it anymore.

"Stop! Something's wrong," I said, and using all my strength, I glanced over at Issy, who was a few feet behind me.

"Mom, I can't take one more step. I can't stand here much longer. I'm going to have to stay outside," she cried.

Hercules rushed to Isolde's side.

"What's wrong, *beautiful girl*?" Adrian asked, concern creasing his face. He was no more than a few feet ahead of me.

"I don't know. It's like gravity is pushing back at me while trying to walk up a steep incline, only worse. I can't take another step. I'm not strong enough. I can't push it out of the way either," I groaned, taking two steps back to relieve the pressure on my chest.

Adrian closed his eyes. His fingers curled in as his knuckles turned white. The blood vessels on the side of his temples rose, and his body began shaking. He turned red and finally released a breath, "I can't shift you. I can't move you from where you are to me."

Cackling laughter filled our minds again. <No, no, no, no! I only play with boys. The girls must stay outside.>

"It's not much different from human stories. Women can't enter her domain. Sorry, Sydney, but it looks like you are staying outside to guard our backs. Rogo and Fedar, you stay with them." Perseus replied.

I shook my head, "No! Take them with you. You need the numbers. We will be fine." I reached for Adrian. He closed the distance and took hold of my hand as if there was nothing in the world stopping him.

He leaned down, and I closed my eyes as his lips met mine. I held my hand to the side of his face just for a moment before he pulled back, and I got a flash of his beautiful blue eyes, "Don't worry, *beautiful girl.* I'll be back. It's fate. right?" He quirked a half-smile at me, knowing I'd be irritated about that.

I huffed and smiled, "You better come back. Otherwise, once fate gets a hold of you, you're a dead man."

He pecked me on the lips and followed the others towards the entrance. I looked at Isolde. Wet lines traced down her cheeks. She wiped them away.

Hercules' large frame trudged up the stairs to his brother. He turned around and yelled so everyone could hear him, "I'll be back, Calla." His eyes shifted over to Adrian, "And I'll bring your step-dad back with me."

She choked out a laugh. "You better, or else I'll never hear the end of it."

I shot her a dirty look.

"There has to be some kind of field being created around this building that's keeping you out. It has to be something that's able to identify females from males. Find it and turn it off, and you'll be able to come inside with the rest of us," One-eye suggested.

I nodded to him and clasped his forearm, which he returned. "You're a brave man. Come back! The universe could use a guy like you. As soon as we figure out how to reverse engineer this genetic serum, I want to make sure you're first in line."

"Fate has already decided whether I die here today or not. My string was measured and cut long ago." He gave me a one-eyed wink and sauntered away.

I took a deep breath. Being surrounded by a bunch of true believers was enough to make me heave. The heat around my eyes wouldn't go away.

They won't all come back.

I already knew that. I rubbed my hand over my face as if to wipe these feelings away.

The rest of One-eye's crew turned and joined the men. Still, Rogo and Fedar lagged behind. They wanted to stay.

They'd be with Adrian, not that he needs anyone to protect him.

I'd seen him fight. He was quite capable of taking care of himself and several people around him.

The team disappeared between the pillars into the giant cavernous space beyond.

If Medusa's palace is anything like the Parthenon, there is plenty of space inside to move around.

CHAPTER 19

HERA

Rhadamanthy left the room not long after our first encounter. Soon, the air crackled with power, a power that I could only attribute to Sydney. She was a force without the use of the forces. She carried a power I couldn't quantify.

The slaves murmured behind their hands and hair. Their eyes were the haunted windows to the downtrodden.

"I can offer you a sheet to wipe your face," a young boy wearing nothing more than a loincloth said.

The other slaves placed trays of food on various surfaces around the room. I reached for something resembling a blue strawberry, yet another slave slapped my hand.

"This is for Rhadamanthy. Your food is there." He pointed to a small bowl on the ground.

The young boy glanced over and shrugged a shy smile at me, then pointed at the sheet of fabric next to the bowl on the floor.

Awe!

The sheet was a napkin.

With his hand, he indicated I should use it to cover my genitals.

I returned his shy smile, with one of equal reserve, as I laid the sheet over my lap. The sheet was large enough to tie around my slim hips as a type of skirt.

Part of me wanted to refuse to cover my body. Rhadamanthy's would assume I was ashamed, which I was not. Yet, my long years with Zeus taught me small-minded men needed to feel they won. Even if the battle wasn't worth winning.

This win is not the war. The war will be won according to Fate.

I'd hardly taken a bite before the building shook. The other slaves in the room shrieked and shrank. A piece of the ceiling fell, shattering on the floor.

I smiled. But the terror on their faces was not what amused me.

Sydney was here. She liked to make an entrance, and this was a tell-tale sign she was here. Her rage would bring this structure down on our heads if she wished to.

"Lady?" the boy asked. "Has Fate arrived on Elysium? Are we to be judged?"

I beckoned him to my side. He ran and knelt next to me, wrapping his arms around my waist as the building shivered again.

Others in the room moved to join us. They huddled in fear.

"Yes, the Fates have arrived," I replied. "And we are here for the Judges."

Every head in the room snapped up to stare at me. I allowed a satisfied smile to fill my visage.

Fate has arrived indeed.

I was more than happy to judge the wicked.

CHAPTER 20

SYDNEY

I took five steps back to stand next to my daughter, then mentally, I began mapping. In front of me, there were seven steps to the no-go field.

"Issy, did you notice where this began?"

Her brow was damp with sweat. The heat of the jungle was wearing in her. She shrugged, "I don't know. Somewhere back there." She waved a hand in the direction we came from. "I didn't really notice it at first. Maybe, I was tired."

"Yeah, me too." I turned around to retrace my steps till I was free of the malaise.

The path we followed to reach the palace changed from a white stone shot through with gray veins similar to Earth's marble to pure white. This wasn't the crystalline Themian technology.

It couldn't be.

Charon discovered that tech after he left this dystopian world. This was something different.

I pulled my gun out and shot the stone slab in front of me. My eyes followed the bullet as it ricocheted, causing little damage.

The stone was one giant slab as if it'd been poured like a piece of concrete. Yet, most concrete carried dividing lines in it, while this was a solid megalithic continuous piece, all the way to the corners.

Issy cocked a moist eyebrow.

"Want to go for a walk?" I asked, and a nervous smile peeled back on my face.

She flipped the safety off, "Sure, mom, I'll take up the rear."

My daughter's reaction was assured with an ease that only came from having faced horrible odds before. A warmth filled my chest. I was proud of her. She was amazing. She knew we could all die, and she still cocked her gun and said, "Let's go."

Maybe I did some things right.

We headed to the left of the palace, following the edge of the field and the slab. It couldn't be one giant solid piece unless they poured white concrete.

This begs the question of - is it the rock or something else underneath it?

We finally reached the corner of the palace foundation. The slab didn't stop. It didn't even have a break or a dividing line, nothing. It simply turned the corner and kept going. The marble slabs from the garden ended, and we were now next to the grass.

"Isolde, tell your brother to send on a shovel."

She quirked a half-smile, "Should I have him send two?"

A moment later, two shovels appeared.

The palm of my hand no longer carried the calluses of a sailor. My skin was now soft. So, even before I wrapped my hand around the handle, I embraced the reality that this was going to hurt. I hadn't done this kind of manual labor in a few years.

The blade of the shovel cut the loamy soil, and I shoved it into the yellow moss-like grass. My back strained with the weight of the dirt, but I tossed it over my shoulder. My back immediately protested as I returned for a new load. However, it helped to take my mind off of what was possibly going on inside the palace.

Adrian mumbled in the back of my mind, but most of it was indistinct as if passing through water.

Whatever this field was, it was blocking everything. I couldn't contact or hear Adrian with my mind, and he couldn't hear us.

The metal of my shovel scraped against the rock slab as I dug. A screech followed every thrust. Once we cut through the moss-like substance that was growing on the surface, it was really all dirt. There weren't any rocks, just fine fluffy soil filled with organic material, perfect for growing plants. The slab continued down into the soil and unhindered a giant block.

Issy and I worked in alternating turns, each digging while the other tossed their load.

"Mom, the hole's 5 feet deep. I don't think whatever we're looking for is here. We could dig to China and still not get through that slab." Issy had shucked her vac suit to her waist and tied the arms around it. The sweat pouring off of her soaked her tank top, leaving stains. She tilted her head back, so her hair fell out of her face.

"China's a mighty far away, Isolde." I huffed and pushed my hair out of my eyes.

I was hot, yet I refused to remove my suit. It was a layer of protection I was unwilling to be caught without.

We both chuckled at the idea of digging to China from the underworld.

"Well, maybe we should walk around the backside. There's got to be a backdoor. She has to get in there somehow." Issy leaned on the handle of her shovel and coughed. I pulled water from the air into my hand and offered her a sip.

"Medusa's not like us, Issy. Her genes are different." I panted to cover for my heavy breathing. "I'm sure that whatever this field is, it's wired to let her through and keep us out." I picked up my shovel and slung it over my left shoulder, holding the long handle for balance with one hand. Both my arms were sore and jelly-like.

I pulled my gun from my holster, keeping it ready at my side. Isolde did the same thing. There was no point leaving the shovels behind.

It may not be a sword, but it is a weapon.

The pointed tip was sharp enough.

We walked for about 10 minutes, heading to the edge of the palace slab, only to be stopped by another slab.

"Something tells me this isn't as easy as trying to find the backdoor." I threw a side-eye at my daughter, then back to our surroundings.

Issy's dirt-smeared face clocked the area, searching for the trouble we both knew had to be out there.

Quiet was not my priority while we were digging. Anyone could have heard us.

Issy turned her back to me, "We should go back. We're supposed to be watching the guys' retreat. We can't do that if we're nowhere near where they come out."

I nodded in agreement. We turned around and headed back towards the garden.

Silence suddenly engulfed the garden. I stopped and began searching for the cause. The palace was nothing more than pillars and walls. The jungle was much the same. Other than the giant hedge with palm trees beyond, all was as we previously found it.

"Mom?" Issy murmured tentatively.

I held up my hand, "Shhh!" My head whipped back and forth, surveying the gardens.

That's when the laughing began. First in my mind, then the air. It was a moment before we were slammed into the field that was keeping us from the palace.

Euryale and Stheno.

CHAPTER 21

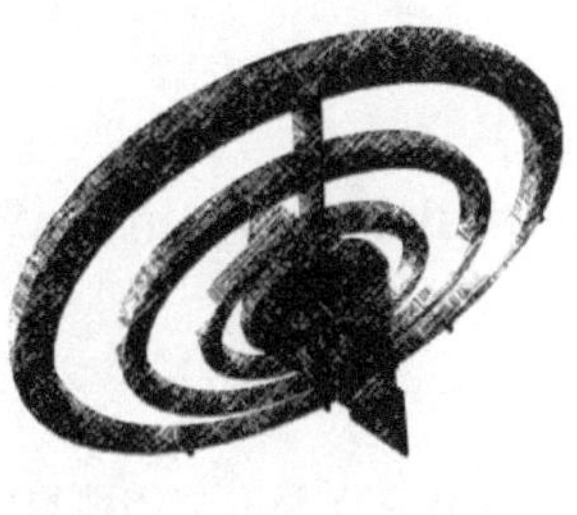

PERSEUS

A large rectangular opening between the columns took the place of an entrance. The columns curved back to reveal white stone walls with no defining characteristics. They created a wall between the edifice and the line of columns.

Our group faltered along with my steps. I unhitched the helmet from my belt loop. Hercules caught my eye, nodded, then pointed to the left, raising four fingers. He touched One-eyes' shoulder and pointed to the left.

On my right, Adrian pointed right and swirled his index finger in the air, indicating he would take the rest.

That leaves me alone to do the hard part.

The helmet slipped over my head with an ease I didn't expect. I double-checked to make sure the kibsis was properly secured on my back.

If we don't have that, we won't be getting her head out of here.

The path left for me was the one straight up the middle.

<And if I want to find you, brother? > Hercules asked.

Something about the cool metal on my head made it impossible for them to even track my sounds.

<If I need you, brother, you'll know.> I replied, hoping I would have no need of him.

<And if I need you?> he chuckled.

Hercules didn't believe he would need me.

<If you must look for me, brother, I'm already dead.> I pulled my shield off my back as my hand gripped Hermes' sword.

Guns are for women and humans.

If you truly want to kill something, you should see the whites of its eyes before you watch the light die in them.

In Medusa's case that would be a death sentence.

I'll just watch her head roll away.

I smiled to myself, as no one else was ever going to see it.

The two groups headed off in different directions.

I stalked a few steps inside the structure to take in my surroundings. The space presented even more columns with exposed beams at various heights within the room. I couldn't tell if the beams were made of wood or stone. Both were white. However, some were shot through with the gray veins like marble, while others carried the red-gold color of orichalcum.

Furniture without legs and low to the ground filled the room in groupings. Pillow-covered reclining beds were scattered around. There were also bowls in varying sizes with and without handles made of various metallic substances I couldn't identify. The bowls sat on tables and littered the floors.

Physically, I could feel *her* presence. I was blocked from everyone else. The sounds of the men here and there, the light touch of footsteps as they moved on either side of the cavernous space, was the only noise breaking up the vacuous space.

The beating of a wing cut the muffled silence, and a giant feather the color of a golden onyx fell in front of me. My instinct was to pick it up. Instead, I examined the room.

In the rafters stood a woman-type creature. A thing. A golden-bronze sheen touched her scales. Giant wings erupted from her back, while long thin snakes trailed down her spine, ending just below the curve of her buttock. Several snake heads were wrapped around her arms. They were so long they touched the rafter she squatted on. The creature braced her weight on the one hand, staring intently at something on the other side of one of the pillars.

"Oh, you've come. Pythia promised a challenger. Is Perseus with you? I want to play with him as none of you are a challenge. Only Perseus." The twang of a sword striking a stone rang from across the room.

I caught a glimpse of some leather straps.

Hercules' *battle skirt* before he disappeared around the side of a column.

I headed in that direction.

Her body took to the air, and her wings snapped open for flight.

"There's more of you?" she marveled, and a wide battle-crazed smile covered her face.

That's when I spied the bow. She didn't carry arrows. The bow wasn't made from wood or metal. The dam thing didn't even have a string. Yet, it glowed with an inner light.

Her left hand was covered with a glove. As she moved into drawing position, the bow's illumination increased. A strand of light appeared between the two ends of the bow, under her drawn fingers. She pulled the light strand back to meet her scaled cheek.

As I watched my prey, I grew transfixed by her grotesque beauty.

With a giggle, she loosed the bolt of energy. It smashed into the pillar above my head.

I flinched, then looked at the rock. There was a giant crater, yet there was no projectile to be found.

What did she fire from that thing?

"She has the *laser bow,*" One-eyes shout echoed around the space. "We only had one. It was a prototype." The sound of his voice drifted to me then ricocheted off the ceiling.

Tracing my way around one column, I stalked up next to Hercules. One-Eye slunk nearby, and I closed the distance to stand behind Hercules. "Brother!"

He jumped out of his skin and gritted his teeth, "Yes."

"She thinks you are me. Lead her to the far end of the room." He nodded his head. Gripping his sword, he turned to the others, and they headed off in the direction of the far end of the room.

Crazed laughter filled the cavernous space, bouncing off the various walls and around the pillars.

"So many players just for me," her words were followed by more laughter. Next, she jumped to the ground and quickly went around one of the pillars. I heard the bloodcurdling scream before the smashing the sound of stones on the floor.

I leaped over the shays lounge, beating my feet to the other side of the room. This was her game. She knew I was here.

She's trying to tire me out.

What was left of Feid laid on the ground in chunks. The white stone of his body was split in different places. His head was intact for the most part. It was cracked from side to side and twisted in terror. More than his body turned to stone, everything he wore or touched. Moreover, his metallic blade was now stone.

She'd instantly petrified everything.

Medusa flew back to the rafters. Dust trickled onto the ground at my feet.

"That's one. Who should the next one be? Your brother? Or maybe I should kill your great-grandson. Perhaps, I should move on and start killing Daphne's child. After all, she wasn't helpful at all. What's his name? Is it Erick, the One-eye?" her head whipped around, making the long snakes fly through the air with the motion. Two snake heads kept watch at her back. Their silvery eyes shined as they tasted the air searching for One-eye. "She sent him to kill me. He definitely took long enough to get here," Medusa chuckled under her breath.

The acoustics of the room caused every little sound to carry. Even the hissing of her hair met my ears. It, too, sounded like laughter, making my skin shiver.

"Or I could whittle your numbers down. Who needs friends anyway? That's, unless you step forward, Perseus. Let's fight this out! Monster to monster." Her manic laughter bounced around the room and seemed to grow with each gusty cackle.

"The only monster here is you!" Hercules shouted. The sound bounced off the various walls as it reverberated. He'd taken the bait.

Dam him to Hades! Why does he have to be such a hot head?

"Oh, no, no, no! I am not the only monster here. I'm sure you'd be happy to know that your two ladies outside are well occupied with my sisters." She jumped down to perch on a large bowl. "Steno and Erythal will be perfectly happy to clean up the garden. This way, I don't have to leave my palace. Anyway, they prefer garden dining."

Fear clutched at my chest. Isolde didn't have any defensive abilities other than being able to hear and alter emotions. She wasn't good with the forces, and she had no chance in a swordfight with a Gorgon. The sisters, on the other hand, had trained their entire lives for this fight. Even with all of Sydney's abilities, I didn't think she could take them out.

And if they have abilities—

"Now, you're wondering whether my sisters have powers," she giggled and coughed.

I hated how easy it was for her to distract my train of thought, leading me down a road of self-doubt. My lungs pulled in a cleaning breath, though before battle, it did little good. Her words had done their work. I now had visions of Isolde and Hercules dead while Sydney and Adrian fought on with rage.

The delicate balance of our small band will fall with just one death.

I gritted my teeth and stalked my way across the room.

"Of course, until I die, you won't be leaving this palace, so you'll never know. Did Rhadamanthy forget to mention that my sisters and I always fight together?" She raised her gloved hand again and drew back the bowstring, and the bolt glowed with a laser-like power.

My eye found her target. It was Adrian. She released the arrow, and a split second before it crashed into Adrian's head, he shifted away.

"He sent you out here to kill me. He failed to mention that Euryale and Stheno would be helping. Everyone here is self-serving. Who's the next player?" The flap of Medusa's wings filled the air again. She dove over the top of the room, crossing to the other side. Her snakes tasted the air for fresh prey.

The scuff of a sandal reached my ears, and she dove for the sound.

At this rate, if she's picking us all off, and the only person who might get out of here is me.

Full-fledged fear gripped my chest. I couldn't let that happen.

Medusa hadn't actually committed a crime. So she, in any way, didn't deserve to die. But everyone must die sometime. She also didn't contribute to the betterment of Elysium. She spent her time obsessing about her blindness and the lack of perfection.

She's a moron! Nobody's perfect. Does she think I was born perfect?

With all of her goading, I was surprised Hercules hadn't tried to leave the palace and go to Isolde. My brother and his group reached the other end of the room. They were whispering about a distraction.

If I can hear them, so can she.

She leaped back to the rafters with her bow swinging from her waistband. Other than that, she was completely naked. Without the weird scaly skin and wings, she might've been a beautiful woman. If you could get past the snakes coming out of her head, of course. She cleaned her nails for a minute, looked around, and took a deep breath, stretching her arms up, "You're boring me. I don't like to be bored. So, come on, boys, make your move."

That's when moisture appeared in the air. It was a warm fog that began floating in drifts here and there. "How lovely, a challenge. My favorite! So, I guess you hybrids have powers too."

I looked over at Hercules. I could see the concentration as well as the bead of sweat on his brow from concentrating. I hadn't tried to pull any of the forces. I didn't think there was a point. But Hercules was right. I dashed over to where I thought Adrian was. The rest of the men spread out one per pillar. He had his shield up against his body and was sort of ready.

<Adrian, start throwing shit.> I murmured.

A squeak of surprise issued from above. I dashed around a pillar. A chaise lounge fell from the rafters only to smash into the floor.

"How did you move that? I'll turn you into 1000 little pieces!" She yelled and pulled her bow to her face, fingers pressed to her cheek. Several different pieces of furniture came at her, shifting in from different parts of the space. She loosed one laser bolt after another, causing each to explode into burning chunks of wood and fabric. Smoke choked the air around her.

Adrian shifted one of the large bowls off of a statue from the other side of the room, but he didn't take the water inside. The liquid drenches the top, creating a puddle on the floor. The statue was once a person, his face contorted in terror. The water running down his cheeks only made him more life-like, as they formed tears that he most assuredly wept before he died.

She changed her fingering on the bow and released a blue net-like laser, cutting the table Adrian tossed at her into chunks.

In the distance, a heavy draw of breath cut the tension in the air. I heard it, and so did Medusa.

Her bolt sailed through the air. Roger never screamed before his blood splattered the floor, along with the different pieces he'd been cut into.

The smoke in the room turned the air acrid. I called for the wind to clear it and push me up to a crossbeam.

This was the closest I ever wanted to be. The snakes in her hair hissed at the scene before us. They tasted the air and shook their heads. One of the snakes hung down, covering one of her eyes, and she pushed him out of the way as if it was nothing more than regular hair. She stared down at her burning domain that was painted in the blood of her victims. The deranged smile never left her face as her wild eyes searched for her next target.

She laughed again. "Doesn't everyone have control of the elements? It's the simplest of things for hybrids. Even the Graeae have the ability to move stone." She lifted her clawed hands and waved them away from each other, pushing all the fog out of the way. "In case you didn't know, I can control water and wind."

The room filled with a whistling sound as the pressure in the space dropped. She stood with one hand clasped in a fist and the other holding her bow.

I grabbed some of the wind and pushed myself onto the same beam as her, holding up my shield. Still, she couldn't look at me, and I wouldn't look into her eyes. I moved toward her and slashed. A bead of blood formed across her exposed breasts.

"Where are you?" She screamed. "I know you're here. I can feel you. I can feel your presence!" Her blood dripped off her breasts. One drop landed on the beam, cutting it in half like a knife. It weakened the structure of the building.

I leaped to another rafter and steadied myself as the building shifted.

She rubbed her hand in the blood and threw it across the room, using the force of the wind to push the droplets. They landed on several other beams. The building shuttered, followed by the sound of stone grinding on stone.

I dove off the beam I perched on and yelled, "Hercules, the building's coming down! Adrian, move us! NOW!"

The roof was never meant to stand without the support beams between the pillars. I could use this in our favor. I grabbed some of the wind she'd forced to whistle around the room, and I used it to push one of the beams towards the center of the room.

Maybe, if we collapse the entire palace, it will somehow break the protective field.

Behind me, the beat of her wings was followed by her feet smacking against the floor. "Perseus," she laughed, "You can destroy this building. I don't care. I can build another one. I'll be here to do it," she giggled, "but you won't."

Something cut the air near my back. I ducked and rolled to get away. A wicked claw missed me by an inch. I rolled into the side of one of the pillars. The building shook again. A stone slab from the roof lost its battle with gravity, careening toward me and the ground. I rolled out of the way, avoiding it slamming into me. Instead, it hit the floor next to my face, creating dust and shooting small chips of stone in every direction. The impact pushed my helmet off my head.

I sneezed.

"There you are!" Medusa remarked. The tone of a laugh lined the tip of her tongue. "And very clever, I see. Pythia is willing to help anyone. Isn't she?"

Keeping my eyes on the ground, I covertly searched for the helmet. It must have rolled away with the impact, and I had no idea where it ended up.

I was fully exposed, and the building was coming down around us. A hand appeared before me.

"Let's go, brother!" Hercules pulled me into a standing position, practically lifting me off my feet as he did.

I moved my shield over my head to protect us from falling debris. Light glimmered off a puddle of water, blinding me. The surface on the underside of my shield reflected the light.

I hate fate! It is unavoidable.

Parts of the outer walls began buckling. The furniture around us spontaneously caught fire, creating black smoke. The visibility decreased with every moment as the smoke took over. Someone coughed, but the smoky room hid their location.

I pressed my lips firmly together, holding back the cough, desperate to escape. I didn't want to reveal my position. I limped out of the smoke.

"Remove her head, and let's be done with this!" Hercules growled through gritted teeth.

"Where are the rest of your men?" I asked and gasped to cover the need to cough.

My brother shook his head as a bloodcurdling scream raced across the room.

One of One-eye's men.

Hercules closed his eyes then reopened them, staring directly at me, "We must finish this now."

He jumped over a downed column, and I followed suit.

A woman's giggle filtered through the smoke. "Fire, fire everywhere and not a drop to drink. Where's our water, man? Don't we need water? He could put out all these fires. I wouldn't want anyone to choke to death on all this smoke?"

"I don't care if she didn't really commit a crime. I hate that fucking woman!" I grumble.

"Issy says her sisters are outside," Herc replied while peeking around the safety of our pillar.

"Tell Isolde to keep them there," I replied, squeezing my eyes shut in an effort to push the acidic smoke from my eyes and clear my vision.

I stared hard at Hercules, knowing what I needed to do.

"Don't overthink it, brother! Just do your part, and I'll do mine." Hercules returned my gaze with the hard sapphire orbs our kind were known for.

My grip on the forces allowed me to pull the wind and push the smoke out of the way, leaving Hercules exposed. I wanted her to see him. He was our bait.

The twinge in my heart lasted but a breath before I pushed forward with my plan.

Now, all I have to do is cut her head off before she kills him.

Back in the shadows and smoke, I lingered, waiting for the sound of beating   wings to come forward.

The wind revealed One-Eye. His eye was scrunched shut, and he swung his sword around in the direction of the beating wings. The hum of the bow filled the background. As I glanced up, her wings beat the smoke into my face.

Medusa drew back and struck One-eye in the leg, who fell to his knees. She landed in front of him. His face creased, keeping his eye closed.

Medusa leaned down, her lips an inch away from his face, "Now come, come! Don't you want to see the monster who's going to kill you?"

The snakes from her head flicked their tongues at his eyelid, tickling his face. The man screamed. The glowing orange from her eyes slowly moved over his body. The snake tounges lifted the edge of his one eye. The bleach white of marble moved from his face down, petrifying every bit.

In slow motion, I moved. If I was going to have a chance, now was the time. With the shield in front of my face, I jumped, slashing at her with my sword. The blade connected, and that grinding sucking sound the body makes when you cut it open issued forth before the heavy thunk of her head hit the floor.

The wings on her body variously flapped, knocking me to the ground.

I scrambled to get out of the way as her torso fell in my direction. I used the shield to push it off course. It released the sickly sound of dead flesh smacking into metal, resonating through the room.

I pulled the kibsis from my waistband and stalked over to the head. It was facing away from me.

I turned the bag inside out, picked up the head by the snakes, and pulled the bag over before cinching it shut.

Only then did I look down to avoid the acid pockmarks forming on the floor.

I checked One-Eye. Only part of his body had been turned to stone. The rest was partially covered in Medusa's blood and was quickly melting away.

My heart clenched. He only came because I asked him to help. I took a deep breath.

A giant stone slab from the ceiling dropped, making a loud crack. Adrian appeared on top of it. "You have her head?"

"Yes, I have her head. One-eye is gone."

Adrian looked over at the half-dead man standing there. "Isn't there anything we can do for him?"

"I think the only person who would've known the answer to that is One-eye, and he's obviously half dead."

Adrian shook his head. I reached down and picked up the sword of Hermes. Three of the Pheadeans survived. One rubbed his face as if to push sweat from his forehead, not tears. I clapped him on the back, as did Hercules.

"Let's go!" Hercules said, "Issy and Sydney are alone."

CHAPTER 22

SYDNEY

My feet pushed me up from the ground against the field, repulsing us as I thumbed the safety off of my gun.

A low clicking filled the air.

My daughter's eyes met mine, and at the same time, we nodded slightly as we crept towards the garden. The remains of the other women turned statues provided cover as we moved. Issy and I shadowed up to each Elysian statue as we went.

I caught a glimpse of a red flash in the jungle, but just as quickly, it was gone.

Maybe it was a bird, like a macaw or some kind of animal.

"Isolde, pick up the pace. I don't want to fight anybody up against this force field." I pointed at a fountain. "Center of the garden."

There was plenty of space around the fountain, and the ground was relatively level. The fountain didn't have a high ledge, so it was easy to jump over. The plaza space was surrounded by more of the Elysian statues of the dead with their gruesome faces. Most importantly, there was water trickling over the sides.

It's Primordium. We can heal!

Having an entire pool of it close by emboldened me.

"Mom, did you see that?" Issy asked.

I glanced in her direction, and around the garden, all was still. I turn back to scanning my section of the garden with my back to the jungle wall.

<No.>

"It was just a flash of something, mostly a bright color."

Daphne hadn't said anything about Medusa's sisters other than their names, Euryale and Stheno.

They might be here.

I mentally kicked myself. She said they weren't a threat, yet every hybrid I'd met was a threat.

I should have asked more questions.

"Do you remember anything about the Gordon Sisters?" I asked, hoping Issy read something.

I bit my lip. The pain amped up my already adrenaline-filled veins.

"No. There wasn't anything about them. They were an afterthought. They were pissed off after Medusa was dead." She heaved a sigh.

"She's not dead, so that's not true," I drolled.

The giant slabs of white rock gave way to the cut stone of the garden paths. Each stone was placed several inches apart, with the grass-like moss growing between them.

I stepped over the cracks to keep my feet on even ground. Issy mirrored my moves from behind.

My stomach sank.

We should have known more.

"Okay, work the problem. Medusa has snakes on her head. I'm sure her sisters do too. Daphne said that the Graeae pulled Medusa's eyes out. So my guess is that they all have snakes for hair."

The clenching in my stomach got tighter with every step, and the fountain seemed miles away.

"I saw something red," I said.

They were toying with us.

Are they herding us?

I whipped my head left and right, hoping to find something of use. I put my back to Isolde's, dropping the shovel and pulling out my second gun. "Listen, honey, send the fear as far as you can. Just don't hit the building," I finished my sentence with the gripping spasm that hits your belly just before you fall off the side of a boat or when you know your car is going to crash and there's nothing you can do to stop it.

I locked my mind up as tight as I could.

The laughing started. One sounded like warm honey, spreading everywhere. The second laugh was more of a dry scoffing as if you've breathed nightclub smoke all night.

"You see what I see, sister?" the honey one asked.

"Oh, yes! It's two women. They look scared," Nightclub coughed in reply.

They were toying with us. We couldn't see them, but they could see us.

"I don't think they are Elysian," Honey's voice oozed.

"What makes you say that?" Nightclub barked.

"One of them is sending out fear as if she could actually penetrate us." They both laughed.

"Silly girl! We send our own fear."

"Now, Euryale, she's not just a girl. She's a hybrid like us."

That's when the beating of two sets of wings filled the air. The scale covered the bodies of two women lowered from above. One was red, the other aquamarine-blue, with the shades only a snake could achieve. Both were naked.

On Earth, one of the defining characteristics of a mammal is hair. Yet, the Gorgons had none, not even covering their genitals.

No wonder their fathers thought they were a mistake.

The reptilian differences made them hideous. Both sported bronze claws protruding from their hands. Each of them smiled wide to reveal sharp teeth, like the fangs of a viper. Their snake hair hung down their backs and shoulders, wrapping around their arms. It was hard to believe they weren't pets.

The blue Gorgon had a snake so long it was wrapped around her waist, constantly slithering its long-forked tongue, tasting the air.

I probably could've stomach all of it, except for the feathered wings. They didn't fold. Instead, they kept them displayed wide, almost like a male bird would when trying to attract a mate.

I pivoted against Issy's shoulder, so we were both facing them. The red one tilted her head towards her sister, narrowing her eyes. "Do you smell what I smell, Euryale?"

The blue one crossed her arms. "Yes. Pythia?"

"They're both of Pythia," she said and spat on the ground. The ground steamed, and the moss-like grass withered away as if it was vinegar or acid.

"The children of Pythia have returned. She said you would come here to save us all. She was always a liar," the blue one scowled at us.

The ground shuddered as a loud crack split the air. I didn't take my eyes off of the two sisters. I simply didn't dare. Both beat their wings and flew into the air.

"But you're not here to save us, are you? You're here to take Medusa's head. Father finally found someone to do his dirty work."

"Don't think you will make it off this island alive. We may not agree with Medusa and everything she does, but blood is thicker than water." Euryale was the bigger of the two, clearly the strongest.

I turned to face her and elbowed Isolde, "Take the red one!"

"The fear isn't working, mom."

I leveled my gun and shot at Euryale. It glanced off her blue scales.

"The fear doesn't work? Pick another emotion! Pick any emotion. Just hit them with whatever you can."

Isolde's gun opened fire alongside mine. Everything glanced off Euryale. It didn't even leave a mark. Nothing damaged her skin.

"What stones are you throwing at me? Didn't Pythia teach you that you can't use rocks to cut our skin?"

My bullets were doing nothing, maybe knocked a few feathers off of her. Choosing another target, I shot at her wings. Some of the feathers drifted to the ground. My bullets glanced off her hard skin, doing nothing more than pissing her off.

She charged me while the red one, Stheno, headed for Isolde.

This isn't good.

I was not ready for hand-to-hand combat. Neither was Issy.

I holstered my left gun. The water in the fountain sang to me. Without another thought, I pulled it from the stone basin and thrust it into Euryale's face forcing her back.

She screamed in irritation, flapping her wings.

It didn't stop her. She continued flexing the muscles of her wings, yet she gained no air.

The ground around was dappled with small water puddles. I gathered them up into an undulating mass of liquid, dancing in the air, and flung it at her sister, saturating her body. It was followed by a scream of protest that rattled my eardrums.

I lost control of the water. It fell to the ground, leaking away between the stones.

I pressed my gun to my right ear, and the meat of my palm right cradled my skull. "Isolde, make it stop! I know you can."

My knees reached the ground a moment before a hand grabbed my hair, "Oh, Stheno, you can stop now. They're in too much pain. They'll be too easy to kill."

The screaming stopped, though the pain still resonated through my skull. A split second later, the gun was ripped from my hand.

"Should we play with them, or should we just kill them?"

"They're hardly even a challenge. You would think Rhadamanthy would've found someone bett—"

The ground shook as a massive portion of the edifice crashed to the ground. It was enough to throw them off.

I picked up two stone slabs and thrust them in different directions with my mind, both of which hit the sisters simultaneously. Euryale was projected over me. Her nails scraped across my skull, pulling hair from my scalp as she went. I screamed in pain, and blood found its way down the back of my neck.

Isolde stood up, and the wind picked up sharp and fast. Her finger twirled in a circle. She moved the air like a tornado.

Her invisible force picked Euryale up and threw her against the ground over and over again as if she was in a washing machine.

Stheno pushed the stone slab off her belly and stomped over to us. Her wings hung at odd angles. The feathers were crushed, and blood oozed from a lost section of down.

Before she could reach me, Isolde leaped in front of me and touched her. "You've been judged!" She proclaimed.

All Stheno's momentum came to a screeching halt. Her eyes glazed over white as she obediently stepped in front of me, and I placed my hand upon her shoulder.

She was a shattered kaleidoscope of a soul - never loved, wanted, or touched; never shown any kindness from anyone but her sisters. The Nymphs did nothing more than poke and prod her for more lifetimes than any mind could live through. She was kept locked and examined for years in the name of science.

A laboratory is not the environment for a child. The trauma never leaves them.

Mentally, she would never be free of that place. Even when she had her freedom, she had no desire to go and find peace, only revenge.

I knew what I had to do, no matter how much pity I had for her or the pain she suffered at the hands of her creators. No amount of Primordium or therapy could save her. She and her sisters were too dangerous to be left alive.

My hand touched her forehead, and her lifeblood boiled, then leaked from her eyes and nose. She slumped to the ground at my feet, finally free from the suffering of a life that was never meant to be.

A bloodcurdling scream bellowed behind me.

"I will rip you apart in front of your child. Pythia was wrong! You will never save anyone. You won't live long enough!" Euryale screamed.

Isolde pulled me to her with the wind and slammed her back down on the ground. I pelted her with his many stones as I could rip out of the walkway, then I pulled the water from the fountain. I fashioned it into a bubble over her head.

I didn't want to judge another Gorgon.

I'd rather just drown her and be done with it.

Venom issued from her snakes into the water, turning it a sour yellow. Euryale opened her mouth to breathe. Instead, she swallowed. Her body convulsed as she drank the poison. Her broken wings flapped against the ground, beating furiously. Her claws dug around her throat, ripping her skin apart. Blood oozed between the deep gouges before her movements slowed and then ceased.

She lay dead on the stones, with her eyes staring up at the golden sky. The warmth from the Elysian sun never reached me.

I'm so tired of death.

It reached me, no matter how far I ran.

I caught Issy's eyes, "How were we able to affect judgment without Hera?" I asked.

Issy shook her head, "I touched her, and she was instantly drawn in. She was judged, and she got her punishment, so did her sister." She wiped a drop of bloody water from her face.

"Yeah, it must really suck dying on your own poison," I remarked and ran my hand over my neck, searching for the rents in her skin on mine. There was only the blood from my head.

The sound of stone crashing against stone drug my eyes away from the two carcasses of the dead Gorgons just in time to see most of the palace roof collapse.

I screamed, "Oh my God! They're all in there." I reached for Isolde's arm, dragging her back from the snakeheads of the dead Gorgons.

She pulled free of my grasp and ran for the palace. At the base of the stone, she tripped, falling on her knees.

"Nooooo," she cried, and her voice cracked. She pounded her fist on the ground.

I grabbed her hands and held them to my chest as she continued hammering. Her eyes were wild with terror, "Adrian, for fuck sake, Adrian." Hot tears poured down my face, and my chest clenched.

"Mom, I can't feel him. I don't know if he's okay." Her face was filled with agony, and her eyes shot through with blood for a moment, then quickly cleared.

"It's okay, we are alive, so they have to be also." I forced her to look at me. I couldn't give in to a fear that wasn't founded in reality.

Issy sniffled, "What if it doesn't work that way for us because we are the Fates?"

Tristan pressed in the back of my mind, but I couldn't let him in.

My body sank to the ground.

This can't be how it ends. There is so much more to do.

I was willing to burn fire across this planet if he didn't walk out of that building. Tears flowed, and Isolde whimpered in my lap.

"Of course, I came back to you, *beautiful girl*."

I turned around, jumped up, and threw myself into his arms, covering his face with kisses, holding his head between my hands.

"I thought you died." He shook his head, releasing a husky laugh in my ear. "If the tsunami didn't get me, do you really think a collapsing building could finish the job?"

I cried with laughter, "Of course not. How silly of me." I could barely make out the mumblings next to me.

Isolde kissed Hercules. I pulled them to me, hugging my child and her husband.

Isolde wiped my tears away and sniffed, "Where's...where's Perseus and One-eye?"

Perseus coughed, "He got his revenge. We got Medusa's head." His voice was tight with pain.

I cleared my throat, "I liked One-eye too. He was a good man."

"He might not be dead," Adrian mumbled.

"What?"

Adrian kicked an imaginary stone. "Only half of him was turned to stone. The other half, I think, might still be alive.

I shifted him to the cryogenic chamber Hades and Persephone were in, and I sealed him inside. Medusa didn't get to finish changing him, so I think he is not really dead. It didn't get any further than part of his skull. The rest of him could be alive. If we can figure out the gene therapy that Charon gave to everyone, maybe we could save him."

I shook my head, "That's a lot of maybes and wishful thinking, Adrian."

Hercules intervened, "We barely made it out. One-eye distracted her while Perseus cut her head off. He did his job. We all knew there was a price going in. For some, it was higher than for the others."

I pulled them all in and hugged them once again. I even took Perseus in my arms.

"Why are you bleeding?" Adrian demanded.

I put my hand to the back of my head. "Euryale scratched my scalp and pulled some hair out. I may have a bald spot."

"You can control wind?" Hercules pulled Isolde to him and gave her a big hug, wrapping his arms around her, "You have control of the forces?"

She nodded her head with a quiet smile. "Well, at least one of them."

"She was awesome. She picked that Gorgon up and smacked her onto the ground like she was plunging a toilet. It was amazing," I said enthusiastically with pride.

"Not as cool as you drowning Stheno in a bubble of water."

I waved her off. "I don't care what you say. Everybody knows what I can do. You, on the other hand, I will not believe you to be so helpless ever again."

Her smile broadened as I collected her chin with my hands and planted a big kiss on her face.

"We're done here. Let's give Rhadamanthy his prize," Perseus remarked.

All eyes turned to Adrian, who announced, "Shifting now."

CHAPTER 23

SYDNEY

We were right back where we started - Rhadamanthy's front garden step. There were 10 times as many people standing in the garden as before. I couldn't tell if they were there to welcome us or watch us.

You'd think with the level of technology that they flaunted, they would've noticed whether or not Medusa was dead, or at least her palace collapsing.

The bulging kibsis hung from Perseus' shoulder. He never let go of his sword. Glancing around, I discovered everyone held a weapon. Even I allowed my hand to lightly play on the handle of a pistol.

I didn't wait to see what Rhadamanthy's next move was. I wasn't interested in playing any of his bullshit games. Speeding up my pace, I wanted to make sure whatever was said to that son of the bitch was said by me.

"You in a hurry, *beautiful girl*?"

He knew I was. I meant to be ahead of everybody.

"Ask me no questions, and I'll tell you no lies, my love."

His deep-throated chuckle wrapped around the back of my spine, tickling my earlobes.

"Ick, God, when we're all done, you can both get a room. But until then can we keep it PG," Isolde intervened.

I shot her a dirty look.

She thought this was playful banter.

What the heck would she do if she found out how dirty I can really be?

<Don't tease the poor girl, sweetheart. No one wants to be that blind.> Adrian snickered.

We were coming up on the main entrance at the base of the stairs. The giant doors to Rhadamanthy palace were firmly closed. It was better than Medusa's.

At least he has a door.

I didn't even reach the top of the steps before pulling the forces and slamming the doors open. The reverberation on the structure was music that I could listen to all day long. The frames holding the massive door cracked with the force of my ability.

I smiled to myself. Rhadamanthy was probably good and ticked off about that.

I. Don't. Give. A. Shit.

Filling my lungs with air, I shouted. "Get your scrawny ass out here, Rhadamanthy! I'm done playing your bullshit games." Loose objects around us tapped with my anger.

"Diplomacy, Sydney, we need to use diplomacy," Adrian muttered.

"I'm not being diplomatic with that scraggly little fucker." All I could see was One-eye and his friends, Liza, and the thousands that came before her. Even his daughter ran away from this planet, practically screaming.

Rhadamanthy lay sprawled across his throne, gaudy clothes and all. He had two prepubescent girls completely naked, feeding him grapes as he lounged over the side of an armrest. He pushed his black hair out of his face and slicked it back over his pate. On most guys, that move would be sexy. With him, it was so calculating I wanted to gag.

Over my shoulder, Isolde sucked in a breath. I offered Issy my hand for comfort. The acid taste on my tongue burned in time with my rage.

The doors behind me rattled.

<We need Hera first, *beautiful girl*.> Adrian reminded me.

<I know.>

The air pressure in the room became oppressive. Issy's lips were set in a firm line. Her nostrils flared, and she fixed her eyes on Rhadamanthy.

"There's no need for name-calling. We are both getting something we want." He sat up, straightening his robes, then waved the children away. They pulled back to cower behind the tables near his throne. Their eyes were wide with fear.

"We fulfilled our end of this twisted deal. Now it's your turn." My teeth hurt from the gritting. The building around us groaned, making my belly quake with the shifting of the structure.

Rhadamanthy moved in his seat. "Very well then. Who needs pleasantries? Show me proof of Medusa's death, then I will give you Hera. A delightful woman and such a beauty. I didn't know hybrids could be so desirable." In a snake-like fashion, he slid his index finger sideways across his lower lip as a smile played over his face, goading all of us.

Hercules took a step forward as if he was going to rise to the bait. Perseus laid his hand on his brother's chest without turning away from the reptilian creature seated before us. For all his beauty, he was ugly to the core.

"Desirable or not, you gave your word. You wanted a head, you have a head. We want Hera. Bring her out so we can assess she is unharmed, then you will receive your heart's desire," Perseus replied, and I let him.

The rage growing in my belly stoked a new fear. I was on the edge of control, and I didn't want to lose it with so many innocents nearby unable to protect themselves.

Rhadamanthy tossed his head back, releasing a dry coughing laugh. "Not my heart's desire. Merely an annoyance. Like a hair that tickles you. Nothing more—" he waved his hand.

Two large men wearing white pleated skirts, similar to an Egyptian-style kilt, and armbands appeared. Each one with a hand on Hera's arms.

A half-smile crept over my face.

What if he realizes that she has the ability to shake them off?

Hera remained stoic and serene. Her white dress didn't cover her breast and flowed in the breeze that slipped through the room, slowly picking up speed.

Issy was beginning to lose control. My smile grew.

"As you can see, the hybrid woman is untouched and in the same manner as when snatched. Now give me Medusa's head. Show me my proof, and I'll release this woman to you."

My desire to kill him where he sat was strong. Yet, my ideas of right and wrong were more blood-thirsty than most. That was my job, and I was willing to go to that dark place so others wouldn't need to.

Turning my head slightly, my eyes grazed over Perseus and smirked, "Give him what he asked for."

Perseus slung the kibsis down and loosed the knot, holding it closed.

<Close your eyes!> Tristan screamed.

As if falling into a feather bed, I closed my eyes and embraced what came next.

A blood-wrenching scream reverberated through the space, crashing into rafters and pillars. It was chased by a deep-throated laugh.

The smile I'd held back took full form. A hearty laugh came with it. I knew he wouldn't let that bastard live. It wasn't a story. We all knew from the moment Rhadamanthy told us what he wanted that he would die.

Pythia. Everywhere I turn, she's there, leaving her little crumbs for us to follow.

She never told the Judges how their fate would come, only that fate would come for them and they would die.

I was happy we got the right end of her stories.

"It's safe. You can now open your eyes," Perseus informed us.

A perfect statue of Rhadamanthy stood before us, pain etched on his face. His fingers clasped the armrest. The details were perfect. Even his eyelashes were white. He was a rock, a whited-out statue of his former self.

My only regret was related to the two guards holding Hera. They could have been standing on the Giza plateau next to a pyramid or perhaps in Saqqara, with wide, unseeing eyes, staring into the room.

"Tell every servant in this palace to stand on the beach. If you have a way of leaving the island, do so. Spread the word ding dong, Rhadamanthy's dead!" I ordered the two girls who were hiding behind the tables. "And put some clothes on."

They scurried away.

Perseus used his sword to knock the hands off the guardian statues holding Hera.

He immediately wrapped his arms around his mother. She beckoned to Hercules, and they all hugged. Then, she murmured in a low voice, "You know I was in no danger. Rhadamanthy might have been immortal, but he was as weak as a newborn baby. He allowed all of his desires to run and control him. He would have never cut me apart. He didn't have the stomach for it."

"That's really not the point," Hercules grumbled.

She patted both of her sons on their cheeks as if to dismiss further arguments. Hera glanced at me and, with a flat bland face, remarked, "I always knew my sons would be impressive," she finished by cocking an eyebrow.

"Why didn't you throw the guard off?" I asked.

Hera thrust her arms out. On each wrist dangled an orichalcum-colored bracelet. I glanced from them, back at her. "They block abilities," she supplied.

Hercules grabbed one, while Perseus took the other and snapped them in half. Before I could say a word, they disappeared.

"Who did that?" I demanded.

<Me.> Tristan demurred.

Hephaestus will have a grand ole time with those.

I mirrored Hera and turned to leave the audience chamber. The fresh air of the gardens welcomed me as the waves lapping on the beach sang their watery siren song. The call soothed me, and I yearned for the comfort of the sea.

Hundreds of the Elysians emptied from the structures, whispering and pointing in our direction.

"Adrian, is it possible to ship some of these people to the mainland? Maybe, near that store we came from?"

He smirked, "Is it really polite to ship someone without their permission?"

I rolled my eyes. He knew how much it irritated the hell out of me.

"This building," I waved my hand at the monstrosity behind us. "I want to tear it down. There won't be anywhere for them to live. Whatever supplies are here will be buried under the rubble. They need to be somewhere they can survive."

"Sydney, some of these people have never lived anywhere else. Generations were spent here, father to son, mother to daughter. All serving the Judge. You'd be taking away the only home they've ever known. Maybe, you don't need to tear the whole thing down." He tilted his head to chide me.

Adrian always took the opposite side of every conversation, forcing me to put it all into perspective.

I wanted to destroy everything Rhadamanthy stood for, and the building was part of it.

Making people homeless wasn't helpful.

But when the supplies run out, what would happen to them then?

"Fine! Only the audience room," I huffed.

The breeze picked up, and I pushed the loose hair from my face.

Adrian ran his hand down my arm and squeezed my hand before stepping away. Issy gave me a mental nudge.

The bedrock of the island answered my call with ease. It lifted one side of the building enough to push all twelve of the pillars off balance. They fell like dominoes. The domino effect didn't end with one column hitting another. The earth underneath ripped open, and the building was swallowed by the island.

Terrified screams came with the building's collapse as people clutched one another in fear.

<Okay, *beautiful girl*, I think you've made your point. They get there's a new sheriff in town.>

Easing back with my mind, I allowed the earth to close and stop moving. All that was left of his audience chamber was the back wall that was free-floating in the air.

A sense of satisfaction rolled over me, "I don't know about the rest of you, but demolition is one of my favorite things," I snickered.

Hercules tilted his head back and belted out a laugh. "Sydney should be called the Goddess of Excitement for things are never dull when she is around."

CHAPTER 24

HERA

"One down two to go," Sydney's smile changed her face from the dark cares she carried daily to one of youth and vigor.

I understood exactly how she felt. The Judges of Elysium were real people at one point. Between time, genetic manipulation, and power, something in them twisted. Rhadamanthy no longer saw anyone as an equal, not even his fellow Judges. The people around him were nothing more than playthings. They weren't even beings with the right to live.

My interaction with Rhadamanthy made it painfully clear to me. Whatever reason the Themians had for leaving this planet, Pythia especially, they'd done the right thing.

"Are you okay, mother?" Perseus asked.

I gave him a tight smile. I couldn't enjoy the moment. Not when all around me the chaos of this world churned under the surface. The emotions of the people beat at me anew. The bracelets gave me a reprieve I'd never experienced before, and the sudden return of my abilities was a battering ram to my psyche.

Perseus was always a thoughtful boy. He'd grown into a thoughtful man, ready and willing to defend all who needed it. As a full-blooded Themian, I never believed I would need him or anyone to defend me.

Against other Themians, I might not be as strong. But from the moment I accepted that I was one of the Fates and had the ability to judge people, good or bad, I accepted a power to rule, similar to the Elysians.

I wield the power of life and death.

Rhadamanthy tortured poor innocent people for pleasure.

I understood a long time ago that trauma forces evolution. I was traumatized by what I'd witnessed. The desire to see every one of the Judges of Elysium pay for their evil pettiness   was a new taste on my tongue.

The weight of Perseus' hand on my shoulder and his searching eyes did nothing to alleviate that desire. "Don't worry yourself, Perseus. I am well. Really, Rhadamanthy did absolutely nothing to me. I am physically, completely unharmed. He was only desperate you should kill Medusa, so he could leave his island paradise."

"Do you think his spirit is floating around, surveying his empire, saying, '*well fuck, this isn't how it was supposed to end*'?" Sydney snickered softly to herself.

That was humorous, and I forced my laughter away.

It was Rhadamanthy's very arrogance that killed him. He wanted Medusa's head so badly, he never once thought to ask himself what would happen when someone gave it to him.

"Hey, do you think he saw it coming?" Issy snickered.

The deep reverberation of Hercules chuckling joined her, "Yeah, I'm pretty sure he saw it coming. Just as soon as her snake-head slipped out of the bag."

Everyone began to laugh, and I joined them. The simple release of mirth eased some of the tension from my shoulders and back.

Perseus wrenched the sack higher up onto his shoulder. "Perhaps, you guys think it is easy to heft this sack? You don't realize how heavy it is."

Adrian burst out, "The human head weighs 10 pounds— "

Adrian, Sydney, and Isolde all threw back their heads, laughing.

I couldn't see the humor in repeating a known fact. Neither could Perseus. "None of us are human, so how would that analogy apply to us?" I remarked.

Isolde covered her mouth with the back of her hand to hold her snickering in.

"It's a movie." He panted for a moment before explaining the joke, "It's a line from a movie. In Jerry Maguire, there's a little kid who says '*the human head weighs 10 pounds.*'"

Perseus opened his mouth, "Oh," yet he clearly didn't understand why it was funny. He'd never seen a human movie.

Although I grasped the concept, and I actually was under the impression that I might've seen the movie, the pure comedy of it was lost on me too.

"Yeah, well, if the human head weighs 10 pounds, I'm pretty sure Medusa's weighs at least 30. All those snakes… they add volume."

That was when the real howling started. I found myself joining in. Sydney was practically crying, and their laughter was contagious.

"Something tells me that Medusa had a fat head." The childish snickering continued mostly from Isolde and Hercules.

After a few moments, my sides hurt, and I stopped to catch my breath. The others quieted down as well.

"Which Lord should we visit next?" Sydney smiled. She narrowed her eyes and glanced from left to right. "Maybe, we should flip a coin? It's a 50-50 chance who we kill next."

I realized that all the Judges had to die, but I didn't like going somewhere with the intention of killing. Not without giving them a chance to redeem themselves anyway.

I believe that is the job of Fate.

"Sydney, do you really believe we must kill all of them? Can we just go with an open mind, and perhaps they'll self-correct?"

Sydney lightly touched my arm, "Hera, one of the things I admire about you is your kind heart. Even when you know someone's evil, you still think you can save them." She gazed off for a second before returning to stare me down. Her deep sapphire blue eyes were as hard as any substance found in the stars. "There is no way these people can be saved! They're not even people. They are creatures, monsters, beasts!" She growled.

Her throat worked as she swallowed. She may have faced the ghost from her past, but the lessons learned there were never far from the surface.

"To hear how Rhadamanthy referred to you… '*I didn't know a hybrid could be so desirable,*' as if you weren't any more than a thing, an object... That is not a healthy mind. He was a truly disturbed individual. We are free moral agents, sentient beings, capable of conscious thought and decision-making. We have incredible powers, just like him."

Her nostrils flared, "Rhadamanthy is a hybrid, or he was right up until he was turned to stone by his own daughter."

She gazed around at our group, "Do you really think his two friends are gonna be any different?"

I took a deep, cleansing breath. Sydney's angry resolve peppered the air with chaos. "I don't know if they're different. Rhadamanthy was evil, and he got what he deserved. I agree. But Minos and Aeakus could be different. Perhaps, they've seen the error of their ways and simply withdrawn from taking part in the evil around them." My alternate point of view was not swaying Sydney at all.

Her eyes blazed, and the ground shook. Sydney was truly terrifying when her back was up.

"Withdraw? There is no way in heaven, earth, and the underworld, the universe, the cosmos, or whatever lies beyond the stars that I would ever stand by and just watch. Not if I have the ability to do something."

The rocks around us were tapping out a rhythm with Sydney's rage. "You're wrong, Hera. However, because I care for you because you are my friend and I respect you, I will try and listen with an open mind and keep myself in check." She turned and began to walk away, then whirled around, "But whatever happens, whether it be by our hands or someone else's, they will be judged."

The idea of someone standing by and watching children having their organs harvested, or turning their own children to scientific experiments while subjugating an entire people and then doing nothing to correct it, struck me as a dilution.

One, I shouldn't hold on to.

Yet I did. The hope that a person could be saved...it was the one fault I couldn't give up. No matter how many times I was proven wrong.

I couldn't help but hold to the chance that people can and do change.

"When good men stand by and do nothing, it makes them just as guilty as the people committing the crimes," Issy quoted her human history to me as if I hadn't heard it many times before. "My mother's right. If there was any good left in the Elysium Judges, even in one of them, he should have defied the other two or died trying."

When good men do nothing...

But what did that say about Pythia and Charon? Their entire crew of Elysians left the planet to become Themians, taking their genetic cure with them?

"But good men did do nothing. They left the planet. They left everyone here to their Fate, leaving the Judges of Elysium intact," I retorted. I didn't cling to my belief blindly. I clung for the one reformed beast that might live among them.

"Being as we don't actually know what really happened on that spaceship or exactly how they got the gene therapy, we can't judge them too harshly," Sydney stopped her retreat.

"Almost all of them are dead. Charon doesn't remember much. Isolde only remembers what he remembers. We don't have anything to go on. Hades wasn't even born at the time they left. He and Poseidon are children of the Exodus. They only know the stories they were told, like everyone else, like you. I think we know by now the game of telephone is misleading, in the extreme."

I closed my eyes for a moment, taking another deep, cleansing breath. I always found it to be the best way to free myself of whatever emotions were swirling around me. I opened my eyes, "Our debate is pointless. Our answers will only be found with Minos and Aeakus, so let's continue our journey."

"Sydney, you want to flip a coin? Heads Minos, tails Aeakus?"

Hercules held a gold coin to display to all its lack of two heads. I'd seen this coin before. It was one of the few minted with Hercules' own visage. He threw it up in the air, allowing it to land on the ground. We all watched it fall and slowly land on tails.

Aeakus.

CHAPTER 25

PERSEUS

"Should we do it now or wait for first light?" I asked. The lapping of waves against shore worked its age-old spell on me. It eased my concerns, so I heaved a sigh of relief and allowed the emotion to flow over me. With that, my eyes drifted closed.

I opened them moments later to take in the beach only to spy my mother. That ease disappeared along with any footprints with each next wave.

The warring inside my mother was there for all to see. She searched for the good inside of others, hoping for some peaceful conclusion. She always did it, even when she knew that war was the only inevitable answer.

When we hunted father, she hoped the good was still there. My one relief — I never saw the light die in her eyes as she realized her love never existed.

Zeus was an evil, cruel man, and I barely had any memory of him. He disappeared not long after I reached manhood. Most of my interactions involved hunting him down to end his reign of terror on the humans.

I took the time to think back and wonder - if I hadn't participated, to begin with, would I have been incarcerated with the rest of my siblings?

However, I never allowed myself to go too deep on that path.

My father was pure evil, and he had to die.

It was necessary. It was one of those inevitable circumstances in which there was only ever one conclusion.

Like a horse with a broken leg... It doesn't matter how you feel about that horse. You must kill it to put it out of its misery.

Zeus was no different. He had to die. I had to put him out of humanity's misery. Even though I hadn't killed him myself, I participated.

To right his many wrongs.

It shaped who I was and how I handled my life - helping the weak, protecting them from the strong and abusive ones.

Zeus treated the weak as if they were insects to be crushed or used as he saw fit. Whether my mother realized it or not, she was one of his victims. His roaming the Earth, raping, pillaging, and seducing every human he could possibly get his hands on. It affected her. I didn't think he could've wormed his way into her affections without her belief there was good in everyone.

That belief made him possible.

The same was true in this case, the Elysian Lords. They believed that they were all-powerful and better than everything and everyone and that no measly pathetic hybrids such as ourselves could ever affect them. Nor that we would be their downfall.

I snapped back to the scene before me and the waves. However, the waves here could barely be called such. They resembled the calm lapping of a lake after a storm. The water moved but nothing like the violent oceans of Earth.

Hercules stripped off all of his clothes, turned, and leaped into the gentle waters. Isolde laughed and stripped her suit down to what I could only assume was some form of human underclothing. She ran after him.

"What the Hades are you doing?" I shouted, yet a smile stole across my face.

Only Hercules can create joy from darkness.

"The water here works like a Primordium pool, Perseus. I'm juicing up before the next fight," he laughed.

My brother seemed carefree even in the worst of times. I longed for that freedom.

"Come, brother! The water is fine. Just stay away from my mate." He winked at me, wrapped his arms around Isolde, and placed a kiss on her forehead.

"Do me a favor, Hercules, get a room!" Adrian intervened. He quickly slipped under the waves before surfacing, moving back to the beach. Adrian sat down, digging his toes in the water to watch.

His experience with water left him happily on the shore. I could not blame him for his wariness. I, too, would find pause from that event.

Sydney stripped down to her undergarments and followed her daughter into the waves.

There was wisdom in Hercules' words. He did have a few brains in that vacant blond head of his. A quick dip in Primordium would heal all our wounds and revitalize all of us.

Though our souls might not be reached so easily.

"Go ahead, Perseus, cleanse yourself. I'll stay with the head," Mother waved me on.

I looked at the kibsis. It moved. The snakes were still alive, even though the host was long dead. Hercules laughing and splashing in the distance overwhelmed the feeling of dread that threatened. The crashing sound of a wave shook me into action. I set the bag down at my mother's feet.

"Whatever you do, mother, don't open that."

"Why would I open it? I don't have a death wish," she retorted with a tight smile and rearranged the fabric of her dress to cover her breast.

Sydney used her control over water to raise the waves, creating a heavy crashing of water.

I unlatched my belt and allowed the leather kilt to fall on the sand. The helmet rolled a short distance away before connecting with a rock, releasing a hollow metallic sound. I loosed the ties of my sandals and pulled my tunic over my head. The cool air of the beach headed off into the water.

CHAPTER 26

HERA

Life comes in moments. You have to take those moments as they are offered to you. Happiness isn't a continual state. It's fleeting, and it only comes with those small moments, much like strife, anger, and pain. They're all moments.

As my new family and friends played in the waves, it, too, was just a moment. If this was all the happiness I would ever receive, I would take this moment and hold tight to the simple joy it had.

The mental guard dividing me from all the feelings and thoughts that swirled around me was nothing more than a wall. But it was gone. It cut me off from the flow of empathy.

I missed the bracelets for the quiet they gave me. I do not miss the utter helplessness.

Elysians couldn't turn off their emotions. Hybrids could, though most simply didn't. Themians naturally operated on a low emotional scale, and therefore blocking is an afterthought.

We were far enough away from the population on this island.

Their internal feelings shouldn't reach me here. And yet...

The emotion attached to the simple pleasure of swimming washed over me, the frolicking in the waves. It worked as a wave itself, smoothing over me again and again. Sydney pushed the water to grow, creating larger waves than the gravitational pull of the moons warranted.

The icy fingers of fear walked up my spine. As humans say, "*someone walked over my grave,*" just like that, the joy of the moment came to an abrupt halt. However, it wasn't a grave walking, but a person.

Somewhere out there was a person in pain. The feeling was weak, barely a vibrational trickle. I closed my eyes and reached out. Yet, it was so faint. There was proximity to the emotion. Someone was quietly suffering not far from here.

The laughing from the beach died, and Sydney was at my side in an instant.

"Isolde, can you feel it?" I asked. The splashing ceased as the power pushing the water died.

"I can. Where is she?" Isolde's lower lip trembled. She felt more than I did.

Interesting.

"Everybody, out of the water! Let's go!" Sydney ordered. She blasted a breeze to dry her hair and threw her clothes and vac-suit on.

They trudged through the low surf and re-dressed as everyone did their best to dry off.

I wasn't waiting for them. I picked up the sack with Medusa's head and headed South on the beach. I didn't bother to watch my feet to see if every step was sure. I couldn't. The pain enveloping the air was too palpable.

"Mother, wait for the rest of us," Perseus called.

I threw the bag over my shoulder, "I've waited for thousands of years. I'm tired of waiting. I'm perfectly capable of defending myself if I so choose," I snapped without knowing why I did it. There was no reason for my reaction. Perseus didn't deserve it.

The emotions coming at me were a blend of terror, anger, bitterness, and complete, utter hopelessness.

I have carried every one of these. They were like a heavy stone, one that you cannot lift but must carry anyway. My mind pounded them back into the recesses where such feelings must remain if one is to survive.

The sound of Perseus's feet slapping against the sand as he dashed to catch up with me drifted over my shoulders.

"I don't feel what you feel, mother, but I can see how it affects and distracts you. Being able to defend yourself is one thing. Being distracted by your emotions is another. And that, in battle, it will get you killed."

I patted him on the shoulder and kept going as if nothing had happened. Wherever this person was, they were suffering. Everything in my being said we must help her.

I wanted to be a good person, the person I'd always believed I was before Zeus, before Poseidon, before all those that died for my mistakes. In order to do that, I had to help others.

Our cove came to an end as we met a rocky outcropping on the far end. Instead of waiting for the others, I used the forces to lift myself off the sand. I peered around the cape of rocks.

Perseus rose next to me.

I relinquished Medusa's head to him. It was his prize, and I had no desire to carry around that creature's head.

"She's close. I can feel her, but I don't see her anywhere," I remarked in frustration. The beating in my chest hit with a fierce rhythm.

He waved my hand away. "Hold on to it. It will only throw my balance off in a fight." The weight of the head pulled my shoulders back as I slung the kibsis. The feel of the seething snake hair sent shivers through my body.

There was nothing but rocks on the beach and the remains of a temple. The small cove held pieces of white stone shot through with the golden orichalcum. The even platform where a building once stood occupied the middle of the cove. Columns laid down on their sides as if the entire area had been struck by an earthquake or tsunami.

"Do you see her? She's here. She's so close," Isolde's voice clawed at me with her desperate need to find whoever this person was. Isolde fed my desperation, transforming us into a self-perpetuation loop, each feeding the other.

I shook my head and searched with my eyes.

Perseus vanished. I allowed the wind to push me over to the foundations of the old temple. I could survey most of the small cove from this vantage point, so I sat down.

The wind picked up, and there was no reason for it to rise.

Sydney and Adrian stood near the breaking waves. The tangy taste of the sea changed, speaking of something amiss. The water roiled with angry waves as the sky darkened, leaving everything with a dull gray pallor.

I scanned the cove for anything awry.

Perseus had disappeared. The only object of significance, besides the fallen building materials, was a statue between two pillars down near the water's edge.

"Where is your brother?" I called. Hercules pointed down at the surf.

Perseus was picking his way along the rocks. He had a sword in one hand   and a shield slung across his back. He jumped with the ease of an acrobat from one giant rock to another never, allowing his feet to touch the sand.

I divined his course. He was heading for the statue.

I closed my eyes, attempting to find the strand Isolde spoke of.

A string that connects you to someone, which you can use to find your way directly to them.

But whatever ability she had, I did not possess.

No strings tied me to others. Whatever web she was connected to, I couldn't access. I opened my eyes and huffed in frustration.

"Isolde, where is she?" I demanded.

Isolde turned towards the water. She raised her arms, letting them hang in the air with her hands wide open as if she was feeling the air. Then her body lifted up and began to move in the direction of the surf.

I pulled on the forces of the wind and followed her, as did Hercules.

<Sydney, Adrian, come!> I ordered.

The pull of my sister Fates, moving in time with me, was a gravity well all its own.

We converged on the beach with the statue at the heart. The closer we came to the focal point, the more agitated the waves and heavier the wind. I set myself down a good 30 feet away from the carving.

To my right stood Isolde while Sydney was on my left, Fates, all in alignment. No matter what happened, the three of us always faced it the same way.

Fate can not be changed.

Perseus almost reached our destination when *it* moved.

A lifting of the shoulders for a quick breath. For all its outward appearance, it seemed like a marble statue. Up close, that illusion faded away, leaving deathly pale skin blanched of its color.

The woman hung with her arms raised by shimmering black chains between two rocks.

She is trapped here.

I could just make out the curve of her cheek. Her hair hung around her in ratted ringlets. Her dress was a drab gray of filth, nothing more than tattered rags.

We moved in tandem, pacing our way around to the front of this woman. The roar of the waves rose higher with each movement.

Her eyes landed on Perseus. "You should flee while there is still time," she said, resignation flowed from her along with a bitter sadness that laced her voice.

My sister Fates and I moved into her line of vision, and her shoulders straightened. She raised her head to an unseen sky, hands open, fingers wide.

"The Fates have come for me. Thank the Judges! I will join my sisters at last."

I froze.

"Who are you? Why are you here?" Sydney's voice sliced the air asking all the questions my chest burst with.

She pushed the waves flat in the cove with a gentle move of her hand. I raised my forces to join with hers and quiet the winds.

Perseus leaped from a nearby rock. His sword cut the massive links holding her in place. Her body slumped to the sand. He landed two feet from her fallen form.

She curled her legs behind her and pushed up into a sitting position at Perseus' feet. My son extended his hand to her, and she took it, before I could stop him.

The blast of blue lightning filled the air around us. It pushed me back, forcing me to pivot and rebalance my weight.

The blast was followed by joy, indescribable joy.

Perseus pulled her into an embrace. There were heavy emotions in the air laced with deep satisfaction.

His lips locked on hers. I had to turn away as the emotional bast was too much for me.

Perseus is finally mated.

The wind returned, turning my tears to cold rivers running down my face. A shadow fell over the cover. The sky was heavy with dark clouds and the taste of rain.

Perseus pulled back from his mate. The moment she opened her eyes, they remained on a fixed location behind us.

I turned toward the shadow that held her attention.

"Holy shit! What is that?" Isolde's voice woke me out of my trance. I moved to Perseus' side, and the rest of our party joined me.

"That is Cetus. He's here to kill us," the woman remarked in a cold tone, never turning away from the water.

A giant serpent-like creature protruded from a heaving sea. Its head was bulbous, with small, deep-set onyx-colored eyes on either side of a gaping maw. The fans, like a dragon's wing, framed a mouth laden with saber-shaped teeth.

It reared its head back, releasing a scream that cut the sky in half. My ears rang with a shrill tone.

I shivered in my own skin at the noise exiting the gaping maw. I lived through Poseidon and Zeus.

I'll not die here, killed by a worm.

I pushed it with the force of the wind and pelted it with stones from the beach. Sydney stepped in the water and pulled herself up onto a watery wall, riding it like only one person I'd ever witnessed before.

The ocean carried her to the center of the cove where she parted the water, and she rode the wave down as she exposed the seafloor and the wiggling tail of Cetus.

Its scream rent the air, cutting into my senses again. The curdling in my blood lessened in power this time.

Fear flowed from Isolde, blanketing the cove. It held Cetus for a moment, but the sea snake reared back, shaking its head to free itself from the hypnotic hold.

Adrian shifted giant stones from the beach to fall on the monster. The pile on its tail grew.

Sydney slapped her hands together, closing the waves over Cetus, battering him as the power of the ocean crushed him.

A yell from behind me rose up in the air as Perseus used the wind to carry himself to the fight. He lashed his shield on and pulled the helmet of darkness from its loop on his belt, then disappeared with his sword raised for the coming battle.

The cornucopia of emotions swirling around the cove buffeted me from all sides, forcing me to rebuild my mental walls.

Isolde threw cannonballs of hail, pelting the monster. No matter what we did, he remained undamaged. The creature weaved from side to side as if dodging an invisible force - Perseus.

All at once, Cetus reared its head back as its tail split into eight tentacles. It was a moment before Sydney crashed the watery walls back over it.

The sea moved back to the shore at a rapid pace. A wall of water rose up, dwarfing my companion and me.

I grabbed the woman next to me, wrapping my arm around her waist. I called to the wind and shot into the air.

<Hera, get out of here!> Sydney's words rang in my ears.

How is it that I am the weakest link?

"You hold our salvation, Hera. You undervalue yourself. Remind them of that," the woman said.

Medusa!

<Sydney, the bag!> My heart was beating out of my chest as the wiggling snakes at my back reminded me of the power I carried.

A tentacle whipped toward me, and I dodged, slipping to the right, then lowered, only to shoot left. I moved in circles around the limb while its hook-lined suckers flexed as they searched for me.

The others weren't doing any better. Every direction I looked, someone was leaping and dodging, trying to get out of Cetus' and his many limbs way.

Hercules slashed at a tentacle as it reached for Isolde. It turned and wrapped around his leg, lifting him into the sky. Cetus reared and lurched to one side. My son raised his sword above his head, all the while pressing his free foot against one of the giant suckers. He flexed, pulling his body into a pike position as his sword dug deep into the limb, exposing blood and muscle.

I watched in horror as his second blow cut the end of the tentacle free, and he fell toward the dry ocean floor.

He won't survive the impact.

Just before my baby met his fate, the waves crashed over him.

Isolde screamed, and a moment later, the tentacle, along with a wet Hercules, appeared near her.

Hercules jumped up. "Come back here, you worm! I'm not done with you." He raged and brandished, his sword then moved in front of Issy, working as a wall.

The next limb slapped the water near them, raising the waves. Hercules pulled Isolde to his side as I used the wind to lift them away from the force of the wave.

Fear gripped me.

We could all die here.

Fury welled up inside me, beginning in my belly and burning its way to my chest.

"Perseus, Adrian, the bag!" The weight on my back lifted as the figure of Perseus appeared in front of Cetus. I turned my face away. My right hand covered my companions' eyes as I lowered us to the ground, where I curled into a ball to protect my son's new mate.

The creature split the air with its death scream. Wet blood flowed from my ears and nose. The scream was cut short and replaced with the crackling of stone.

The roar of the waves subsided, as did the wind, only to be replaced a moment later by laughter.

"Mother, he's dead." Hercules removed my hands from my eyes. He had one arm around Issy's waist. He pulled me from my crouch, kissed my temple, then turned to his mate and kissed her lips.

Relief washed over me, yet the fury was still there.

Who would leave such a creature to run wild?

"Hera, brilliant call!" Sydney hugged me, slapping my back, just before Adrian pulled her from me and planted a deep kiss on her.

Perseus floated in front of the monster, the cords from Medusa's bag gripped tight in one hand and his sword in the other. He raised his blade and stabbed it into the stony chest of Cetus. Spider web cracks formed out from the impact point of the blade. It crumbled into the sea with a low rumble.

"Does she have a name, or shall we call her your woman? Like the cavemen of Earth?" Sydney asked with a chuckle, looking at our new group member

Perseus pulled her into his arms and embraced her with all that he was. The sucking sound of lips breaking turned into laughter. "Andromeda is my name."

Sydney hacked a few times until Adrian smacked her on the back. "Of course, you're Andromeda. Who else would you be?"

Issy and Adrian snickered with her. I did see the humor in her statement, but the sarcasm was unnecessary.

"Why were you chained?" Adrian asked.

"My father lives in fear that Pythia's vision would come true. He chained me here to be guarded for all time by Cetus. Before you came, all who entered the coved were doomed."

Pythia! It all goes back to Pythia.

"Who is your father? Rhadamanthys?" Perseus never took his hand from hers but kissed it gently.

"Pythia called Rhadamanthys - Ray. It was a joke we had. Ray as in a ray of sunshine. He has never been a bright light in our lives. Nor was Aeakus."

Issy covered her lips with the back of her hand, pushing back a giggle.

"You are the daughter of one of the Judges of Elysium? Who is Pythia to you?" Sydney never missed a beat.

"She is—" she stopped, took a deep breath, and shuttered. "If you are here, she *was* my sister."

CHAPTER 27

SYDNEY

"Send her to Odyssey. I don't want her with us. Aeakus and Minos need not know she's free. We have enough problems," I ordered.

I was not worried about young love.

"We can't be parted," Perseus' words cut me.

I knew that feeling, the first moments of the mating when you need to be with the other person every second of the day. "Adrian and I were parted, as you say, for over 30 years, and we survived. You will, too. The Judges know how many are in our party. They also know our names. Don't you think you will be missed? You stay, she goes. If you can't trust your brothers and sisters to protect her, who can you trust?" I shrugged.

I couldn't even trust my brothers. Cousins? Hell, no!

Fuck, my family's a mess.

His eyes still burned into me. I wasn't sure if he was going to smash me in the face with his sword or not. I did, however, know the blow would never land. Adrian would make sure of that.

"She goes to Ares," he gritted out through his teeth, "he'll protect her with his life. I want Ixis to —" His words barely left his mouth before Adrian completed the shift.

Perseus dove and the sound of slapping leather filled the air. Adrian blinked away before he landed. Perseus' foot smashed into the stone, echoing around the cove. Perseus lost his footing on some rubble and tumbled head over tail, catching Adrian off guard and knocking him off his feet. Before Adrian could hit the stone, he was back at my side.

"You can't win against a shifter." Adrian chuckled, slicking his golden hair back and winking at me.

I cocked an eyebrow at him. <Stop!>

He brandished his sword for show. I rolled my eyes since guy dick swinging made me crazy.

"I will end your portion of my bloodline," Perseus snarled, then he moved forward, "You never should have moved my mate without my leave." He bared his teeth and growled as he gripped his sword. He pulled the wind to him and slammed Adrian into the rock pillars that once held Andromeda.

Adrian coughed and shifted Perseus three feet in the air and dropped him. Perseus kipped up, "Face me without the forces, like a man of my line would."

Adrian shifted to stand a few feet away from the angry Demi-god.

I spread my hand over Perseus' chest and pushed him back. "She's safe. Don't lose your shit over it. What is our objective here, Perseus?" I yelled at him.

Adrian shifted Perseus to face me.

Hot eyes bore into mine. The muscles in his jaws worked over the bone, grinding his teeth, "To eliminate the Judges of Elysium." He straightened, clenching his fists. The hilt of his sword took the brunt of his anger.

"Then, let's get to it. The sooner we reach Aeakus, the more likely the news of Medusa's death didn't reach him. We need that advantage," I growled.

I stepped closer to him and stared him down. Yet, I didn't dare touch him. I didn't want the hand of Fate to step in and take his choice away.

"Shifting now." Adrian's words bled into my mind as the pressure around us changed. The world turned upside and down, then right side up. The shift was clumsy, and the pressure on my skull was tight.

<What was that?>

Adrian shrugged, and his eyes rolled down. He turned away from Perseus and me. Adrian didn't often fight or act cocky. This was for show. Perseus was acting like an overprotective ass, and Adrian took the bait.

<Keep the male posturing to a minimum will, ya?> I asked.

He winked at me, and a moment later, we reached Aegina.

Another island, another Judge.

It, too, was covered in tropical foliage, the air heavy with water and heat.

I wondered what Aeakus looked like. The Themians said he was the Judge of the people of Europe. Was there a Europe here, or was that another human bit of telephone?

Knowing where you need to be and finding the exact spot is not the same thing.

We were definitely not in the right place.

The only sounds reaching our party were birds and the humming of insects. We didn't even have One-eye to use as a reference.

Rather than trudging through the brush like we did with the Gorgons, I closed my mind to my body. Pulling out, I rose and floated. The scene below me seemed frozen. Adrian held my hand, though the feeling of it never reached me.

The soul moves with the speed of the light from a star. It leaves all physicality behind to delve into the cosmos that surrounds us. And so, the movement of space and time continued.

Life forms moved at an unbelievably slow pace. It was as if I'd stepped out of that dimension and into another. This wasn't the subspace of a shift. It was a different existence.

In the blink of an eye, I covered the entire island. The location of the palace was all I needed. Fixing it in my mind, I slid back into my body. My skin was heavy and awkward. A shiver rolled over me in an attempt to settle my soul.

<Adrian?> I sent him my vision. A mental lethargy clouded my world. The lapping of the calm waves called to me, and I dipped my toes into the water for energy. Primordium worked like the elixir of life, pushing back the drain of my out-of-body experience.

"Shifting now!" He winked at me, and the pressure changed.

CHAPTER 28

SYDNEY

The edifice in front of me was similar to all the other palaces we'd visited on this planet, done all in the Greek style.

Err, Elysian style.

Why was there such a divergence from the Greek style on Delphi? I didn't know. The rest of the Themian culture clearly adopted and kept it.

Large columns supported an edifice with arched openings into the interior colonnade. Carved statues of women and men in variations of forms of dressed and undressed sat in each archway. Through the grand opening, you could just make out the courtyard beyond and what appeared to be a fountain.

Though we were surrounded by the sounds of the tropical rainforest, birds and insects twittering and chirping. The tinkle of the water falling from the fountain played in the background. I couldn't hear them. Instead, I listened for the enemy I expected to be here.

The floors were covered with mosaic stones, pictures depicting various creatures. One of them showed the Gorgons. In another section was the Graeae.

Our steps carried us deeper into the palace. The shadow from the colonnades fell across the floors, dappling the surrounding area.

"This courtyard reminds you of anything?" Issy murmured.

Other than the floors...

Yes, yes, it does. Delphi and Sashat's statue!

This could have been the same place.

Fuck!

Inside, the main archway revealed a wall mural of three normal women. One on the left resembled Andromeda. The woman to the right resembled the others in the set of her eyes. Though, I didn't know her name. The woman in the center had piercing blue eyes and golden hair. The set of her lips and nose niggled the back of my mind.

I'd seen her before, somewhere. Many mosaics and murals had titles or words set to them. The creatures were labeled. The bottom of this mural was damaged, the names removed. I tried to recall any names associated with Pythia and Andromeda. However, I came up empty.

When I glanced at Hera, she shook her head. She, too, was at a loss.

The size of the tiles was minuscule. The painstaking craftsmanship and attention to detail were mind-blowing.

How many slaves had worked in this palace? How many had died? Did they get to enjoy for a moment the fruits of their labors?

I had no idea how old this palace could possibly be.

There were hundreds of creatures depicted, not just the genetic mutations the Elysium Judges called their children.

There were also creatures that resembled Cetus and something similar to a hippocampus. They were creatures from earth's stories.

Perhaps, Poseidon spoke of them?

Hera, herself, told me stories of Elysium. They were Themian folktales.

Poseidon sounded like an awful person, no better than the Elysium Judges. I still cringed when thinking of him dominating humans and Themians into unnatural shapes and creatures.

Anger rose from my belly to my throat. It burned like bile. The sudden rush of fury shocked me. Tasting the bitterness that coated my mouth scared me.

<What is it, beautiful girl?>

I swallowed it back. Whatever it was, I didn't have time for it. Not right now.

<I'm okay. Let's just keep moving.>

Yet, it didn't go away. No matter how hard I pushed, it lurked, smoldering in the background of my psyche.

The courtyard was a garden of shrubs and flowers surrounded by channels of water that spilled from the fountain in the center. The twittering of birds that lived in the dwarfed trees and the chitterlings of a rodent or lizard echoed off the colonnades, drowning out all other sounds, leaving us deaf to anyone's approach. It left me to rely on my other abilities, and I didn't like that one bit.

The palace itself reminded me of a villa with the dwarf lemon trees scattered around the courtyard. The only difference was that it wasn't overlooking the Mediterranean Sea.

A moment later, Elysium slaves appeared and waved us through the colonnade, deeper into the palace.

My eyes strayed to each person in our group individually. We all knew this was going to be a big facade, so we each had to play our parts perfectly. The only loose cannon was Perseus.

Under the surface, he's seething.

His mating had given him access to knowledge, and he wasn't sharing it with the rest of us. It ate at him.

<Perseus.>

<Yes, *beautiful girl*.> he answered ironically.

Hera shot nervous looks of concern in his direction. Isolde chose to walk as far away from him as possible. He must be throwing off a tremendous amount of emotional energy if Issy was giving him a wide berth.

It didn't strike me at first that Isolde's irritation might be directed at the Elysium Lord himself. I finally took a look at the slaves leading us to their master and realized the males were barely covered in loincloths. The females wore sheer cloth that left little to the imagination.

That wasn't what really bothered me. It was the clear sign of healed scars from lashings. They covered the bodies of each and every one.

The two male warrior types' scars were chopped up. They also bore them on their arms and legs. The taller of the two carried a scar that ran down the side of his face. His eyes were still good.

I guess he got lucky.

The edge of the scar dug into his jawline, marring what was once a handsome face.

Isolde scowled. Everything about this place raised her hackles.

Something hummed deep in the background.

Was I the only one who felt it?

We approached a sheer curtain, and each of our escorts held them open so we could enter an anti-chamber. Before us was a giant bowl filled with water which poured over the side in an even flow. The water fell into a rock-covered cistern that fed a channel surrounding the room beyond.

"You must sanctify yourself and bath. None may face a Judge clothed. Remove your outer covering, so you may not hide your sins." The warrior stared straight ahead, avoiding eye contact. His speech came with the practice of many years.

For the sake of peace, I dipped my fingers in the basin and crossed myself as if that meant anything here, then dashed the curtain that was separating the main chamber from us, open and strolled in, clothed and unafraid.

A chaise lounge sat in the middle of the room with a naked man lounging on it.

Rhadamanthys looked like he was barely out of his 20s. This man, on the other hand, was mid to late 40s. He was still in excellent shape, but the graying wings had already started the march over his pate and down his chest.

The man blinked his light blue eyes. His eyes were so light they were practically devoid of color, and like Rhadamanthys', his eyes were also cold. He yawned and rolled to face us, his flaccid dick flopping over onto his leg. Gray laced his pubic hair and his chest.

Yuck, cover that shit, for fuck sake!

<I'd rather not lose my lunch before we kill this guy. Dignity is so hard to come by.> Adrian gagged.

We took up our various positions with myself and my sister Fates in the center. Adrian was on my right, while Hercules watched our back and Perseus to the left of his mother. We moved in unison in our choreographed dance.

"So you've managed to kill my daughter, Medusa. And you come here seeking what from me? Forgiveness? A new task? Do you think that you're going to succeed?" the man said with little care for the answer as he barely gave us the once-over.

Why is he in such a hurry to show his hand?

"We completed the task Rhadamanthys asked of us. If you have an issue with the death of your daughter, perhaps you should take it up with him. After all, he's been asking someone to kill her for thousands of years. If you want an apology, very well. I apologize. I'm sorry I killed your murderous, mutant daughter," I said.

His laugh was dry, "You cannot apologize for a sin that you did not commit."

That was it! He knew I couldn't kill Medusa.

We only just figured out that women couldn't enter her palace. The force field was all another excuse for the Elysium Judges to continue on with their rule.

If a powerful woman came to them, asking for something, they would send her on a mission to kill Medusa. She would never succeed. The Gorgon sisters would tear her apart before she got inside the palace.

Layers upon layers, they'd spent so much time thinking about how to foil any progress for their people. The sheer scope of their devious behavior was unimaginable.

Perseus was barely holding on. The muscles in his jaw worked over the bone. He clenched and unclenched his fists. One hand played upon the pommel of his sword.

"You wish me to apologize for killing your daughter?" he spat, "I don't apologize. I'm not sorry. She was a freak of nature designed by you. I'm not sorry to free this world from her and her sisters."

Perseus repositioned his stance with his feet a little wider and his arms loose. "I am just sorry that I didn't get here sooner to kill her."

Aeakus lurched forward before recovering himself. His jaw hardened, and he snapped his fingers. The fabric covering our bodies disintegrated, leaving only the leather of belts and kilts. My vac-suit covered my goods but left my tits out for the world to see.

"You must appear before your Judge naked so that you may not hide your sins behind the trappings of the clothes. Remove those articles before you speak another word!" he demanded.

This was the real judge, not the lounging old guy we walked in on. Lounging was a cover for his piety. He believed the hype.

Ugh.

"What Perseus is trying to say is that Medusa was not made quite right." Hera's clothes were barely there, to begin with, and now she was naked, "And I'm sorry I killed your daughter, and for your loss. We came to treat with the Judges of Elysium for the safety of our people on a small plot of land. If you could possibly provide us with a task to win your favor, we would be forever grateful," she offered, then, in true Hera fashion, she bowed to the vile thing. She timed her bow to allow her reddish-golden hair to fall and catch the light. When she brought her head up, she shook her hair, so the long tresses tickled over her breast and shoulders.

Bile burned in the back of my throat, along with anger. Yet, I took my cue from Hera and plastered a giant fake smile across my face. I even threw in a little bow just to make him happy.

<That was extremely well done. We should have Hera address the next guy too. I'm surprised you didn't throw up just listening to her.> Adrian mentally smirked, then began shucking his kilt.

<Well, the bullshit fest isn't over yet. I might still yak, so watch yourself. And put your leather skirt back on. My daughter is standing right there!> I barked.

<Issy is my daughter too. We are going to get more with a little skin, so strip *beautiful girl*.>

I groaned. Hercules unbelted his kilt and let everything drop but the cross straps that held his sword. Issy, on the other hand, locked her hands on her hips and refused to budge. Perseus, too, didn't remove his clothes. I wasn't inclined to stand naked for the old guy to shake his dick at.

This ain't Plato's Retreat, so fuck that!

Aeakus covertly spied the crowd. His eyes lingered on Issy a little too long, and he licked his lips at Hera. But she wasn't wearing much more than a smile.

"Very well! You wish to have another task and win my favor? My daughter Andromeda is trapped on Rhadamanthys island. Free her." He leaned back and allowed one of the slave girls to pop a grape into his mouth. His hand cupped his pecker as he drug the back of his nails across his balls repeatedly.

I was internally gagging.

What is it with these guys? They lay around all day eating fruit with naked children feeding them — weirdos.

"Why did he imprison her?" Issy asked, and it sounded innocent enough.

Aeakus' head lazily turned toward us, "I don't know. Something to do with a prophecy he didn't like. So he imprisoned her. Now, I want her back."

I felt it before I heard it.

The wind pressure in the room changed, "What will you give us if we do indeed free her?"

Perseus!

I wanted to slap my hand over my forehead. He just couldn't let any of it go.

Aeakus stood up, "Why? I would be willing to give one of you my daughter's hand in marriage. You're welcome to have her if you can free her. That will make you my heir." He ran his hand over his chest.

The lies in his words were apparent for anyone in the room. You could smell it, like rotten flesh, sitting in the sun for too long.

"Very well, I will have you know that I freed your daughter yesterday," Perseus said and crossed his arms.

I inwardly groaned and outwardly kept my peace, all the while shooting Perseus a look of *shut the fuck up or I will kill you.*

"Andromeda? She's free?"

Isolde hissed, "You doubt our word?"

"No. I simply wish to see her for myself." The stench of his lies grew to the point where I almost wanted to gag from the putrid flavor of it.

"No, you will never see your daughter again. She's mine, and I intend to keep her!" Perseus changed his footing and wrapped his hand around the hilt of his sword.

Aeakos ground his teeth and sat up. By doing so, his junk rolled around and flopped.

Saliva pooled in my mouth.

"How did you accomplish this feat? She was guarded by a monster! Show me how you killed it."

Before Perseus could jump to the conclusion he wanted from the moment we entered this room, I stepped in front of him. "Tell us why you locked your daughter away in that cove. Tell us about the prophecy, and then we'll share with you how we killed it," I intervened.

Aeakos tilted his head to one side and smirked, "Pythia, Andromeda, and Demeter were all born with the power of prophecy -- seers. Each one gave a prophecy for their chosen father. Pythia and Demeter escaped. As soon as Andromeda pronounced her prophecy, I tricked her into walking down by the beach. I let her believe I would change and indeed become a better father." A cruel, clever smile curved his lips.

He is the cat that ate the canary.

"I would be kinder to the people." He continued, waving his hand around to indicate the slaves serving him. "She told me that if I changed my ways, I would live. I had to give up being one of the Elysium Judges and become a regular man. You can understand how that didn't work for me," he took a pause only to continue, "I led her down to the beach where I chained her. I called forth my sea creature, Cestus, and I had a field installed around the cove. Cestus could neither leave, and no one else could enter without dying by him. I left the beach never to return." He smiled and clapped to signal the end of his story. The slaves clapped to indicate their approval.

It was so automatic, making it laughable.

"Perseus, don't you just love it when they monologue right before you kill them?" I asked.

Perseus' eyes narrowed as his lips broke into a broad smile. He stopped fiddling with the pommel of his sword and instead took the kibsis off his back and slowly opened it.

"What do you mean before you kill me? You cannot kill me! I am immortal. I'm a God! I'm a Judge of Elysium! I will never die! You, on the other hand, are nothing but pathetic hybrids, part human, part Elysium. You are nothing." He took to his feet, shaking with rage.

My guess was that it had been a while since someone pissed him off.

"You say you killed Medusa? You must've tricked her somehow. How many men did you lose just to get to her? No matter. You will never kill me." He was shouting and shaking.

The putrid rot of his lies burned away to reveal the scent of fear. He was shaking with fear. His robes trembled, as did his hands.

"You will never reach my throne! I have fields all around me. Go ahead! Do your dirtiest. You will still never kill me." A dry laugh escaped his lips. There was no conviction behind it. With every word he uttered, the tannic scent of fear grew. However, the brave words washed over me, cold and calculated.

He really believed his bullshit. He really believed that he was impervious, and we couldn't kill him.

I guess when you're the most powerful being on your planet, having devised your immortality, you get drunk on your own stupidity.

I nodded to Perseus, "Well, Aeakos, you wanted to see how we killed Cestus. Here you go!"

I turned away, as did the rest. Using the wind, Isolde and Hera pushed the servant in the room down while I blocked doors and turned bodies.

Perseus drug Medusa's head from the bag. I pressed my eyes shut. The crackling of stone-forming permeated the background, along with the hissing of the snakes.

"This is how we killed Cestus. Medusa was a terrible creature in life but a fabulous weapon in death," Perseus remarked with glee. The rustling of fabric and the cinching of ropes   was followed by, "it's safe."

I opened my eyes only to find the shocked expression on Aeakos face.

"Do you think he saw it coming?" Perseus asked.

We all snickered. It was cheesy, but I couldn't help myself.

"He wanted to see how we did it," Herc continued and shrugged, flipping his long hair back.

I shook my head, between Perseus and Hercules they could probably go on and on all day.

"Perseus, the next time we go somewhere, and you go off half-cocked, I'll have Adrian shift you out so fast, you'll never know what hit you. When we get back to Prometheus, you'll be scrubbing floors with your own toothbrush," I stopped them.

"What's a toothbrush?" Herc asked.

I glanced at Hercules and then Isolde, "You're kissing him, and he doesn't know what a toothbrush is?" I shivered.

Gross!

The light dawned in Hercules' eyes, "I clean my teeth. I don't use a brush. But I really do clean them. I'm not disgusting. My breath is good. It's...it's minty fresh. I swear!"

I shook my head and put my hand up to stop his protestations, "Hercules, really, I don't need to smell your breath to know whether you're giving my daughter halitosis. I don't care."

Perseus turned to his mother. "I'm not sure if I'm the best choice to continue on this journey with you anymore, mother. My mating has clouded my reason. Sydney's right. I went off half-cocked, as she said. My anger for what he did to Andromeda won over my reason." He slung the bag over his shoulder. "I wanted him as dead as she did. He chained her there because she saw this day. She told him the Fates would come and judge him and that he would be wanting." He shook his head, "She told him that if he didn't change his ways, he would never survive. She gave him the chance to change. He didn't. He became worse."

Hera patted his shoulder, her blue eyes softened as a small smile played on her lips, "I understand. It is all right if you wish to go and be with your mate." She stepped back, giving him the space he needed for a shift, then raised her chin, "Anyway, this is something we must complete. There is only one Judge left. Hopefully, we've already completed the hard tasks," she said.

One of her hands fingered the material of her dress. It was her tell. She was nervous and didn't want to sway his choice.

CHAPTER 29

SYDNEY

"No, mother, I will stay until the end," Perseus replied in a low tone.

"Ask your new mate to help keep your emotions in check while you're at it, would you?" I requested.

The slaves cowered around the room in disarray. They now had no purpose and didn't understand what to do with their day. Issy herded the children to one side, offering them cloth for coverings. They soon disappeared.

She and Tristan must have picked a place for them and sent them there.

Hera made her rounds in the room, opening doors and inspecting the adjoining spaces. More people who entered were handed the ruminates of the hanging curtains, only to disappear into thin air seconds later.

It was a repeat of our previous clean-up. Adrian murmured in my mind to Ixis about our next destination. I suddenly felt useless. For all the power I wield, cleaning up wasn't my strong suit. I didn't interact well with others. I wasn't personable. I was the blunt weapon you brought for safety, not the blanket that offers comfort.

Do I want to comfort others?

For me, removing the impediments to your choices was a comfort in itself. The ability to maneuver your own path through life was the greatest comfort I could offer. The lack of choice was a death sentence I would not wish on others.

The sniffling and movement in the room lessened, and the itch under my skin for forwarding momentum reared its head again. It was the need to push on and find something just out of reach. It grew with each passing moment.

Hera used the last of the sheer curtains to fashion a Delphinian dress around her chest and a cowl around her neck to cover her breasts. She tucked and folded, creating a beautiful vision of flowing fabric and grace.

Perseus and Hercules replaced the lost fabric from under their kilts, belting whatever they scrounged from the adjoining rooms.

<Adrian, are we ready to go?> I inquired.

Whatever Minos had for us, I was ready to seek it head-on and be done with this.

<We have a location, but we can't.> the answer came.

<What do you mean, we can't?> I asked.

Sweat dripped down my bareback. My clothes were gone. The only covering left to me was the vac-suit, and it was hot in there. I scratched the back of my neck, hoping to ease some of the moisture from my skin. All that did was cause the liquid to run down my chest between my breasts, and that itched even worse.

<I mean, something is blocking me. Whatever it was at Medusa's palace, Minos has something similar surrounding his entire island. As if he knew we were coming.> Adrian remarked.

"What's the holdup, mom?" Issy intervened. Her eyes widened as it sunk in that feeling when something wasn't right.

"Minos has shielding we can't shift in," Adrian told her. A bead of sweat trickled from his brow, down the side of his face, and into the collar of the vac-suit he'd shifted in.

"Why don't we just have Tristan give us a ship and fly in?" Hercules asked. He slicked his blond hair back and shook his head.

The sound of running water ceased. I turned back to the cleaning bowl. It sat silent since the water no longer slipped over the sides onto the rocks below.

Hera laid a hand on my shoulder, and I met her inquiring stare.

"There is something not right here. We should go," she murmured and tilted her head towards what was left of the servants. They, too, were covered in sweat.

When we arrived, the room was temperate. Now, it was slowly becoming an inferno.

<Tristan, move the rest of the servants off this island now!> I ordered.

Adrian cocked an eyebrow at me, <Shifting a ship would be the easiest way.>

<I know it would be easiest, but that doesn't mean Minos wouldn't shoot us out of the sky.> I remarked and rubbed my temples. My fingers came away wet.

<They do not have projectile weapons here. The Judges are so arrogant they think no one will confront them.> Adrian informed me while. pushing his hair back with one hand and wiping it off on the couch that was dominating the center of the room.

<If that was true, why would Minos have a shield?> I asked.

I tilted my head and pushed the sweat from my brow back into my hairline, working it back to my nape. My hair was soaking wet.

<Okay, you got me there.>

"Hey, want to share your conversation with the rest of the class?" Issy remarked, then crossed her arms, staring me down. Her underarms were ringed in fresh sweat stains. She pulled a light breeze to her, which cooled us but was not enough.

"I'm not sure flying in is a good idea," I said while plucking at the closure on my vac suit. Part of me wanted to rip the thing open and strip down to my toes.

But that won't be any different than what Aeakos wanted to begin with.

There was no way I was doing that.

"When in doubt, call Ares out." All heads swiveled in Hercules' direction, who shrugged, "What? I'm sure you have poetry and rhyming on earth. They did when I was last there," he finished and put his hands out.

I was still in shock about the rhyming.

Hercules cocked a half-smile. "I know most of you think I'm a big dummy even though I'm not. There's a reason why there are so many stories about me. I have a way with words."

"I realized that having all the stories about you, which you have, you must have some ability to entrance people with your stupidity. However, I just didn't know you were into rhyming on the spot," I snickered.

He shook his head and shifted his shoulders. "What can I say? It's a talent."

Everyone laughed. Hercules and talent was not exactly something I would think would go together, but he had a good idea. Calling Ares was the right thing to do. Ares already had most of his ships outfitted with weapons.

I gave Adrian the sign. At the very least, we needed to leave. There was something going on here, and I didn't want to stick around and see what it was.

A swift pressure change and a pop later, and we were standing on the bridge of the Argos with Ares in front of me with his black hair and blue eyes alight, arms crossed and legs wide. But most importantly, with the oppressive heat gone.

"Who in the name of Hades thought it would be okay to shift me without my permission?" His eyes bored into Adrian.

"I did. Either you're my general and the leader of our armies or you're just a petulant child who hasn't grown up yet and needs me to put him in his place," I argued, and he immediately shifted his rage to me.

"A child? I am 10 times older than you."

"I don't care what you call yourself these days - God of War, the Demigod of War, or whatever it is that you consider yourself." I waved my hand, "You understand the chain of command, don't you? I'm in command. I've shifted you here, and now you'll do my bidding."

His eyes locked on Hera. She didn't breathe a word, yet something passed between them.

Through gritted teeth, he seethed, "Commander!"

A moment later, the clouds on the surface of the planet changed. There was a circle over the top of Aeakos island.

"What was that?" Issy whispered.

She knew, and so did I. The island was no more, and the power of the explosion created a tsunami.

A whimper erupted from Issy, "Is there any way to stop it?" she mourned.

"Poseidon could have stopped it," Hera said.

I wiped around and snarled at her. "He is not my father—" A moment later, I was on my boat, Calypso, and a giant wave was moving toward me.

"Whose fucking idea was this?" I shouted into the roar of the wave.

I ran to the bow of the boat and jumped over the safety line into the agitated water. The ocean pulled the residual heat from my body and drug me down by the heavy vac-suit. For a moment, I embraced oneness with Primordium. The power of the water electrified me, and I turned that energy around, allowing it to heal all that hurt.

The water came from underneath and pushed my body to the surface. I was in control of this element and emerged on my feet. The sheer power of water rolled over me, working like the tsunami coming at me. I raised my hands into the air and closed my eyes. The kinetic energy of the wave pounded into my soul. I mapped it in my mind and closed my hands on the power. There was no way to stop the wave, only direct it.

<Where can I send this thing?> I shouted to anyone who could hear me.

<Back to its maker.> Tristan supplied.

I whipped the wave around and released it back to the epicenter of the explosion. Setting that much power free pounded me back, and I hit my head against the port-side pontoon of Calypso.

<Whose idea was it to shift the fucking boat down here?>

No one responded, which meant it was the kids.

I rubbed my stinging head and came away with blood on my hand. While treading water, I surveyed the water around me. Blood in water was always bad. No matter what planet you were on. Though the water would heal me fast, the scent of blood would linger. I dove under the boat and swam for the stern and a sugar-scoop. The dive ladder was clipped up, so I used the water to lift me up onto the steps.

I stood on deck for a moment and enjoyed the wind blowing over my skin. The wheel was in my hand, and I was ready to sail to my next port. It was as easy as breathing. The muscle memory was simple.

My life had become so difficult, and for just a moment, I was back on the water. For a moment, I was free. I was me, the me I remember, not this leader or the freedom fighter I turned into. For a moment, I was just a woman in a boat, crossing an ocean.

<You are crossing an ocean. It isn't blue, but it is an ocean. We can come back, beautiful girl. >

The moment was gone, and the weight of what needed to be done was back. I heaved a sigh.

The pressure of the shift took over, and Calypso and I were back on Odyssey. I stared out at the Biodome. The fake horizon was a sad comparison to the golden glow of Elysium's star. The holo-panels lining the ceiling gave off a light similar to Alexandria. Elysium reminded me more of Earth.

Adrian shifted me back to the Argos and to the next problem. I didn't complain about him not warning me or that I was still wet. I sucked it up because that was what I have always done. I turned to face everything head-on.

"Minos has some kind of defensive shield. We need to either get through it or take it out" my voice startled everyone in the room. All eyes were turned to me.

Issy barreled into me. "Oh, Mom, think of how many people you saved." She pulled back to smile up at me with tear-filled eyes. I kissed her forehead and looked at Ares.

"Well, if you're thinking of shifting down there immediately, he may have more than a shield," Perseus remarked.

"We need to send some scouting drones. And I have just the thing. Adrian, come with me," Ares barely had time to breathe before the both of them disappeared.

"We've been at this for days, and no one really had any sleep. Take a break. Whatever Minos has planned, it can wait at least a couple hours. Perseus, go see your new wife." Hera was always level-headed and practical.

She embraced her newlywed son, and a moment later, he, too, shifted out of the room along with Hercules and Isolde, leaving me behind with Hera.

"Three down, five to go?" She smiled.

My mouth fell open at the implication. I slicked the water out of my hair, and rivulets ran down my neck into my suit.

"What? You're halfway there," she chided, and finger brushed her hair, easing tangles out.

"What about you? You think you'll ever find someone?" I asked.

She had never let on that she was interested in anyone or that she was feeling lonely. But I was sure that there was no way she could be satisfied alone forever.

"You know, in the story of the Fates, there's the maiden, the mother, and the crone. An old crone does not marry. She simply stays with her family, wreaking all kinds of havoc." Her shy smile edged her lips, hiding the truth.

"I don't think so. First of all, you don't look old enough to be a crone. And second of all, I find it hard to believe that you'd go through all of this and end up with nothing." I shook my head to remove the thought. It made me sad to think she'd be alone for as long as we survive.

"If you think, I've always ended up with nothing, Sydney. Then you do not know what truly has value," she remarked. "I have gained the universe, and it's filled with everything I could ever have wanted."

She pushed me toward the companionway, and I hoped for dry clothes.

CHAPTER 30

HERA

Dread filled my belly over the next step. Facing the judges was easy, too easy. There had to be more, something we were missing. Pythia could have used Anu and Charon to kill the Judges easily. Instead, she boarded a ship and left with the brightest minds of Elysium.

If our job as Fates was to bring justice to Elysium, then why was the High Council so afraid of us?

There was only one Judge left, and my heart told me we would come out victorious with him too. Yet, a deep foreboding lined my mind and colored my world.

Is this all we were meant to accomplish?

It ate at me like ants on a carcass, nibbling away until only the sun-bleached bones remained.

Ares and the rest of the men discussed the best way to reach Minos, each taking their turn to poke holes in the other's plan.

I let their words wash over me. Strategy was not my forte. People were my domain. I stared out at the viewport on Argos. The cloud cover over Aeakos island was still shaped like a perfect circle, yet even that would fade with every turn.

This world, like the rest of the cosmos, would go on and find its equilibrium. I had to be satisfied with that. Yet, I couldn't. Sydney, too, tapped her fingers or bit her lip with pent-up energy as if there was a greater fight just around the corner.

She was an explosion waiting to happen. I, too, was becoming an internal supernova.

Issy was the only one that was not on edge. Since her mating with Hercules, she was no longer the Fate from before. She was more controlled.

"We've got a plan," Hercules announced and gave his bride a winning smile.

"Hit me with it!" Sydney replied. She took to her feet as if standing would make it better.

"We shift to the island but land in the water. Then swim in," Perseus said.

Sydney looked to Adrian and back to Ares. "Is that it? What if we can't pass through the shield?" She bit her lip and stared out the viewport before turning back to the group.

"We need to bring one civilian," Ares remarked with his arms crossed. He looked so like his father this way. It squeezed my heart. Ares carried all the best of Zeus, and for that, I was grateful.

"What? No way," Sydney said. Even though she was now dry, her hair was still damp, and the back of her shirt was too. She turned away to pace before pivoting and pacing back. For some reason, I watched the damp shirt as she moved.

"We have a volunteer," Adrian offered. He'd changed from the vac-suit to a leather kilt. He dressed more Themian than human with the leather straps crossing his chest to hold his Khimera horn-blades. He could be mistaken for Perseus easily. His time on Alethea honed him into a Demigod.

I'd like to think I played a part in that. Emmaline really took all the credit since my background string-pulling was an unseen influence I preferred to keep to myself.

Sydney shook her head. "I'm not taking a normal person to that island. If we fail, they might never get out."

The Nymph, Daphne, crowded into the cockpit. "My son is dead. I am unaltered. I will pass through the shield. I want to see the last of the Judges face his fate. Erik was my only child."

Sydney stared her down with her unyielding blue eyes. Daphne lifted her chin even as she shook to face her.

"You may not survive," Sydney remarked and began pacing around her, inspecting her reaction.

Daphne nodded her head in understanding.

"Say it for everyone to hear. I don't want anyone running around, claiming I tricked you."

"I am dead already. I died the day Erick spoke to Rhadamanthy. There was no going back." Her lips quivered, and a single tear traced its way down her cheek.

I wanted to give her hope and tell her we had what was left of Erik, the One-eye in stasis. However, that hope was too thin to hang a breath from. Distracting her with a hope that was nothing more than a dream wasn't wise.

Sydney gave her a curt nod of acceptance.

"What happens after we pass through the barrier?" Sydney asked.

Ares replied, "Do you need me to attend you? Otherwise, you are on your own. I'm sure my brothers will provide ample protection, along with your mate."

Sydney groaned. This wasn't the answer she was looking for.

I glanced at Daphne, "Have you seen the inside of Minos palace?"

"No, the only people who visit the Judges are tributes and petitioners, and they never return. If a Judge wishes to contact the Nymphs, they send an envoy." She glanced around, "And an envoy arrived yesterday from Minos."

"Where is he?" Sydney demanded, pushing her hair out of her face.

"She is out cold on Prometheus with your son."

I opened my mind. My citadel of windows appeared in my mind's eye. The windows were closed. Some rattled, others sucked in and out as if breathing. They came in every color the cosmos carried while some were blank.

Show me Tristan! I called to my mind.

His window resolved in front of me, and I opened the door and stepped through.

*****

<I was wondering when you would come.> Tristan remarked. His body was stiff. Tristan was not a relaxed person.

<I came to dreamwalk you, with your permission.>

<You don't normally ask.> Tristan said.

<In the past, it was common practice for a dreamwalker to ask. Our needs have outweighed the propriety of my training. Do you give your leave? It will be a drain. >

He didn't respond, only tilted his head and turned away. Tristan bemused me. He held himself apart from the rest of our group, choosing solitude over brotherhood. His main contact was his sister and Adrian.

That line of thought will need to be investigated another time.

I pushed into the dreamwalk world. The fuzzy outer edges of the dreamwalk were the only telltale sign of my reality.

My body materialized on Prometheus, and I took a breath.

"Where is she?"

He waved me down the companionway toward my room and Charon's old cell. I took a moment to change my clothes into something less revealing and more in line with my personal tastes. Themian fabric flowed with a soft hand to the fibers. The sheets from Aeakos palace were sheer and rough on my skin. As soon as I was dressed, my hand moved to clasp a small amount of the fabric between two fingers. I rubbed the threads, testing the feel. It soothed me, and I clung to that comfort before leaving the room.

The door was firmly shut with the security locks in place. They didn't need all of this. Elysians weren't able to cause any harm.

I shook my head and pressed the mechanism to release the door. It pulled into the wall to reveal my quarry.

<Hera?> Sydney called.

<I am retrieving the information you need. I am the only one who can.>

She didn't respond. I was going to mind diving this woman. Part of me pushed at that truth. Another part, the survivalist I'd grown into, understood the need to do what was necessary. The Judges needed to be stopped, and I had no doubt we were the only ones who could stop them.

The woman sat in a chair like a statue. Her eyes stared off into the bulkhead at the gray walls covered in the black spider-like crystalline circuitry.

She was beautiful.

The Judges only take the lovely into their service.

Her hair was the color of chestnuts, and her eyes hazel. It was her lack of response that bothered me most. I stepped into her line of sight, hoping for a reaction. Yet, there was none.

I leaned over, placing a hand on either side of her face. Her eyes blinked, she refocused on me.

"Minos, the Judge of the final vote, and son to Zeus."

I drew in a breath.

This is not possible.

I quickly pushed my fears aside.

He speaks of another Zeus, of course. My Zeus is long dead.

"Invite the Fates to his palace to treat and share a meal," the woman quit speaking.

That could not have been the message she was meant to deliver to the Nymphs. Rather than wait for her to wake from her mental prison, I clasped either side of her head and invaded.

The dreamwalk moved from her reality to her mind.

She was a blank slate, without even a name. The corners of her mind sat empty. There were no flower-gathering moments of happiness from childhood. The golden star that shone on Elysian soil didn't shine in her mind. She carried no memories of friends or family. No matter where I searched, all I found was Minos.

There is no part of her life without Minos.

I danced through her life as Minos' possession. She was his sex-toy and slave. Minos surrounded himself with people just like her.

Wiped minds and hollowed bodies.

She carried no emotions. The hollow shell of her mind surrounded me, but it was an empty and cold husk.

I couldn't stop the tears as they found their way down my cheeks. They, too, were cold, and I shivered as I realized if we failed, Minos would only do this to more people.

I pulled back from her mind and into the dreamwalk of Prometheus. Tristan stood by my side.

His hand cupped my shoulder, and I turned into the comfort he offered and cried. Tristan murmured into my hair as he petted my head. I couldn't make out the words.

What had been done to that woman was no different from what Poseidon did to other Themians on Alethea when this all began. I shuddered with fear, and the pain in my chest took over.

"It's okay, Hera." Tristan pulled my face away from his chest and forced me to look at him.

I sniffled and swallowed back a fresh round of tears.

"Whoever that woman was, she isn't there anymore, and there is nothing you can do about that. But you can stop Minos, and you must. My mother can't do it alone." He nodded, and I nodded with him.

"I am in control." I stepped back and wiped the tears from my cheeks. My dress was rumpled. I used that as an excuse to smooth the fabric. I patted my hair back into place and glanced at Tristan.

His clear blue eyes stared me down. I tilted my head to reassure him. He returned the move with a small smile. I released the dreamwalk and faded from the ship.

Sydney stood over me, her face clothed with concern.

"What did you learn?" she asked.

"Minos controls an army on the other side of that shield. But he is the only one there with abilities. He can dominate minds." I stopped and looked around at our group. We all understood how that worked. The hard walls of mental protection slammed into place, closing off all emotions on the ship but Daphne's. She blinked at me, unaware of the danger.

I'd learned enough from the nameless woman that Minos couldn't dominate a person without touching them first. Minos wiped millions in his lifetime, luring each person to his side with the promise of favoritism and love before taking all that made them special.

Even now, the vision roiled in my belly. I flared my nostrils, filling my chest with fresh air from Argos, washing the vision from my mind.

CHAPTER 31

SYDNEY

Hera held something back. I could see it in the set of her shoulders and the line of her jaw.

She wouldn't keep anything important to herself.

But it was something.

She'd told us all we needed to know - Minos had an army, and we would have to fight to reach him.

Ares gave all of us as many weapons as we could each hold safely and hugged his mother. He laid a hand on his brother's shoulders to say goodbye. They each returned the pose. Yet, none of them said anything out loud.

Ares turned to Adrian, "Good hunting!" Adrian thrust out his hand, and Ares clasped his forearm.

"Take care of my son," was all Adrian said before he shifted us.

The cool water surrounded my legs, and I soaked up the feeling with joy. It would be my last chance to reveal in the one force I truly had command over.

My dress grew damp around the hem from the ocean, and I moved forward with the rest of our group, focusing on the wavering shield before me.

Daphne sauntered ahead of us and walked right through. She stopped just on the other side. All I could make out was a blurred outline of her body. The shield resembled a piece of medieval glass, wavy with distortions.

Isolde lingered at the back of our group, and I stepped ahead of her to keep pace with Hera.

For once, Hera was in the lead. She moved with a purpose unlike I'd seen before.

"You want to stay with the class?" I asked.

Hera glanced over and returned her attention to the shield and Daphne on the other side. We reached the wavering air, and she reached through, pulling Daphne back to our side.

"That answers your question," Hercules remarked.

"Tristan, take her!" Hera called, and Daphne disappeared.

"That wasn't part of the plan," I hissed.

Hera wheeled on me. "I will not risk an innocent for our fight!" She screamed.

"Whoa, hold up, lady! I don't know what's got you stewing, but I am not your enemy," I said and pushed a stray hair out of my face.

Hera's hand fidgeted with the fabric of her dress. "He wipes them," she replied.

"You said that."

"NO! He wipes them clean. HE leaves nothing behind. They don't even remember their names. We will be killing an army of mindless, innocent people!" She shouted.

Perseus pulled her back from the shield, "Mother, innocents die all the time. We will end this, so no more is claimed by this fate."

The crazed look in her eyes told me there must be more to this. This was deeper than Minos erasing people. This visceral fear was in her soul.

"You could stay here," Hercules offered.

She shook her head. "No! He must be judged. He cannot go free."

I took her hand and laced my fingers with hers. "He won't." Her mouth fell into a grim line, but she didn't reply.

Adrian, Perseus, and Hercules moved ahead of us. Isolde gripped Hera's other hand, "He can't escape what he's done." A tight smile covered her face, and the three of us stepped through to the dry land of Larissa.

The island looked much like all the other ones in this world. It was tropical and covered in plants. The edges of the beach were made up of sugar sand, white with fine granules. The sand clung to my skin and the sides of my feet, making me regret wearing sandals.

A little sand wasn't going to stop me. So, we moved off the beach and into the dense foliage.

The ground was covered in vines and roots, along with the insects that call this island home. The guys used their swords as machetes to clear the leaves and vines As I stepped over an ant-type trail.

I had no wish to piss off an insect hive. On Earth, there were ants that could clean a body from its bones in minutes. I could only imagine something similar had to exist here as well.

The white of the stone building cut off the green wall of plants ahead of us. For a moment, the sound of feet slapping on stone drifted to us.

I swallowed back my desire. I wanted to save them. However, Hera said they were empty, meaning there was no moral person to reach out and convince of our good intent, no soul left to plead with, and no inner child to save.

They were zombies without the brain-eating part.

Alive, but dead.

I had to think of them that way. Would I want to live if all I was, was a vessel for a mad man?

I didn't know if this was true for everyone, but as I stepped over the last of the plant life between us and the army, it was what I had to believe. Otherwise, I couldn't do what was needed to reach my real enemy.

A row of men lined the battlements of the palace. They had knocked their arrows in readiness for an attack.

My heart rate leaped as I gazed up at the sheer amount of men standing there. A hum of electricity ignited next to me, setting my teeth on edge.

Isolde had Medusa's power bow. She didn't wait. Instead, she loosed a round at the wall. It blew a hole in the curtain wall, and the men above collapsed into the hole. The rest released their arrows.

I opened my hand and batted a large swath out of the sky. Hera roared and pulled the wind, pushing the arrows into the ground. The high-pitched whining of the arrows ended with their impact into the ground, only to be replaced by a fresh round.

Issy released round after round until nothing of the wall stood, and all the men who had been on top were dead.

We climbed the rubble, jumping over debris and dodging around projectiles being lobbed our way.

Adrian shifted his way to the top of the pile and moved the lot of us to the other side.

I was expecting another garden. It was a bathing area. There were pools of all sizes here, and they steamed and boiled. The dividing paths for each pool were lined with men. They all carried swords.

I wasn't sure automatons could make good fighters. Rather than wait and find out, I pushed most of them into the hot water.

The air filled with screams.

<Sydney!> Adrian yelled.

He shifted every man in sight out, even the cooked ones, to the beach.

I wanted to duck my head. My response was all knee-jerk, yet I held my head high and continued to the structure. Men began running out of the building like water from a hose. Minos was sending everybody he had at us.

Most of them weren't even armed. Perseus and Hercules began cutting them down in great swathes. Adrian shifted and fought, alternating between how close they were.

Hera pushed bodies into the walls with such force they fell down dead or out cold. I swatted them out of my way with little care for their safety. I couldn't focus on the life part, only the man behind all of this.

My face grew wet with tears, and I pushed them back. Isolde was weeping with each bolt she released. She blasted a hole in the side of the building, gaining us a foothold.

I pushed the rubble to the side, allowing us a level floor to fight on as we moved into the structure.

Hera still stood outside, and Perseus moved in front of her, cutting down every body that came within his reach. Hera's eyes were open, but she was fully in the dreamwalk world.

She raised a hand with splayed fingers and yelled, "Stop!"

All the slaves around us ceased to move.

"Go to sleep!" She instructed

They laid down and closed their eyes on the spot. Hera blinked and brushed past me.

"What did you do?" I asked with awe.

"I broke my vow. That's what I did," she replied.

I wiped my face. Adrian tried to meet my eyes, but I avoided him. He knew I wouldn't stop, and so did Hera. I made her stop me.

She dominated them to stop me from killing them. Because I would have.

The building was clear. Other than all the sleeping slaves, no one offered any form of resistance. The only sounds were those of the slaves snoring. Hera led the way, and I hung back, letting her. She'd seen the inside of the minds here.

Perseus followed on his mother's heels while Hercules and Isolde brought up the rear.

<Neither of you are wrong, *beautiful girl.* >

<No. I should have dominated them so she wouldn't need to. I could have stopped all those people.> I scoffed.

My guilt over this whole situation would eat me alive if I didn't find a better way to deal with this.

I couldn't just bust in guns blazing.

Hera stopped outside a modest set of doors. "Minos is in this room. He's waiting for us."

As soon as Hercules and Isolde stopped, I slammed the doors open. The floor was covered in sleeping slaves. On a dais sat a gorgeous man with blonde hair and blue eyes.

Hera, Hercules and Perseus gasped.

It was the man from the statue, sort of. He *was* a little different. He smiled at me, and all my breath disappeared.

CHAPTER 32

SYDNEY

"I have waited for generations for the Moirai to come. I have hidden here, on Larissa, for many thousands of years, yet I always knew they would find me. " His voice was like thick chocolate laced with hot pepper.

"The day my daughter disappeared was the day I knew my death was a foregone conclusion. So, which of you is her grandchild? Make it quick as I have no wish for my death to be drawn out." He stood and stepped away from his throne.

The dais added 6 feet to his height, allowing him to tower above us. His eyebrows were pulled tight over his nose, creating a deep crease while his blue eyes burned into me. I recognized the straight nose and wavy hair. There could be no doubt whose father he was.

The Oracle had fled Elysium. She'd run from him and into the arms of her own fate. I glanced from Minos to Isolde. There was a slight resemblance.

Minos' eyes seized on Issy. "Well, girl, is it you?"

Issy took a step back, and Hercules placed his hand on her back, holding her steady. Issy couldn't retreat. None of us could.

A flash from Adrian's mind with my face hit me.

<It's you, *beautiful girl*. I can see it, and so can he. His mind races with how you will kill him. Put a stop to his torture.>

My belly clenched as my eyes burned with tears. Why did everyone related to me have to be evil?

Am I evil too?

<You aren't evil. You just have to stamp all that evil out. That is your fate. Now, stand up and do your job!> He urged with his horned swords at the ready.

I sniffed, <Yes, I will.>

Blinking back the tears, Hera stepped forward, as did Isolde.

"The Fates have come to judge you," I calmly stated.

A satisfied tight-lipped smile covered his face. "You are as beautiful as my daughter was. I am ready. Do what you must." There was no fight in his words. Only an unavoidable resolve.

It felt easy.

Too easy.

We mounted the steps to the dais and took our places in front of him. He puffed his shoulders out, allowing his arms to hang loose and free at his sides. He didn't look like a man about to die.

I wanted to stop the judging. I opened my mouth —.

"I will judge you first," Hera announced and laid her hand on his shoulder. Her eyes went wide and white. Both their bodies trembled, and a fine sheen of sweat formed. Blood began to leak from Hera's nose. A corresponding trickle leaked from Minos' nose, creating a mirrored effect.

Perseus yelled something in Greek, and Hercules moved to touch Minos. But Hera backhanded Hercules, and he fell to the floor asleep.

Adrian held his head and cried out in pain. I threw up my shields, blocking them all out. I couldn't let her judgment color my own. The battle between them needed to stay between those two.

Perseus raised his sword to strike Minos down and never moved another muscle. He locked up stiff as a statue with the sword over his head.

Internally I trembled. Hera had never had such a reaction to judging.

Finally, Hera lowered her shaking hand, then collapsed to the floor. Perseus stumbled forward before regaining his balance. He dropped the sword and pulled her body into his arms, rocking back and forth.

He patted the side of her face. "Mother, wake up." His eyes blazed with rage. Perseus inclined his head to Hera's, peppering her with kisses and tears.

She whispered, "You have passed." The words were as light as a feather floating from her lips.

Minos blanched in front of Isolde. "You are my great-great-grand-daughter?" He asked.

With tight lips, she inclined her head. Issy didn't waste a word on the old man but placed her hand on his right shoulder. They froze in statuette form. His eyes became a milky white reflection of hers, and neither of them moved. Sweat poured from Issy's skin, dripping onto the marble-like stone.

In my locked state, I couldn't help her. My stomach turned, wringing me out. My turn was close, and I feared the evil that was buried in his mind.

How long had he sat here, looking down his nose at the Elysian people? Subjugating them, with his foot on the back of their necks. Playing masters of this tiny Universe. The walls began to shake with my rage.

He had hurt people.

The only shining light in my family line was Pythia. How had she survived this place, this man?

My heart rate ramped up, beating like a drum. I was psyching myself out.

Blood leaked from Isolde's ears. She began to whimper while keeping her lips pressed firmly closed. When she broke from the old man, she screamed while thrusting him away with such force, he fell into his throne.

"You are evil," she shouted, "I hope my mother judges you with extreme prejudice," with that, she spat on the floor.

Hercules rolled over and blinked up at her. She sank to the floor, and he took her in his arms. Issy was aggressively shaking as she wept.

Minos drew a labored breath into the barreled chest that carried his lungs. He leaned forward, leveraging his upper body to stand. He looked years older than when we'd entered the room.

His body is becoming weak with the fight.

Minos' eyes twinkled as he stood to face me. A smirk covered him. He still believed he could beat us. Pythia told him about the Fates but never explained what we did. Perhaps she didn't know herself.

Ignorance is an excuse the guilty use to defend their evil.

I wanted to get this over with. Adrian shifted me in front of him. With relief, I placed my hand on his forehead.

I swallowed back all my fears over myself or my family. This man was no blood to me. He gave up my bloodline when he condemned Pythia to death. My lungs pulled in a cleansing breath, and I released it slowly. My heart rate slowed with my breathing, "For all you have done, Fate judges you." Then I dove in.

His mind was a tar-black ocean of hate, fear, and need.

"It all started out so innocent," he mused, flashing a vision of himself as a youth, with bright eyes lacking in guile.

I pushed that visage away. "The road to Hell is paved with good intentions. I imagine the path to the underworld is no different."

My words made him chuckle.

A movie of good intentions began. This was his play - to woo me with his heartfelt desire to help right wrongs.

Elysium was not much different from the earth of my time. Technology was in its infancy, and the Elysians fought wars amongst themselves that paled next to Earth's. Minos was a warrior. He fought alongside many friends who all died.

I understood the pain of loss and the need to fix the cause of the problem. That didn't change what he'd become.

Minos rose in the ranks with three other men.

I recognized two of them as Aeakos and Rhadamanthys. The third, Triptolemos, was a mystery.

They hatched a plan to end the bloodshed by taking over the world. Minos was the ringleader. He controlled the technology sector and the Nymphs. He was one himself. Rhadamanthys ran economics and trade, leaving the Armies to Aeakos while Triptolemos worked with Minos, inspecting the dead.

"Triptolemos was the first to postulate our life extension. Initially, he isolated cells in the blood of the young and transferred them to us," he offered the tidbit up as if he didn't think I could dig it out for myself.

He left out the parts of how many children Triptolemos bled dry to perform this life extension treatment or how they sold it to the highest bidder for their allegiance.

He bought them, and when they lost their usefulness, he tossed them to the side.

Like trash.

The next example of altruism came at me, and I bit back a scream. They exterminated the weak to make room for the strong.

"It was an act of kindness," he remarked, "Most would have only drug out their existence in pain and misery. We allowed them to die for the greater good with dignity."

This, too, was only to cover how they used those people for genetic testing and allowed for the exclusion of undesirable genetic illnesses.

The deeper I dug into his mind, the more aggressive the transgressions. After thousands of years, the Judges were no longer known under their names. They went only with the title of *Judge*. The people they controlled were nothing more than ants crawling across a table, and they quashed them at will for sport.

Minos was too blind to see how far he'd moved away from the rest of Elysium. He cared for no one, only for power and greed. His baser desires took over his world. The game of keeping the masses underfoot was fun, and they took joy in it.

I allowed him to flash all these scenes through my mind until a face I recognized came into view.

Charon and the man from the statue on Delphi.

His green eyes tore through me to the bone as if he saw what others could never reach.

"Stop!" I shouted.

The scene came to a screeching halt. The man was magnificent. Other than the mechanical leg, he resembled what can only be described as a God.

"What, little one? Have I tempted you? do you now see the greater good I have done?" Minos asked.

I ignored his stupid questions, "Who is the man with Charon?"

"A most remarkable man by the name of Anu. They worked together. They created the treatment," Minos chuckled. "You like him?"

"Hard to like a dead guy," I retorted.

I was tired of this back and forth. Minos showed no remorse. He was completely incapable of it. My tip-toeing through his mind was a waste. I was allowing him to have his say. He wasn't fighting me.

"Tell me about Anu!" I mentally pulled the strings of his neural pathways, separating out Pythia and Anu from the rest of the sludge that poisoned his psyche.

"I loved my family," he flashed images of people that resembled him, "We were close. They all died in the wars," he bellowed, deflecting as the vision of their dead bodies splashed across my mind. Blood covered faces with weapons of some variety in their hands while their broken bodies slumped on the ground.

"You loved your family?" I scoffed, "You used your children as guinea pigs for life extension treatments. That isn't love." The putrid taste of partially digested food climbed my insides. "What about Pythia? Did you love her?"

The vision hit me, and I lifted my chin to face it as my stomach fell into my shoes.

The woman resembled me. The main difference was our eyes. Hers were a blue-green like the man in my visions. Like those of Poseidon and Hades. Mine were clear unflinching blue with a dark ring.

Her name came as a whisper in the wind.

Pythia.

He flashed images of her playing in the ocean and dancing in this room. She was all light and joy. The child created most of the art in the palace and the mosaics around the world. Pythia left her mark everywhere in this world. She shared her golden dream of peace with everyone. Then everything changed.

She became a woman with serious eyes and a sad smile. She trained with the Nymphs.

Minos flashed an image of Anu staring at Pythia each other. The hungry chemistry was obvious.

They *liked each other.*

"Anu destroyed her!" he bellowed. "She was never meant to have an ability to see the future." His emotional rage shook me.

"What about you? Were you meant to have abilities?" I shouted back. All those people he wiped danced before me.

The distortion in his face resembled Edward's— my father. When he came up against a fight he couldn't win, his emotions took over, too. I threw her sadness back in his face. It was a weapon.

"All you had to do was change. That is all she asked for," I tossed the emotional hand grenade at him.

"I had to kill her. She was already pregnant. Her grandchild was going to kill me. I had to keep her from having that child. And yet, here you are." His mind pushed back. The mental cudgel battered at me.

His mind flashed to a human-sized box, floating away with the tide. I swallowed back the terror that suddenly gripped me.

He ripped control of my mind away from me. I was locked in that dark box, the water filtering in through the little cracks. My chest tightened with fear. I gulped in the air as if it was soon going to be at a premium.

This isn't real!

I knew it, but I couldn't get past the terror it brought.

This isn't like Erebus.

That wasn't a replay of my fears and life experiences. This was Minos giving me every bit of terror he'd ever witnessed or dished out. I had to claw my way out of this.

I dug at the vision, scrapping my nails on the imaginary walls. The tips broke off, and my finger bled. I cried as the flesh on my fingertips ripped away. The longer I dug, the bloodier my hand became until the bones in my fingers were all that was left.

The taste of terror was metallic, with an electric zing to round it out. I sucked the marrow from the bone of terror and began to chew it up, turning it into a paste. I added worthlessness and misery to the mix and what came out of my mental oven resembled a suicide tea biscuit.

I metaphorically leaped on Minos' chest, pinning his arms to his sides, and shoved the biscuit down his throat.

"She loved you!" I screamed, "and you tossed her into the ocean in a box to drown her."

His mind moved in and began to hammer at me, "Yes, and I would do it again to rid myself of you," he reached in and pulled at my guts, "To get rid of your child and that woman." He mentally pointed at Hera. "I will continue on! I am a Judge!"

He pulled up visions from my past. "You are just like me." The slaves were standing by the pools. "See all the people you killed to reach me? How are you any different?" he demanded, showing me the slaves. I pushed into walls and rubble, breaking their necks.

So this is his game - domination.

He didn't understand how fate worked and that our fight would never be over until I ended it.

"I am eternal!" He shouted as if he thought he was close to winning.

"No, you're not, mother fucker!" I took my hand and slammed it against his forehead, and let my ability do the work.

The quaking started in his torso at the base of his spine. It was a continual vibration of every muscle in his body. His eyes rolled into the back of his head, and blood began seeping from his ears. My hand slicked over his forehead to his cheek as my other hand clasped the other side of his face.

His blue eyes stared at me. I glared back at him. His brow crinkled in the center, pulling down as my heart rate grew.

"Why? I brought peace to my world?" he moaned, and spittle lined his lips, "What have you done?" Sweat soaked his hairline and trailed down the edges of his face to his neck.

"It's not about the outcome. It's every step on the journey." My Confucius quote coated him like an oil slick, sliding over the surface but never sinking into his core.

"I contemplated every step. There was no other way." Blood trickled out of his nose and lined the corners of his eyes. It leaked down to his lips and trailed around his lip line, only to run down his chin.

"There is always another way!" I shouted.

My ability as Fate closed in on him. He shuttered and screamed. His eyes closed as the corners leaked the red viscous fluid of life.

"Pythia..." he called.

I closed my eyes as he called for his child.

Even his love for her couldn't sway him from the path he'd chosen. There was no repentance. He couldn't see the forest for the trees. And now the trees had come to consume him whole.

CHAPTER 33

HERA

The lids covering my eyes were heavy. Minos bled from every orifice, leaking out thick as if cooked on a spit. His eyes were the white of a cooked egg.

I closed my eyes on the scene. It turned my stomach to see the power Sydney wielded. I naturally wanted to save everyone, even those that could not be saved. On the other hand, Sydney fought the battles no one wanted to fight, meting out justice. I was grateful that no one looked to me for that kind of justice.

Perseus, Hercules, and Adrian disappeared while I was out.

"Hera?" Isolde asked while patting my face. There was dried blood around her ears. She scratched at places on her neck where the blood had caked.

"I'm awake and whole," I said and sat up.

My nose and lips itched. I ran my hand across my upper lip and came away with congealed blood.

"Mom has it around her eyes," Isolde informed me.

My eyes found their way to Sydney, who was wiping her face off on her sleeve. I didn't think all of it was blood because she sniffled and turned away from our prying eyes.

Adrian shifted to her side and wrapped his arms around her.

"The shield is down. We can start transporting these slaves to a medical facility," Hephaestus announced. "Mother?" he knelt next to me and cupped my cheek.

"I am well," I stated, though I was not sure it was true. I felt different. The press of fate wasn't as strong. It was as if the bleeding freed me from that obligation.

My son's black hair fell into his eyes, and he glanced at me through the curtain, "I have to go," he stated.

I gave him a tight smile and patted the back of his hand. A moment later, he was gone with a shift, as were half the slaves in the room.

"Isolde?" I called.

She moved to my side. "I feel different," I whispered.

She nodded and pulled on her lower lip as if to stop herself from biting it. "I feel something too. I think I feel free?" She remarked with wonder.

Sydney's shoulders shook. Perhaps the lifted weight freed her in a way she'd never been before. I took to my feet and went to her side. Adrian released her and shifted from the room.

"I don't feel it. Whatever you guys are feeling, I don't. I'm just mad, and I don't know why," she cried. Her tears were pink with blood. She raised her face to gaze upon me, and her eyes were blood red.

I recoiled.

"Your eyes," I murmured.

"I know!" She shouted. The throne tore from the floor and crashed into a wall, shattering into a thousand pieces.

With no other possible outcome but pain, I wrapped her in my arms and began to rock her. "What does it mean?" She whimpered. Her tears grew redder with each moan.

"I don't know," I murmured into her hair.

"I want to destroy something." She pulled out of my embrace, taking a few steps away.

"What happens when the Fates' job is done?" She asked.

"I don't think it works that way. The job of fate never goes away. It only fades into the background," I supplied, yet I didn't know for sure.

It could be our job of fate was done.

Perhaps, by ridding the cosmos of the Judges, we completed our mission?

Perseus stalked into the room, took one look at Sydney, and said, "You better come with me." He extended his hand to me. I clasped it, and he pulled me into a standing position.

The three of us followed him down many passages until we came to a human-type theater. The lights were lowered, and playing on the screen was a vision of the throne room we'd just left.

"Start it over!" Perseus yelled.

*****

The scene began again. Pythia stood before her father in a loincloth. Her eyes were dark with secrets. She looked so like Sydney I ached with it.

"If you don't change your ways and embrace peace, the Moiria will come for you, and they will show you the same amount of mercy you have shown your people. Father, all you must do is change," she pleaded.

He laughed and rejected her words. The conversation went back and forth, with neither side giving an inch. I watched with the interest of a scientist as the two of them bantered. The moment Pythia told Minos the end would come in the form of his grandchild, his demeanor changed.

He acted as if he was listening. He even stated he would change and wanted to speak more on the matter the next day. She left, and Minos instructed his slaves to build a box.

The video played at a high rate until the next day. Pythia was dragged before Minos.

"What are you doing, father?" She asked with a calm there was no reason to feel.

"I am saving myself, of course. If your grandchild kills me, then I must assure myself it is never born. The physicians inform me you are already with child. As much as I love you, I cannot allow that child to be born. I can't sterilize you, for the Primordium will only heal you. That leaves me with only one choice. I must kill you. It is the only way." His reasoning was as cold as the stone on the floor.

"Do what you must," she replied.

My blood ran cold. I looked at Sydney and back to the visage of Pythia.

Mary said the same thing when she handed Sydney over to Edward.

The video moved out to the beach, where an ornate box, big enough to hold Pythia laying down, sat in the lapping waves. Minos pointed at the box, and his slaves drug her toward the yawning opening.

"Father, this will not be the end. The Moiria will come, and when they are done, they will set the Erinyes free to cleanse the Universe of all who treat others as you do. They will set right the natural order of things."

Minos laughed in her face. The slaves shoved her in the box and locked the lid closed. They pushed the box into the sea, with Minos giving the last shove as it floated away.

*****

"Turn it off, for fuck sakes! I don't want to watch anymore!" Sydney screamed. She landed in the nearest chair hard and quickly placed her hands on both sides of her head to cry.

Adrian appeared and waved everyone out, closing the doors firmly behind us.

Hades stood outside the room alone. There was a myriad of questions I wanted to ask him, none of which could find their way to my lips.

"The Nymphs have agreed that I shall lead the changeover from the Judges. We shall transform this into a peaceful Republic," he stated. His black hair gleamed in the sunlight that streamed in the windows. His bride was nowhere to be seen.

"What about our people?" Isolde demanded.

"The islands of the Judges along with Medusa's island are all empty, and none wish to live there. The Nymphs have given them over for our kind as a refuge as long as we agree to stay there. We aren't welcome anywhere else on the planet."

I nodded my head in understanding. They were afraid.

We have powers like the judges, and they don't want more of all that.

This wasn't a home.

"What about the Fates?" I asked as my hand rubbed the fabric of my dress between my fingers.

"They have asked that you leave. They don't want the Fates here." He didn't look away, only stared us down.

His answer wasn't a shock. Actually, I'd expected it.

Who wants fate breathing down the back of your neck, watching your every move? No one wants that.

Part of me was relieved. We couldn't do any more harm to these people if we didn't stay around. Another part was saddened. The Elysian light and all its golden hope turned from a warm embrace to a cold shoulder. They were grateful but scared.

CHAPTER 34

SYDNEY

The bright light on the beach should have blinded me after the viewing room, but it didn't. I soaked it in. Hades had struck a deal that didn't include the Fates hanging out on the beach, and I had to get my fill of the ocean before I left.

I blinked back my bloody tears and dove into the water. The light salt content burned at the edges of my eyes. The salinity of Elysium reminded me of the Aegean Sea, and I let my skin drink it in. I burst through the surface and sucked in the fresh air, enjoying the tangy taste of salt and sea. Elysium carried a little something different from Earth. It was wholly unique to this world. I liked it.

I'll miss it.

I moved to the shore. It was time to go, and I couldn't put it off anymore. I slicked the water in my hair back and sluiced it down my neck. I licked my lips and wrapped the sheet of fabric I'd brought with me around my hips.

<I'm ready.> I informed Adrian.

<Shifting you now!>

I appeared in my stateroom on Odyssey. Our side of the ship was facing the star in this system. The blue of the Elysian rings gave off their soothing glow. I sat down on my bed and stared at it.

This will be as close as I am ever going to come to the Isle of the Blessed.

Maybe, it was right.

I did kill everyone on my way to get here.

Maybe, I didn't have the right to see the promised land. I'd forever be Moses, staring into Canaan from the wilderness.

<What drivel! This isn't the promised land, *beautiful girl*. It's a hunk of rock floating around in the cosmos, and there are plenty of those.> Adrian scoffed.

I turned to look at him.

"You could stay if you wanted to."

"Are you kidding? I'm not interested in any place that you aren't." He jumped onto the bed and stomped across, then plopped down behind me. "I'm not dreamwalking you again for sex ever. I want the real thing." He kissed the back of my neck and nibbled down to my shoulder.

"Stop! I'm trying to be real here. How many people are leaving the ship to stay?" I asked and shivered.

"None."

"None?" I asked in shock.

"We may be a ragtag group of misfits, but we are a tight one. Everyone here is with us. If they can't accept all of us, then they don't deserve any of us. Dewy was incensed that they wouldn't let you stay." Adrian leaned back and cocked his head to the side.

"Dewy. I've only met the guy a few times."

"Well, he's my great uncle, and he was angry. Said they were a bunch of ingrates. You should have heard Emmaline. She was worse."

I laughed.

Emmaline, I'm sure, was more colorful with her words.

"Does anyone know about my eyes?" I asked.

"No, but it's mostly gone now. Maybe, it was just from the fight and nothing more." Adrian peppered a few more kisses down my neck.

"I don't think so. It felt different, like something more. I can't explain it." I leaned back into his embrace and let him pull my wet towel off.

His hands found my breasts, and I turned into his waiting lips. "Come to bed, *beautiful girl*. Whatever else is going to happen can wait."

I moaned into his mouth as his fingers trailed down to my wet folds and forgot about everything but him.

CHAPTER 35

SYDNEY

Melinda mentally paged me, and I ignored her.

I'm on hiatus, for fuck sake. Can't a girl enjoy the afterglow of sex and a job well done?

<Sydney!> she yelled.

Her mental calls never stopped. I was about to talk to her when I was shifted.

Someone will get an ear full later.

The lab ring was empty, other than Melinda. At least, whoever shifted me gave me clothes. Jeans and a t-shirt worked for me.

"She's gone, and I don't know for how long." Melinda was huffing as if she'd run a race. "I've looked everywhere." She ran her hand over her face and pressed her fingers over her mouth.

"I don't even know when she disappeared." She stopped and turned to me with bloodshot eyes.

She stared as if I should know what she was talking about or who. Her eyes narrowed for a moment at my eyes before she continued.

"Do you know what I'm talking about?" she demanded. Her voice grew louder with each word.

"No, I have no fucking idea. What's got your panties in a twist?" I shouted back at her.

"Mary!" she shouted, "Mary's gone. God!" Melinda placed a hand on her hip and turned to look through the crystalline walls of the lab ring.

I followed her gaze. The glass did nothing more than create an optical illusion, allowing you to see the curvature of the ring itself.

Melinda whipped back around. "I put a tracker on her when I first let her out. To know where she is and keep an eye on her."

I really wasn't following her and my brows pulled down in confusion.

"Your mother, you moron! Mary, your mother, Edward's sister! The woman who gave birth to you!" She shouted, spraying a little spittle in my face.

"I don't understand. She clearly is here somewhere. We just need to find her," I shrugged, then wiped my face in disgust.

"No! She's not, and neither are your brothers!" She was practically screaming now. Her hair was a mess like she hadn't brushed it in days. Her bloodshot eyes spoke of lack of sleep. Her lab coat was covered in coffee stains. She hadn't showered.

How long has she been like this?

I stepped back and ran into a wall.

"T, what about T?" I asked as my worries tore through me with the dawn of the truth. But Melinda wasn't listening.

I left the lab running. I stepped into the main companionway connecting room, and the base gravity pull changed. I fell hard onto the flooring, sliding a few feet. My feet met the floor anew, and I found a fresh purchase.

The stretch of my legs as I powered down the corridor was fueled by my fear.

T has to be here.

I reached the cafeteria and came to a screeching halt as I swung around the corner into the room.

T was always here. I searched for Dewy or his kids. I didn't know what they looked like, but they had to look somewhat like Emmaline and Dewy.

Then the tell-tale black hair came into view. T turned—

<Shifting now.> Adrian announced.

The pressure changed, and I was standing, staring back out the viewport in Melinda's lab.

"No, T is fine. She just took the younger boys, *her* sons," Melinda remarked as if I hadn't even left the room.

My eyes snapped back to her face. "What did you say?"

Melinda waved me off. "T is Edward's son. Of course, she didn't take him. Mathew and Edward jr. are Mary's."

"That's not possible!" I breathed, "I saw Anne pregnant."

Melinda laughed, "The only kid she carried to term was T. Mary had the other two. Good old Ed only brought them home. That is beside the point. Mary is gone, and so are they. I've had this ship searched from top to bottom. They Are Gone! There is only one way off this ship, Sydney!"

Melinda reached into a case while shaking her head and pulled out a cigarette, snapped a lighter to life, and took a nice long drag.

The reality of what she was trying to say hit like a ton of bricks.

"When did she shift?" I asked with a dry mouth.

The words from the St Mary's hospital file came back to me.

They found her outside, and there was no way she could have gotten there.

A thousand visions rushed through my mind.

Where did they go? Why did she leave?

I glanced up at Melinda and narrowed my eyes. "Why didn't you tell me about Matt and Ed Jr.?"

"Pasha, would it have mattered? You didn't like them, and they hated you." Melinda waved her hand as if to close the discussion about my siblings, then continued with what she thought mattered, "I put a tracker on Mary. She was talking to someone and didn't want us to know." She raised a hand to stifle my response.

"I believe in privacy, but there is a ton of talk about you being the daughter of the '*God of the Sea.*' Mary had all three of you while on a funny farm, with no men around. So she is clearly mated to someone." She leaned back, took another drag, and let the smoke curl out of her nose.

She and Emmaline must be teaching each other bad habits.

"It is someone who doesn't want us to know who they are. Mary got rid of her tracker somewhere around the asteroid field near Cerberus. That was the last time I had a chance to check on her. I haven't seen her since."

Melinda tapped her ash out into a petri dish with a few butts already quashed out in it.

"Why would she leave?" I asked.

"I'll tell you one reason - *love*. And it ain't for you." She snorted and released a bitter laugh, "Maybe, what you should be asking is where did she go?"

I didn't need speculation. I needed proof, tangible evidence.

I needed to talk to T.

<Shifting now!> Adrian's voice informed me.

The black hair of my brother appeared before me, "T!" I croaked before looking around. T encircled me in his arms as I shook.

"Where are we, and what is wrong?" He asked.

I stepped back to explain, only to stop short. T's face drained of color as he stared over my head. I turned around in the small space. It was stark but for the writing on the walls. One word written over and over again covered every inch of space. Nothing was left untouched.

Tartarus.

All the blood coloring my eyes drained from my head. Tartarus was written in the Themian dialect used on Delphi. I'd seen it in the books about the great division.

We needed to leave.

A shifter embedded with the Titans changes the dynamics in the cosmos.

<Hera!> I mentally shouted.

<Yes, we must go. Poseidon will kill us all.> Hera responded.

For once, she sounded scared.

The end

KILLING GODS

VII

POSEIDON

If you've enjoyed what you've read here please give it a little love and leave a review or feel free to follow me on Amazon

Or send me an email slmason1889@gmail.com or follow me on Instagram @s.l.mason_author

More from S.L. Mason

These Hallowed Hills

Trick of Fae

Test of Fae

Thorns of Fae

Twist of Fae

Traits of Fae

Thief of Fae

Other stories

Twin Lives

Vella

Whisper

www.ingramcontent.com/pod-product-compliance
Lightning Source LLC
Chambersburg PA
CBHW061207190726
48288CB00001B/95